Jessamine: any of numerous often climbing shrubs (genus *Jasminum*) of the olive family that usually have extremely fragrant flowers.

When professor Neil Boehm arrives at Jessamine Grove to take on the task of tutoring a precocious child, he does not know that, like the flower for which it's named, the picturesque jazz-age estate harbors deadly secrets beneath its glamorous façade.

As Neil unravels the twisted vines of Jessamine Grove's past and the pain and suffering that were their fruits, he reexamines his own past and life choices and draws unsettling parallels between the history of the Grove and that of his own family history.

Uncovering old sins leads him to hope he can paint a brighter picture for his future.

JESSAMINE GROVE

D.J. Blankenship

A NineStar Press Publication
www.ninestarpress.com

Jessamine Grove

© 2024 D.J. Blankenship

Cover Art © 2024 Melody Pond

Edited by BJ Toth

First Edition, April 2024

ISBN: 978-1-64890-754-8

Also available in eBook, ISBN: 978-1-64890-753-1

CONTENT WARNING:

This book contains sexual fade-to-black content, which may only be suitable for mature readers. Depictions of discussion of past suicide and/or murder and mention of abortion.

Chapter One

Florentina Bay

December

ALONG WITH SARAH'S letter came an exquisite origami Christmas ornament. Not having a tree upon which to hang it, I attached the multicolored
star to the toggle of my rucksack. Now, as I opened the bag, I admired it
once more. I tried origami when I was a kid. Unfortunately, I never managed to produce anything that resembled the intended object. What other
creative projects had I put my hand to? Shadow boxes, model rockets, the
iconic "science project," and finally, painting. All failures. Not for lack of
intelligence or skill, but for a surfeit of impatience. I wanted everything I
did to be perfect. Instantly. When it was not, I stomped on, tore up, or
otherwise destroyed it.

Now, with the wisdom of maturity, I looked upon Sarah's handiwork with more admiration than envy. I had learned to accept there were certain things I could not do—or do well—and it was a waste of time and energy to dwell on failures rather than concentrate on and hone strengths. This mindset had served me well in my career as an educator.

Sarah had bested me in artistic creativity, applying her crafty little hands successfully to everything from sewing and knitting to creating beautiful greeting cards and handbound notebooks. In her skill with, and love of, teaching, Sarah had been my equal.

As I pulled my thermos and the letter from my bag, I marveled at the passage of time. Almost thirty years since Sarah Lewis and I began work at Allerton Academy. The venerable Connecticut institution was in precarious financial straits when we were hired, holding tenaciously (or foolishly, depending on one's perspective) to its old-fashioned curriculum and strict code of discipline while the outside world moved inexorably forward, and more successful private schools adopted contemporary education models. The anachronism of Allerton initially captured our shared romanticism— the feeling of having been hired as principles in a costume drama—and the reality of Allerton's prestige and high standards that kept us on. From the start, Sarah and I entertained no false hopes that our honeymoon with Allerton would last forever, so we were both surprised the school managed to hang on for more than a quarter of a century.

With Allerton in its final death throes, Sarah, and I—and a few colleagues whose tenures matched or exceeded our own—faced the unenviable fate of being middle-aged and unemployed. Some, like I, chose early retirement. Others, without the luxury of a private income, scrambled to find positions commensurate with their experience working in an old-fashioned boy's boarding school. Some found work abroad. A few, like Sarah, took positions as private tutors.

"Why?" I had asked Sarah, truly baffled.

Sarah had a promising new life awaiting her outside Allerton—a long suffering lover who had finally convinced her to accept his everlasting marriage proposal and follow him to wedded bliss and retirement in Italy. Instead, Sarah had opted for a two-year stint tutoring the precocious child of a wealthy Florida power couple.

"I can't quit cold turkey," Sarah reasoned. "I need some sort of transition. And I could use the extra cash. The Willoughbys are paying handsomely for the Allerton pedigree."

When she divulged the figure, I was floored.

"Jesus. I can't blame you for accepting. But what about Victor?"

Victor was the long-suffering boyfriend.

"His reaction was rather like yours," she said, adding a few cubes of ice and a dash of scotch to her empty glass. "Victor has agreed to a compromise. He's going to rent a condo nearby, and we'll spend our holidays in Italy. When my contract is up, we'll move for good."

Halfway through the first year of that contract, Mrs. Willoughby passed away, and Sarah soon found herself reconsidering the wisdom of continuing in her position.

> "I won't be sad to leave this place," *Sarah had said in her letter to me,* "but I worry about the boy."

The boy. Max Willoughby.

> How often, over the years, have we had that discussion
> about why some people choose to be parents? Ezra isn't

a bad man, really. But his parenting skills leave a lot to be desired.

Anyway, I've had enough. And despite his assurances to the contrary, I know Victor is getting antsy. For so many years, I used Allerton and my career to avoid a true, live-in commitment to Victor. I won't do that anymore. I want to spend every moment of the rest of my life with the man I love.

And yet...

I don't want to leave Max without knowing there is someone there for him. Someone to advocate for him. Someone to care for him. He's certainly no day at the county fair, but there's something about him. Sometimes when I'm with him I recall what you've told me about your own childhood. It's the young Neil Boehm I see when Max rips up a perfectly good essay or kicks his easel to the ground when I offer the slightest constructive criticism about a work in progress. He has much creative potential but lacks a proper sense of self-worth—of confidence.

Though he denies it, the death of Mrs. Willoughby has affected Max deeply, and he turns to me more and more as a surrogate mother.

What I believe Max really needs at this stage in his life is someone who can be a mentor as well as both a mother and father figure. A buddy, a confidant. Ezra—though I do not doubt his love for his son—seems afraid of gentleness, of kindness, of, perhaps, showing himself as weak. He often forgets Max is a child, not a military cadet.

You've already guessed where I'm going with this, of course.

You'd start after the New Year.

Please, Neil. At least consider it seriously. Ezra has practically made up his mind to send his son to a boarding school in France. I think this would be disastrous for Max. If you agree, we'll talk about it in more detail later.

I've already told Mr. Ezra about you—and he's checked you out and is suitably impressed. And he seems, much to my feminist chagrin, to assume you would be less likely to run off and get married.

Would you? I wonder.

Details enclosed.

Love,

Sarah

I received the contract from Ezra Willoughby even before I met him via video conference. Despite the feeling I was being railroaded—gently by Sarah, imperiously by Willoughby—I accepted the offer. The charm of the lifestyle of an aging beach bum was beginning to wear off, and as much as I cherished the pleasant memories sparked by my return to Florentina Bay, other, darker memories overshadowed them and made remaining there untenable.

Allerton Academy had been my home for more than half of my adult life. Where would I live out the rest of it? Perhaps a leap of faith was in order.

*

I WAS MET at Jacksonville International Airport by a stern-looking, white-haired Willoughby employee named Ned, who led me from baggage claim to a waiting black SUV. The casual attire of my escort—polo and chinos—and the budget model of my ride were letdowns.

The drive was pleasant, since the modest interior of the vehicle was spalike after so many hours in an airplane, and the driver made no attempts at small talk. I applied myself to the final chapter of the novel I had started during the flight and had just begun to nod off when the driver announced our arrival at our destination.

"Here we are, Mr. Boehm," he said, lowering the right passenger window for a better view, "Jessamine Grove."

A bizarre pastiche of Andalusian and Pueblo-style architecture, the house built by Harrison Willoughby in 1925 still managed to impress with the sheer chutzpa of its design. Although Willoughby's dreams of a planned community for his fellow tycoons died with the Crash of 1929, the Grove survived. While other historic properties in nearby Old Saint Augustine had been converted to museums or hotels, the Grove remained private property.

As we approached the house, I looked about, puzzled. The driver, noting my consternation, laughed, and said, "There aren't any."

"I beg your pardon?"

"Jessamine vines. You were lookin' for 'em, right? Everybody does. Time was, they covered nearly the entire estate. The scent was somethin', I'll tell ya. But the Señora took a dislike to them. Had them all ripped out. I'll never forget the day she sent Nessa down to give the order. Too high and mighty to tell me directly. Nearly a hundred years of tradition gone in one fell swoop. Surprised she didn't change the name of the place, to boot."

"The Señora?"

"Fabiola Willoughby. Mr. Willoughby's late wife. South American. That's why we all called her the Señora. Some of the Spanish-speaking folk, they called her *La Patrona*. I don't know much Spanish, but I know what that means. Can't say they sounded like they said it with much respect though. But what do I know?"

Not a peep from the man for over an hour, and now he was showing himself to be an old gossip. "How long have you worked at the Grove?" I asked.

"Since I came back from Vietnam. My daddy was head gardener then. I wasn't fit for much else, so old Mr. Willoughby was kind enough to take me on as my daddy's apprentice. Been the head honcho since the old man passed on. Don't live on the estate no more though. Our little house went the way of the jessamine."

After being afforded the tourist view of the spectacular tiled fountain that was the centerpiece of the circular front drive, Ned escorted me to the rear of the main house, where he handed me off to a uniformed household staff member.

"See you around, Mr. Boehm," said Ned, giving me a salute over his shoulder as he walked back to his vehicle.

I was led up the back stairs and thence deposited in my chamber in what I rightly assumed were the servants' quarters.

"Mr. Willoughby should return sometime this evening," said my guide, smiling for the first time. She was a diminutive young woman in her late teens to early twenties, with an elfin appearance accentuated by bobbed black hair neatly swept behind slightly pointed ears. "My name is Rosanie. Mrs. Hanson, the housekeeper, will introduce you to everyone else…the daily staff, and all that…eventually."

Having lived for so many years in an institution that was run like clockwork, I found Rosanie's lack of certainty irritating.

"And where can I find this Mrs. Hanson?" I asked, my voice sounding supercilious even to my own ears.

"Um…" Rosanie glanced from side to side, as if the housekeeper might suddenly pop out from some dark corner of the room, "She's off today… I think."

You think?

Rosanie must have read the incredulity in my expression.

"I mean," she continued, "Mrs. Hanson is usually off on Tuesdays and today is Tuesday, so"–Rosanie shrugged–"she must be off."

She's not the only one.

"Thank you for the clarification, Rosanie. You really have no idea at what time I can expect to meet Mr. Willoughby?"

"Um...after six?"

God, give me strength.

"Thank you, Rosanie," I said with what I hoped would be interpreted as a tone of dismissal.

Rosanie remained where she stood, looking down at the floor.

"This was *her* room," she muttered, turning her gaze from the floor to me, her dark eyes looking on the verge of tears. "Miss Sarah's room."

Of course. Why wouldn't I be assigned the same room?

"She was such a nice lady," added Rosanie, fidgeting with the hem of her apron. "I miss her."

I felt a pang of tenderness toward this young woman I had written off as an irritating nitwit. If she had liked Sarah, she couldn't be all that bad.

"Yes," I agreed, "She was. I miss her too."

Rosanie smiled, wiped her eyes with the back of her hand, then made an awkward gesture somewhere between a bow and a curtesy.

"Well, um...if you need anything, Mr. Boehm, just ask. I'll be in the kitchen. At the bottom of the stairs, down the hall to the left."

"Thank you again, Rosanie."

And with that, I was left alone in my new digs.

I was pleasantly surprised. The apartment consisted of a small living room and adjacent bedroom. The furniture was a quirky hodge-podge of periods from Art Deco to contemporary—all good quality—that managed to coexist in a manner pleasing to the eye. Along the wall to the left of the bedroom door was a small but high-end kitchenette. In the bedroom, there was a sleigh bed, a highboy, and a dressing table worthy of a 1930s film star.

A spacious Jack and Jill bathroom led to what must once have been a matching suite, but now appeared to serve as a storeroom.

As I unpacked, stowed, and hung my belongings, I thought of Sarah doing the same on her first day of employment. I imagined the personal touches she would have brought to her temporary quarters: scented candles, African violets, or a fern (her favorite houseplants), and her monthly journals—handmade of bits and bobs from the Allerton art department scrap heap and bound with ribbon from her vast collection of holiday paraphernalia.

My personal touch was a collection of beloved books—a vintage copy of Jules Verne's *Twenty Thousand Leagues Under the Sea*, Shakespeare's sonnets, a 1920 printing of the *Victrola Book of the Opera*, *The Count of Monte Cristo*, and *The Wind in the Willows* among others–that I endeavored to arrange in order of size on the small marble fireplace mantel.

"Sarah had a clock there."

Startled by the sound of the voice, I let Kenneth Graham's masterpiece slip from my hand, and it hit the floor with a thud, disheveling the dust jacket and sending several folded letters I'd tucked within its pages—my memento mori—flying.

"Sorry."

I reclaimed the childhood birthday gift from my mother, replaced the letters, and smoothed the creased cover.

Maximillian Willoughby's apology was perfunctory. He could not have known how much the damage to the book bothered me. Understandably, he was more attuned to the absence of Sarah than to the feelings of the usurper of her domain.

Sarah had described Max as the "skater boy" type. The kid who stood in the doorway of my room wearing a misshapen grey T-shirt, baggy wide-legged jeans, and worn tennis shoes fit her description perfectly. The only thing lacking was the board.

"An eighteenth-century French ormolu clock?" I asked, as I placed the book next to its brothers. Max nodded. "I was with Sarah when she bought it at a flea market in Manhattan years ago. She stole the darned thing, really. The gentleman who owned the stall was clueless."

I smiled at the remembrance of the trips to New York City that had been a staple of my friendship with Sarah. "Jaunts to civilization" Sarah called them.

"You must be Maximillian," I said, walking toward the boy, my right hand outstretched in greeting. "I'm—"

"Neil Boehm," interrupted Max. "I know. And yes, I *must* be Maximillian. Unless, of course, my parents adopted twins and the one they've kept locked in the basement managed to escape."

I retracted my hand and clasped it to my other behind my back—my nonthreatening at-ease pose—Max having ignored the offer of a hand-shake. "Like *The Man in the Iron Mask?*"

Max smiled and I felt relief at having scored an early point. "Yeah. Dumas is awesome."

"My favorite is *The Count of Monte Cristo*," I said. "Have you read it?"

"Not yet. Just *The Three Musketeers* and *The Man in the Iron Mask.*"

"Good. We can read it together."

Max's smile broadened.

"And then you can write an essay on it."

Adios to the smile.

"Okay," I said, putting my hands up in a placating gesture, "we'll read that one for fun. I'll save the essay assignment for something more tedious."

"Gee, thanks, professor."

Max had advanced into the room during our conversation, and he now stood next to me examining the books on the mantle. Mr. Willoughby told me that Max had been bullied at school. Seeing Max up close, I thought I understood part of the reason why. It was often a curse for a boy of Max's age.

Though gangly in build and awkward in gait, Maximillian Willoughby had a face worthy of the study of a Renaissance master: a mass of curly black hair, wide brown eyes framed with long lashes, well-defined cheek-bones, and a cherubic mouth.

While I despised bullying, I reminded myself of Sarah's assessment of Max as "hardly a day at the county fair." I needed to get to know Max before jumping to facile conclusions.

"Please call me Neil," I said, breaking the habit of formal teacher-pupil relations acquired at Allerton.

"Sarah said the same thing," murmured Max, turning away from the books and toward me. "I mean, not Neil, obviously, but…"

"I get it."

"How about Prof?"

"That will do nicely," I said.

"Is that your real voice?" Max asked, as he removed my hardbound copy of *The Count of Monte Cristo* from the shelf without asking permission. He was testing me. I should have reprimanded him, but I did not. "You sound like a British actor or something."

"I'll take that as a compliment," I replied, putting my hand out for the book. "Thank you." I replaced the book on the shelf. "When I was your age, I used to like to mimic people—singers, actors, teachers. I was intrigued by the sound of voices, of different languages. One day, I discovered the musical *My Fair Lady*, and from that day, I was hooked on elocution."

"Elocution?"

"Yes. The art of speaking properly and clearly. The story of the musical comes from a play by George Bernard Shaw about a phonetician—a speech professor—who endeavors to teach an uneducated girl how to speak proper English and pass her off as an aristocrat."

"Why?"

"To prove his theory of the power of language and comportment— that if you speak and act properly, people will assume that you are sophisticated, intelligent, and cultured, even if you aren't."

"Does it work?"

"Well," I said with a shrug, "It worked for me."

Max smiled. "Sarah said you were the only person she knew who could be silly and serious at the same time. She called you 'seriously silly.'"

"I shall do my best to live down the moniker."

Max's smile faded, to be replaced with a dejected look.

"I miss Sarah," Max said, moving to the window and sitting in a slouch on the narrow sill.

"I understand, Max," I said. "Losing your mother, and then Sarah…"

"No," said Max looking up sharply. "You don't understand. Nobody does. And Fabiola was not my *real* mother. I don't care that she's dead. I hated her."

I did not have a response for this. No one can fully understand the grief of another, and anger is part of the grieving process. Max being an adopted child added yet another challenging dimension to the scenario. I wondered if I was out of my depth. There was no guidance counselor to whom I could send Max, no school psychiatrist, no minister. Throughout my career, I had found myself in all those roles at one time or another. But never all of them at once.

"If you want," said Max, changing the subject with the jarring facility of the young, "I can show you around the house and grounds." He hopped down from the windowsill and followed me into the bedroom as I hung the last of my clothes. "Mrs. Hanson doesn't come in on Tuesdays. And Rosanie doesn't know anything. About the house, I mean. Even though she's lived here, like, forever."

"I'd enjoy that very much," I said. "Where is your father? I thought I would meet him when I arrived."

Max sighed heavily, and I wondered if the gesture was informed by garden variety preteen drama or actual exasperation with his father.

"Dad is at some fundraising committee thing."

Dad. Interesting. Though Ezra Willoughby was no more Max's *real* father than Fabiola Willoughby had been his *real* mother. The late Mrs. Willoughby was Fabiola, not *Mom.*

"So, you have the run of the castle?"

"More or less. Without Hideous Hanson breathing down my back."

It was my turn to smile.

"All right, then. Lead on, McDuff."

*

"UNLIKE THE DOCTOR'S TARDIS," said Max as he led me through french doors into the central great room of the Grove, "it's smaller on the inside."

I understood what he meant. The grounds Max had shown me were extensive, and the architect had obviously worked closely with the landscape designer to create a visual impact that suggested a rambling, multi-tiered property. There were ornamental ponds, follies, balconies extending from almost every room, an Olympic-sized swimming pool ensconced in an elaborate porticoed shelter. Yet, the main house was modest in size by my idea of a mansion. What the Grove lacked in square footage, it made up for in grandeur and detail.

"My dad says the dolphin mosaic at the bottom of the pool was stolen from an archeological dig on the island of Delos," said Max, his tone of voice indicating a degree of misplaced pride.

"It would not surprise me, Max," I replied as I followed Max up a sweeping marble staircase with gold filigree balusters and wrought iron banisters on the way to his attic room. "In your grandfather's time, the laws and the attitudes relating to archaeological excavations were quite different than they are today."

"My dad says the world's museums are full of stolen shit," continued Max.

So that was how the land lay. I had a future of "my dad says" moments to look forward to.

"Stolen *property*. I don't tolerate vulgarity."

"Yes, Prof."

"And your father is correct, unfortunately."

I was tempted to argue that art of dubious provenance on display at the Louvre or the Met was not quite the same as a Hellenistic masterpiece in your backyard pool, but I restrained myself.

The second-floor landing was dominated by a grand piano. I let out an involuntary whistle of appreciation as I noted the make and took a guess at the age.

"Do you play?" I asked Max as I caught up with him as he lopped along to the end of the west hall.

A quick, negative shake of Max's head.

"I'm not allowed."

What? Not allowed to play piano?

Maybe Max meant that *specific* piano. Something in his tone of voice told me otherwise.

Max looked back at me as he mounted a precarious-looking spiral staircase. He must have noticed the dubious look on my face before I willed it away.

"Do you have vertigo, or something? Fabiola was scared of heights."

"No."

I did not suffer from vertigo, but I did have a dislike of twisting, narrow staircases.

I made a cautious ascent behind my guide, who scrambled effortlessly over the iron treads. At the center of the landing was the entrance to Max's bedroom. A large barn-style door was rolled to the side, revealing the interior.

The overall impression I had formed of the Willoughby residence thus far was one of overstated, impersonal expense. The hand of a zealous interior designer with a mania for art deco and chinoiserie was clearly behind the color of every wall, the placement of each piece of furniture, the effect of every mirror or chandelier. The house was like a vintage grand hotel: beautiful and impressive but lacking the unique touches of a family home. It seemed the house had been painstakingly preserved in its entirety from the days of its original owner.

Almost monastic in its simplicity—if not its size—Max's room stood in stark contrast to the rest of the house. Though bare of all but the essentials in the way of furniture—a bed, a desk, a bureau that might have come from a second-hand store—the walls and surfaces were decorated with an eclectic collection of paintings and *objet d'art*. The windows—all open to receive the cool afternoon breeze—were large and numerous and the sun shone through onto every surface. Stepping into Max's room was, quite literally, a breath of fresh air.

"Is that an original Kahlo?" I asked, not bothering to hide the awe in my voice as I eyed the self-portrait of the artist that hung above Max's bed.

"Yes."

"You have excellent taste, young man," I said, feeling instinctively that Max, not a decorator had chosen that painting. The same applied to the exquisite reproductions (or where they?) of pre-Columbian pottery I spied on Max's desk and atop his bureau.

"Thank you, sir. Well, this concludes our tour. On your way out, please take a moment to visit the gift shop. The price of your ticket includes a fifteen percent discount on all merchandise. We hope to see you again soon at the Willoughby Memorial Museum."

"An excellent tour," I said. "But there was one glaring omission."

Max raised his eyebrows. "Really?"

"Yes. Where is our classroom?"

"Oh, that," said Max, as if I should have somehow known. "It depends. Sarah did the art classes outside in good weather, here in bad weather—because of the light—and history, science, and math in the library. I hate math, by the way. I don't see the point of it when we have computers and stuff to do it for us. I mean, unless you're a math nerd or something."

Of course, I could not admit to Max that I shared his aversion to mathematics. I had hoped that he *would* be a math nerd. It would have been so much easier.

"And language classes? I understand you're fluent in Spanish and Sarah told me you excel in French and English."

Max eased up a bit on his habitual slouch, pride straightening his shoulders.

"Usually the library. Sometimes here. I like the sound of French. The verbs suck. I really like English literature and ancient history."

Thank you, Lord.

"Good. I'll be introducing you to Latin. The Latin will help you with French and enrich your knowledge of English and ancient history."

I tried not to laugh at the fleeting look of horror that passed over Max's face at the mention of Latin. I had seen it innumerable times on an equal number of young faces.

"I'll put Greek on hold until I see how you progress."

"Greek??"

"Just kidding." Sarah had told me of Max's talent for photography and drawing. I was curious to see his work and decided that it might be a good moment to request a viewing. "Where do you keep *your* work?" I asked, glancing around the room. "I'd love to see it. May I?"

"No."

I'd expected modest prevarication or eager assent. Max's immediate refusal to my request both irritated and puzzled me. "All right, then. Perhaps some other time?"

Max turned away from me and put his attention to rearranging some items on his desk.

It was clearly a dismissal, and I accepted it as such. Teaching could often be a battle and I was willing to let the first round go to Max. At Allerton, I would never have allowed such insolent behavior to go unchecked. But this was not Allerton. This was Max's home. I was in uncharted territory, and I had little idea how to navigate it. How would I wield authority and earn respect without overstepping invisible boundaries?

"I'll see you later, then," I said. Max responded with a half turn of his shoulders and a nod.

Descending the stairs, I wondered at Max's behavior. Was he being intentionally provocative? I knew how to deal with that. Having an attitude was normal for boys his age. But Max's vacillation between open friendliness and cold rudeness concerned me. However, neither Sarah nor Ezra Willoughby had said or suggested that Max suffered from any emotional or psychological disorder. I put his behavior down to the effects of loneliness and grief upon an adolescent psyche. Still, I wished that I'd had more time to speak with Sarah professionally about Max.

"You know how I dislike talking about anything important over the phone," Sarah had said, stating what was obvious to me or anyone who knew her even casually. Sarah disliked talking on the phone. Period.

"Important? Is there something particular I should know about Max—or his father—before I sign on the dotted line?"

"Well… No, of course not, Neil. I wouldn't have suggested you take the job if that were the case. I mean, Max isn't the anti-Christ or anything. And, as I said in my letter, Ezra Willoughby is a decent man, and he does try. It's just… When I see you, we'll talk, okay?"

The uncharacteristic hesitancy in Sarah's voice had set off alarm bells, but I was so eager for a new start that I was deaf to their clamor. "All right. I'll see you in a few weeks. And tell Victor I expect him to welcome me with his fabulous Bolognese."

"I will."

But there was to be no talk, no pasta. I met Victor briefly after Sarah's funeral and then flew back to California to hastily arrange my departure and begin the next stage in my life.

*

THE BARONIAL STYLE of the dining room suited Ezra Willoughby. Seated at the head of an enormous mahogany table, which could comfortably accommodate sixteen people, Willoughby looked every inch the dominus of Jessamine Grove. His beautifully tailored, charcoal gray suit, pale pink tie with its crisp oriental knot, and snow-white shirt were the perfect complements to his naturally sun-tanned skin. His face was clean-shaven but sported a heavy five o'clock shadow, intimating that his silver, Caesar-cut hair had once been black as pitch. His eyes, like my own, were blue but watery rather than bright. In contrast to my typically Germanic broad-nosed and round-chinned face, Ezra Willoughby's was a strong-boned, horsey visage that reflected his English and Iberian blood lines. It was an interesting face that reminded me in some way of Max. Like Max, I suspected that in his youth Ezra Willoughby may have had something of his adopted son's prettiness. Many times, during my years at Allerton, I witnessed the transformation from boyish beauty to manly distinctiveness. I was certain I was looking at the result of such a transformation.

I was also staring.

"Is something wrong, Boehm?" asked Ezra Willoughby, snapping me out of my physiognomic ruminations.

"No, sir. I'm sorry. I was thinking that you remind me of your son in some ways."

Willoughby laughed goodhumoredly. "I've heard that many times. And I take it as a compliment. He's a good-looking boy. Unfortunately, it's done him more harm than good, so far. Went through the same thing myself when I was Max's age—bullying, name calling, ostracization from the "in crowd." But he's a tough kid. He'll pull through. Just like I did."

"I don't doubt it," I said, not as certain as I claimed to be. "He definitely has a strong personality," I added, intentionally vague. Willoughby smiled, and I understood that he also took this as a compliment.

"The apple doesn't fall far from the tree, eh?" said Willoughby. "Max's mother was a force of nature, and I've always held my own and then some. We tried to raise our son to value the principles of hard work and discipline. Most kids today are more interested in wasting time on the internet—social media and all that garbage—as if a person's value is based on how many followers he has. It's a mad world we live in, Boehm."

Having previously met Ezra Willoughby only via pseudo-scripted video conferences, I decided at that moment that I liked him. He was a straight shooter, and I admired people who spoke their mind. That he was also handsome and charismatic only added to my appreciation of the man. However, I had not been so wooed that I could resist a mild riposte to his comments.

"Mr. Willoughby, I believe that *empathy* is the bedrock of the successful education of young people—empathy combined with expectations that are high but not unattainable and discipline that is consistent and not unreasonable. Discipline alone doesn't shape a maturing mind. And hard work is only fruitful if one is working toward a goal that is within the scope of one's intellect. Work for the sake of work is either a waste of time or an unfortunate necessity. I hope that you agree neither scenario should apply in your son's case."

Though I appeared calm as I reached for my wine, my heart was hammering under my ribs. Had I overstepped?

"And what's your opinion of social media?" asked Ezra Willoughby mildly, as he topped up my glass.

He appreciates honesty. Go for it.

"I must admit I'm of a dual mind on that subject, Mr. Willoughby. I have no personal use for what you call garbage, yet I am open-minded enough to appreciate the potential efficacy of social media platforms in certain circumstances and the inevitability of their existence in the lives of young people. Like the old saying goes, you can't keep them down on the farm once they've seen Par-ee."

"And what if they never see Par-ee?"

"I don't consider that an option. Keeping a young person completely cut off from the grid would do more harm than good. At the same time, parents and educators have a responsibility to serve and protect. From what I've observed of Max thus far, I would say that you and the late Mrs. Willoughby have done an excellent job of both."

Willoughby considered this for a moment, swirling his Shiraz. "Thank you. Your predecessor wasn't quite so...*fulsome* in her praise of our parenting skills."

"Well," I replied, "I did say 'thus far.'"

Willoughby chuckled, and I was relieved that he seemed to appreciate sarcastic humor and subtlety. If Sarah had one fault, it was a lack of self-censoring. I imagined that Willoughby might have found the quality refreshing.

"I'm glad I decided to take you on," said Willoughby. "Ms. Lewis must have mentioned to you that it was initially my intention to send Max to a boarding school in France?" I nodded. "*L'institut Belliveau.* You've heard of it, I'm sure."

Dear God, yes.

Though it sounded more like a psychiatric hospital than an exclusive boy's school, Belliveau counted princes, world leaders and captains of industry among its alumni. It was also one of the few schools in France to openly condone corporal punishment and although the stories of its hazing rituals were apocryphal, they were nevertheless disturbing.

"Belliveau has quite a reputation," I said, noncommittally. "But, as we discussed in our virtual meetings, I think home schooling is the right choice for Max at this juncture, and I am honored to have been chosen as his mentor."

Willoughby inclined his head, and I took the gesture for approval, feeling the weight of responsibility upon me anew.

"I will do my utmost for your son, Mr. Willoughby."

"I believe you will."

Rodrigo, the distinguished gentleman who'd served our appetizer and main course—and whom I learned was the father of Rosanie—served dessert. Although I disliked flan and almost all eggy confections, having lived for a time in Spain, I could appreciate that it was perfectly executed, and I managed to clean my plate and give my praise to the chef.

"After dinner drink, Boehm?" asked Willoughby as we finished our coffee. He suggested an aged rum, which proved to be delicious.

"Excellent, sir. Thank you."

"Glad you appreciate it."

We savored the rich liquor silently before I said, "Mr. Willoughby, your taste in rum is equaled by your taste in antique musical instruments. The piano on the second-floor landing is spectacular."

Willoughby's hitherto jovial expression hardened for a moment before he managed to restore a shadow of its former good humor. "A lucky find, I thought," he said, more to himself than to me. "But a bad investment in the end."

"How so?"

Willoughby finished his rum with a quaff and refilled his glass. He added more to mine without asking if I wanted it.

"I keep it as a reminder," Willoughby said.

"I see." I did not, but Willoughby was clearly unwilling to expand on the topic. "Since I've brought up the subject of music," I continued after a sip of rum, "I'd like to propose adding music appreciation and music theory to Max's curriculum. I thought—"

"No."

"Sir?"

"I said no. No music. Maximillian has no musical talent, and he wastes enough time drawing, taking pictures, and playing chess."

"Sir, if I could only—"

"I said *no*. End of discussion."

I'd been well and truly put in my place. I felt a rush of indignation but stifled it. I was no longer a headmaster. Ezra Willoughby was my employer, and I was handsomely compensated for my loyalty.

"Of course. As you wish."

An uncomfortable silence dragged on.

"I'm sorry," Willoughby said at length. "I was rude. You're a profes-sional, and I respect you. It's just…I…" Willoughby ran a hand over his smooth hair, then swiped it across his cheek and neck. He took a deep breath. "Just no music. Understood, Boehm?"

"Of course." What else could I say? Clearly, some unexplained aversion lay behind Willoughby's unusual stricture, but I was in no position to press for reasons. Perhaps, in time, he would offer an explanation by his own volition—though I doubted it. I had taken his dinner invitation as a good omen as to how our relationship might proceed. Yet, by the end of the meal we were still on formal terms. I left Mr. Willoughby feeling secure in my employment, but uncertain as to my position in the household.

Like the governesses of bygone years and the au pairs and nannies of the contemporary world, did a live-in private tutor exist in a state of limbo between employee and pseudo-family member? I had no point of reference. Sarah had never discussed this topic with me directly, but she often referred to the Willoughbys as Ezra and Fabiola, suggesting some degree of intimacy. Nonetheless, I suspected that to Ezra Willoughby I might always be "Boehm".

Would the invitation to dine at the family table be renewed? Or was I expected to have meals alone in my room or communally with the rest of the help? Perhaps the late Mrs. Willoughby had seen to these details. And, of course, Sarah had been a woman. There should have been no "of course" to it. However, in the minds of many, mine was a woman's job. I was an oddity in a job widely considered an anachronism.

Chapter Two

I PASSED MY first night at Jessamine Grove alternating between sleep crowded with weird dreams and semi-wakeful periods during which I worried over my uncharacteristically cavalier decision to accept my new job. I had acted in response to pressing boredom and from feelings of responsibility, fulfilling what had turned out to be Sarah's dying wish. I owed it to her spirit to do my best.

Sarah's spirit. I felt the press of it. Her presence.

Neil, you need to sleep. You're hallucinating.

No, I did feel her with me. This had been her room for almost a year. Something clung to the atmosphere. Rosanie had felt it; so had Max. The lingering presence of one recently departed.

Willoughby may have thought it was kind to assign me the room of my deceased friend, but as I lay staring at the ceiling, shedding silent tears, I questioned his choice. It was a classic two-edged sword. Knowing Sarah had occupied this room, slept in this bed, afforded a degree of comfort, of connection. Yet, that same sensation of connection made it more difficult for me to anchor myself, establish my own imprint. I felt like an interloper in the Willoughby home, in Max's life.

Give yourself a break. You've been here less than twenty-four hours.

True. I was letting panic set in. That would not do. I plumped my pillows and determined to finish the novel I'd started. It had served as a sleep-inducer on my ride from the airport to the Grove. Perhaps it would work its magic again. I cracked open the book, but my attention was drawn not to the words on the page, but to the fireplace mantel in the sitting room which was just in my line of sight through the open bedroom door.

"Sarah had a clock there."

Max's words had stirred bittersweet memories, and I revisited them as I conjured the clock there on the mantel and I recalled an autumn afternoon in 1996.

*

"DON'T YOU FEEL like a thief?" I had demanded of Sarah, as we walked away from the flea market on twenty-sixth Street. I had just disclosed to her my appraisal of the value of the clock she'd purchased.

"Me? Why should I?"

"That guy has no idea what he just lost."

"And your heart goes out to him? Imagine how many people he's screwed over the years." She lifted the paper bag containing the ormolu clock. "This, mister, is payback."

"I see. So, you're going to resell the clock and distribute your winnings to the poor?"

"Like hell."

"Okay. Then you're buying lunch." I suggested a small, charming, and exorbitantly expensive bistro on Eighth Avenue just off twenty-first Street.

"You're buying the cocktails," countered Sarah in a mock-sour tone.

We strolled along Sixth Avenue in silence for a while, content in each other's company. As we turned west on twenty-first, Sarah exclaimed, "I haven't been down this street in years."

"What's so special about it?"

"The cemetery." Sarah pointed to the opposite side of the street where a wrought iron gate enclosed a rather run-down looking burial ground wedged between two buildings. Sarah crossed the street and I followed, reading the plaque at the top of the gate as I did so.

THE THIRD CEMETARY

OF THE

SPANISH AND PORTUGUESE SYNAGOGUE

SHEARITH ISREAL

IN THE CITY OF NEW YORK

1829-1851

"My grandmother brought me here for the first time when I was a little girl," said Sarah, grabbing hold of the iron bars and peering in as if she were a child again. "She wanted me to know my family's history."

"Your family?" Sarah was an Episcopalian of English and African-American descent. Or so I had believed.

"Well, some of them. My grandmother explained to me that her ancestors were Black Portuguese Jews from Brazil who came to New York in the early seventeenth century. She thought some of their descendants might be buried here. She'd learned the story from her father, but the family converted to Christianity so long ago, that it was more legend than fact. Unfortunately, we have no written records. I've always wished I could know more about them."

I stared through the gate at the sad-looking remains of tombstones and thought of my own family history. "Be careful what you wish for." I didn't realize I'd said the words aloud until I turned to see Sarah regarding me with a baffled look.

"What do you mean?" Sarah asked. "Aren't you curious about your ancestors?"

"No."

Sarah laughed, taking my tone as deadpan sarcasm. "Why? Afraid you might find a slave trader or two in the Boehm family closet? I'll bet I've got some on my father's side. Come on, Neil, it's normal. All families have skeletons." Sarah looked at me askance, then added in a stage whisper, "Unless your great grandfather was Jack the Ripper."

"Please don't joke, Sarah," I said, turning away from my contemplation of the cemetery and looking at my friend. "It's not funny. Not in my case, at least."

"I'm sorry."

How could I possibly explain to Sarah how this happenstance of walking past the cemetery and Sarah's revelation of her ancestry had affected me so deeply—and why. Now was not the time, and I doubted the time would ever come. A wall had come between us, visible only to me.

"Vampires," I said, attempting an impression of Bela Lugosi. "I come from a family of the undead."

Sarah laughed and slapped my shoulder. "Damn it, Neil, you had me there for a moment. I was ready to believe your great grandfather really was a serial killer. Do not do that to me again."

"I promise."

"Good. Let's go. Martinis are calling."

Sarah would never know how close she had been to the truth.

*

I GRUNTED WITH frustration and sat up, pushing aside the duvet. I shivered and regretted declining Rosanie's bedtime offer of a fire in the small hearth.

A fire in Florida?

Big mistake. For all its surface glamour, the Grove was nearly a hundred years old and had obviously not been completely updated to twenty-first century standards.

I grabbed my robe from the foot of the bed, deciding that I might as well work if I could not sleep. I parked myself at the desk, opened my laptop, and began to review Max's curriculum for the coming week. I had arrived at Wednesday when my eyelids began to droop.

Great. I can't sleep in the damned bed, but ten minutes at the computer and I'm snoring.

Slapping the machine closed, I lay my head upon its surface. My two-thousand-dollar black pillow.

I was halfway to dreamland when I heard the music. At first, I thought I *was* dreaming, so incongruous was it to hear *"Mon coeur s'ouvre à ta voix"* being played on a piano at four thirty in the morning. For a few moments, I simply lay there, letting the beautiful melody wash over me.

Then I sat up, walked to my bedroom door, and pressed an ear to the wood—just to convince myself I was *not* dreaming. The music from Sain-Saens's *Samson et Delila* seemed quite real.

Barefoot and still a bit fuzzy in my head, I opened the door and followed the sound of the music. I needed no guide, as I believed there could only be one source. As I made my way in the darkness, the chill air cleared the cobwebs from my brain, and I asked myself what the hell I was doing. If someone in the Willoughby household chose to play piano in the wee hours of the morning, what concern was it of mine?

I was halfway up the central staircase when I tripped on the trailing belt of my robe; defensive reflexes saving me from a concussion. Or worse.

"Shit!" I hissed as I righted myself, rubbing the part of my left arm where I knew a bruise would bloom later that day. By the time I tied the sash and resumed my ascent, the music had stopped. I gained the landing and beheld the piano.

There was no one there. Not a figure or a shadow of one in either wing of the hallway. The house was silent except for the tick-tock of the grandfather clock in the foyer below.

You're losing it, Neil.

I approached the antique instrument. The bench was aligned perfectly, the music rack was empty.

A part of me felt the urge to sit down and play—to spite the phantom pianist. But good sense held sway. I padded silently along to the entrance to Max's domain and looked up through the spiral of iron. No light shown through the darkness from behind the barn door.

Why had I immediately thought of Max?

Do you play?

I'm not allowed.

I realized my question and Max's response had been in my mind from the moment I had first heard the music. I'd expected to find him there, head of messy curls bent over the keys.

Why?

Max has no musical talent.

No music. Understood, Boehm?

So, who was the phantom pianist?

Phantom pianist.

Could I have imagined it? Had the aria been part of a dream? Was I still dreaming?

Maybe.

Just try to get some sleep and forget about it.

*

"IT'S NOT MUMBO jumbo," said Rosanie, with an edge to her voice. "It's *cartomancia*. People have used the cards for divination since ancient times."

I watched as Rosanie shuffled her tarot deck with the skill of an expert while a statuesque, severe-looking woman—whom I assumed was Mrs. Hanson—looked on with a sour expression on her face.

"Actually," I said, startling both women with my otherwise silent entrance to the kitchen, "The use of tarot cards for the purpose of divination dates only to the eighteenth century, while the use of the cards as a game can be traced to fourteenth century Egypt."

Mrs. Hanson laughed and cast a haughty glance at her junior.

"You, see?" she said, folding the towel she held and placing it neatly on the marble countertop. "Complete nonsense."

Mrs. Hanson approached me with a smile and an outstretched hand. "Nessa Hanson. Pleased to meet you, Mr. Boehm."

"Thank you. The pleasure is mine."

Unlike the gorgon I'd envisioned from Max's "Hideous Hanson" moniker, Nessa Hanson—notwithstanding the scar that ran the length of her left cheek—was a very attractive woman of middle age with warm olive skin, eyes of deep ebony, and steel gray hair styled in a masculine crew cut. Her utilitarian gray-and-white uniform failed to hide her well-proportioned figure.

"Waffles suit you?" asked Mrs. Hanson as she waved me to a place at the large island.

"Yes, thank you."

The aroma of hot, buttered waffles and fresh coffee was intoxicating.

Mrs. Hanson's timing and her knowledge of my favorite breakfast food was uncanny, and I told her so as she put a steaming plate before me and filled a mug with black coffee.

Nessa Hanson laughed and tapped my shoulder.

"I didn't need to consult Rosanie's cards, Mr. Boehm," she said. "Sarah talked about you all the time—about your lives at Allerton Academy. So, I know you love waffles and take your coffee black. As to the timing, well, the Young Master's lessons have always started at ten, so it was just a matter of keeping the iron at the ready."

The waffles and the coffee were excellent, and I accepted extra servings of both.

"I like a person with a healthy appetite," said Mrs. Hanson as she collected my clean plate. "The late Mr. Hanson only ate raw vegetables and look where that got him."

"I'm sorry," I replied out of habit rather than understanding.

"No need to be. He was also a first-class bastard."

"Don't get her started," murmured Rosanie over her coffee mug.

"I heard that, Ro."

I smiled at the easy camaraderie, then asked, "How long have you worked at the Grove?" I looked to Rosanie and then to Mrs. Hanson. The latter answered for both.

"I'm here eleven years in June. Rosanie was born here."

"Not quite," corrected Rosanie. "My parents were with Mrs. Willoughby before her marriage to Mr. Willoughby. My dad and I moved here around the same time as Mrs. Hanson. I sort of grew up into this job."

I was interested to know more about the late Mr. Hanson and what had become of Rosanie's mother, but did not wish to puncture the bubble of kindness and potential friendship I found myself in.

"Would you like a reading, Mr. Boehm?" asked Rosanie as she spread the cards.

"Ro!"

"It's all right, Mrs. Hanson. I'm sure Rosanie will tell me that I'm about to embark upon a new chapter in my life, I'll soon meet a dark handsome man, and my future is undecided."

Rosanie studied the cards before her, then looked up at me with a smile.

"I *do* see a dark handsome man."

"Don't encourage her, Mr. Boehm," said Nessa Hanson glancing at her watch. "And you've got better things to do, Rosanie."

"Yes, ma'am."

Rosanie gathered her cards and wrapped them in a purple cloth embroidered with gold pentagrams, then rose to depart. As she passed me, she put a hand on my shoulder, leaned in close to my ear, and said, "I really *did* see a dark handsome man, and—"

"Rosanie!

With a huff and an annoyed glance at Mrs. Hanson, Rosanie stuffed her tarot deck into her tote bag and flounced out of the kitchen.

"She's a good kid," said Mrs. Hanson, "when she's not spouting superstitious nonsense."

"You don't believe in the power of the cards?"

"I believe in prayer and hard work."

I chose not to point out that there were those who considered prayer a superstition.

"I agree that the tarot deck has no power in and of itself," I said. "It was created as a card game, after all. But I do believe there are people who possess genuine psychic abilities. For them, the cards are a way of organizing—putting thoughts and impressions into an orderly construct."

Mrs. Hanson folded her dish towel over the oven door handle and turned to me with an incredulous look on her face.

"And you, a professor from a highfalutin school!"

"Highfalutin schools, at their best, encourage open minds."

Mrs. Hanson rubbed her chin and scrunched up her face as if considering. Then she smiled.

"I think I might like you, Mr. Boehm."

"The feeling is mutual, Mrs. Hanson."

As I savored my coffee, Mrs. Hanson began to put me up to speed on household routines—such as they were.

"Mr. and Mrs. Willoughby used to keep all sorts of hours," said Mrs.

Hanson. "She, with that TV show of hers and he with his art collecting and sitting on committees and whatnot. Now, Mr. Willoughby is rarely at home. It's as if he's afraid of the place. Can you blame him? Losing his wife that way? Not that they were blissfully wedded. I know I sound like a gossip, but it was common knowledge. Sometimes, I wonder why they ever—" Mrs. Hanson cut herself off with a sigh.

"Why they ever what?"

Mrs. Hanson poured herself a cup of coffee and leaned against the sink, her arms folded under her bosom. "A conversation for another day, Mr. Boehm." She looked at her watch. "It's nearly ten."

I gulped the rest of my coffee.

"Yes, ma'am," I said, parroting Rosanie.

"Nessa, to you."

"Thank you. Please, call me Neil."

Nessa nodded acceptance, took a sip of her coffee, and said, *"In bocca al lupo."*

Momentarily thrown by Nessa's use of the old Italian idiom for "good luck," it took a few beats before I replied, *"Grazie,"* and took my leave.

Italian was not in my planed curriculum for Max, though I spoke it fluently. How had Mrs. Hanson known? Sarah must have mentioned my love of the language along with my coffee and breakfast preferences. That made sense. But as I embarked on my first day of work at the Grove, I could not shake the feeling that Nessa Hanson's words were more a warning than an expression of well wishes.

*

SINCE THE WILLOUGHBY household lacked structure, I imposed my own. Beginning on the second day of my tenure, I rescheduled the start of Max's school day to 8:30 a.m. There would be a fifteen-minute break beginning at 10:30 a.m., one half-hour break for lunch (served in the kitchen) at noon, then dismissal at 3:00 p.m. Although Max made the expected faces and noises when I laid out my plan, he admitted to being an early riser and appreciated the advantage of more free time in the afternoon. I met no opposition from Mr. Willoughby when I requisitioned the library as a dedicated schoolroom.

"Why not?" said Willoughby, "There's nothing in there but old books."

So, the new routine was adopted and ran smoothly for the first few weeks.

Max proved to be exceptionally intelligent and eager to learn. He picked up Latin with surprising ease, his English grammar was excellent, and he took a genuine interest in geography and physical science. By the end of the third week, I allowed myself to savor a degree of satisfaction in the progress of my pupil.

Then came the day when Max threw the book at me.

Literally.

I had been warned, so I should not have been completely surprised when Max hurled his copy of *The Epic of Gilgamesh* across the library toward my desk, declaring it boring and pointless. The fact that the epic had been the subject of my doctoral thesis made his actions that much more galling. And perhaps I had misjudged his level of intellectual maturity.

As I retrieved the book and moved toward Max's desk, I noted the classic butter-wouldn't-melt-in-his-mouth look on his face and an alternative occurred to me. One I did not care for at all. It dawned on me with certainty that Max had chosen to dismiss this work precisely because of its personal significance to me.

"I must congratulate you on the thoroughness of your research into my life," I said. "I shudder to think what other information you have in my dossier."

Max held my gaze for a second, then looked away.

Bingo!

I slapped the paperback down on Max's desk with as much force as I could muster.

Max flinched.

Good.

"You may act the petulant child as much as you like, but you are an intelligent young man, and I shall continue to treat you as such. You will complete your first reading of The Epic today. Tomorrow, we will begin our analysis of the work's principal themes."

With that, I left Max alone to study and stew.

I had been at the Grove for almost a month, yet I felt I had made little headway in my understanding of the Willoughby family dynamic— both past and present. Father and son appeared to live separate lives. Had it always been so? I considered the animosity Sarah had felt toward Mrs. Willoughby, and Sarah's vague confessions to me about something not quite right in the household. Sarah had been a romantic at heart, and I had to wonder if perhaps she had been influenced by Ezra Willoughby's charm, the atmosphere of the Grove and what I had come to learn had been a less than happy relationship between Mr. and Mrs. Willoughby. Hadn't I also experienced the gravitational force of Ezra Willoughby's sex appeal? Could that force have affected Sarah's decision to leave?

Putting aside my musings on what may or may not have transpired in the recent past, I reminded myself that it was Max who mattered in the here and now. Despite his tantrums and mood swings, Max Willoughby was beginning to grow on me. And I felt the pull of being necessary—needed—though I had yet to understand exactly what form it was that that necessity would take beyond my function as a teacher and mentor.

Chapter Three

WHOEVER DUBBED FLORIDA "the Sunshine State" had clearly never been to Saint Augustine in winter. I shivered slightly as the sudden cloud cover darkened the foliage to a sinister gray-green and a chill wind whipped across my bare neck. Disoriented by the abrupt extinguishing of light, I found myself stumbling through the thick vegetation, relying on the algal stench of the lake to guide my return to the waterfront path from which I'd strayed. I gazed across the shore and was surprised to find that I had come farther than I realized, the roofline of the Grove just visible over the tops of the trees. I looked out over the tranquil water, standing close to where Sarah had stood in the last moments of her life. Although I'd moved beyond the denial stage of my grief, I still found it hard to accept that Sarah had died so suddenly.

"I guess you've discovered why it's called Snake Lake."

I started at the sound of the deep voice coming from behind me, interrupting my thoughts.

"It's public land, this side of the lake," the stranger continued. "The way the lake twists and turns, it can be hard to tell exactly which side is which. Especially since the owners chose not to mar the landscape with fences, satisfying themselves with dainty little private property signs staked here and there."

The man who owned the voice was well over six feet tall and thickset. Not fat. What they used to call husky. My age, maybe younger. Latino, I guessed, with longish, gray-streaked, black hair and a face with features that taken individually might have been considered ugly, but in composite were strikingly handsome. He wore snug, faded jeans, a white oxford shirt, and a faun-colored linen blazer.

"Thanks for the lesson in local topography."

"*De nada*," he said.

He advanced toward me and extended his hand.

"Dean Chaves."

"Neil Boehm," I said, accepting his firm, warm grip.

"I know. The new nanny."

"Tutor. And who are you, Mr. Chaves? The local psychic?"

"No," Chaves replied. "My *abuela* had the gift though. Maybe some of it was passed down. But me, I prefer to rely on the facts and leave intuition for those times when the facts are few and far between."

Chaves turned his gaze from me to the lake.

"Did you know her well?" he asked.

"I beg your pardon?"

"Sarah Lewis. Your late colleague. She used to walk here too."

There was an air of authority about Chaves. When the wind caused his jacket to flap open and reveal the gun holstered beneath it, the pieces fell into place.

"You're one of Mr. Willoughby's security guards."

"Might have been a better career choice, pay wise," he said, reaching into his breast pocket and removing what resembled a passport case, then opening it for my inspection. "I'm a private dick."

I let out a snort as I looked from the ID to Chaves's face.

"You love to say that don't you?"

"It works as an icebreaker."

"What's to detect?" I asked, looking down at the slight slope of the shoreline. "Sarah died from a stroke."

"Please accept my sympathy for your loss," said Chaves. "But it's not Ms. Lewis's death that keeps bringing me back to this place. It's the death of her employer, Fabiola Willoughby."

*

AS I RAISED my glass of pinot grigio to my lips, I tried to recall the last time I had dined in a cozy restaurant with a man I'd just met. I could not. Hell, I could not recall the last time I had dined in a cozy restaurant with *any* man. I'd lived under a rock at Allerton but hadn't been so painfully aware of that circumstance until now.

In the defused light of La Cocina on Aviles Street in old Saint Augustine, Dean Chaves looked younger and even more attractive than I had judged him at our earlier meeting at Snake Lake. I prayed that the soft illumination of the restaurant flattered me equally.

"Nice place," I said sincerely, taking in the low-ceilinged, timber-beamed dining room with its whitewashed walls and pitted, plank flooring.

"It's the best Colombian restaurant north of Dade County," said Chaves. "And one of the few intact structures in town dating back to the original Spanish colony. So much of this place is fake, it's amazing that it manages to avoid looking like 'Conquistador Land' at a theme park."

"Just barely," I allowed, then kicked myself, not having considered that Chaves might have been a native.

Chaves smiled over his beer.

"Seriously," he said. "I mean, it's great that they try to preserve the history, but it's sad that so much of it is reconstruction."

I pondered this for a moment, taking another sip of wine.

"I don't know," I said eventually. "Wouldn't it be amazing to see the Roman Forum reconstructed? Or Pompei, or the Coliseum?"

"Maybe," conceded Chaves. "In some sort of virtual reality 'holodeck' kind of thing. But brick and mortar? That would be an insult to history. Take the Coliseum. The fact that it still stands—even in partial ruins—is a testament to its importance, its significance. It's a magnificent symbol of the lasting cultural influence of the Roman Empire."

Chaves made a good point.

"Are you from around here?" I asked.

"No," Chaves replied. "Born and raised in Oregon. I worked as a cop there for a few years, then in Miami. Eventually, I ended up in Saint Augustine. My folks were still around then, living here. I wanted to be close to them again before…well…you know." I nodded understanding. "After they passed, I retired from the force and went into the private sector."

"What about the late Mrs. Willoughby? Why is it that you wander the grounds of the Grove, wondering about her death?"

"I wonder as I wander?" asked Chaves. "Thanks for sticking that awful Christmas song in my head. It was Ms. Lewis who started me wondering. A semi-long story. How about we eat first?"

It was a good suggestion. The empanadas and patacones smelled delicious and their taste followed through on the promise of their aroma. We munched in silence for a while. When I paused to sip my wine and lay my knife and fork neatly on my empty plate, Chaves laughed and said, "Do you eat fries with a knife and fork too?"

My fastidious habit was one I'd been ribbed about for most of my life. I answered Chaves honestly. "No. Just a fork."

Chaves shook his head, and I was certain he thought I was being sarcastic. He then proceeded to suck a bit of stray chimichurri from his middle finger, as if to prove his unspoken point that some things were meant to be eaten with one's hands.

The waiter returned with our entrees. When we had worked through our shared dishes and relaxed, sipping our aguardiente-laced coffee, Chaves held forth.

"It was about three months ago that Ms. Lewis first contacted me. She said she'd chosen me not by reputation but by opening the yellow pages to private detectives, closing her eyes, and poking her finger blindly at the listings. My name was the closest to the tip of her nail when she opened her eyes, so she chose me."

I smiled. The method of selection suited Sarah.

"Anyway," continued Chaves, "Ms. Lewis told me she believed that she was being followed. Stalked. Oftentimes, this sort of case turns out to be nothing but the result of a vivid imagination and a persecution complex. Ms. Lewis, however, was straightforward and genuine. Whatever was going on, I was sure she wasn't imagining it. My hackles went up, as the saying goes, but when she told me about her living situation and the names of her employers, I was relieved—even if it meant a loss of income.

"I explained to Ms. Lewis that people like the Willoughbys were understandably concerned about security—might even be a bit overzealous. Truth is, security at the Grove is on the lax side. Anyway, I said I would not have been surprised if the Willoughbys had all their employees under surveillance. She was shocked by this and went into a mild rant about it being a breach of professional trust."

I nodded understanding. I had felt the same sense of intrusion and distrust when I'd mistaken Chaves for a member of Willoughby's security detail. Sarah had been a naturally trusting person and had expected the same of others. To have been continually watched, spied upon, would have been galling to her sensibilities.

"I thought that was the end of it," said Chaves softly.

I examined Chaves's rugged face as best I could through the shadows of the mood lighting. Was that anxiety or deep thought that accentuated the fine lines at the corner of his eyes? Chaves satisfied my curiosity quickly enough.

"I *wanted* it to be the end. But there was *something*. Something about Ms. Lewis's conviction, her feeling of wrongness. It rubbed off on me, I suppose. Stuck with me. She told me she was worried about the kid—Max. If it had anything to do with the stalking or with Mrs. Willoughby's death, I don't know. Maybe I never will. But, like I said, there was something about Ms. Lewis's suspicions, feelings… She had a magnetic personality, you know?"

I nodded. "You asked me earlier if Sarah and I were close. The answer is yes. Sometimes I felt as if we were siblings."

There were some things I could never bring myself to share with Sarah. Since her death, I'd come to regret my reticence—believing that I had been unfair in our exchanges of personal information. I'd never quite met her halfway in trust.

"How about we get out of here," said Chaves, signaling the waiter for our check. "Go for a walk, maybe? Looks like the sun's finally coming out."

"Sounds like a plan."

*

WE ENDED UP on the green between Cathedral Place and King Street, eating ice cream and taking in the view of the Bridge of Lions and the play of winter light on the Matanzas River.

"Of course," said Chaves, taking a break from his childlike consumption of his frozen treat, "you do realize that this was a test."

"A test?"

Chaves looked pointedly at my cup of ice cream and spoon, then shifted his gaze to his half-consumed waffle cone.

"I thought I could catch you out with your utensil fetish. I was itching to see you try and politely wriggle out of my suggestion of ice cream once you realized you'd have to use your hands. Forgot they did cups."

"It's not a fetish," I replied coolly. "It's called fastidiousness. By the way, your desire to see me wriggle could easily be defined as sadism."

Chaves smirked and looked away toward the river. I followed his gaze, and we sat in silence for several minutes.

"So," I said, finally. "Sarah and Max. The Grove. Mrs. Willoughby. How does it all fit together? What do you think Sarah was trying to tell you?"

Chaves was slow in answering, and when he did, it was with a question.

"Have you been to Castillo de San Marcos?"

"Not yet."

"Good. Then I'll take you on your next day off. It's impressive, even if you're not into military history. It has four bastions. The chief use of these structures was to house cannons. But they could also be used as conning stations because of their strategic locations."

Chaves polished off his cone before continuing.

"The Willoughby estate—compound is probably a better word—is like a fort," said Chaves. "Or a medieval demesne with a protective moat."

"Snake Lake?"

"Yes. Before Ponce de Leon Shores developed around it, Willoughby Grove was entirely isolated. A private fantasy land for the eccentric industrialist who built it."

I resisted the urge to push Chaves to get to the point. Already, it was clear to me that Chaves was the type who preferred the circuitous route over the direct. Plus, I liked the sound of his voice.

"A fort's obvious function is to protect," continued Chaves, "but a fort can also be a prison. Jessamine Grove has bastions and turrets. Tower rooms. Locks and keys. Granted, they were designed for effect rather than function, but imagine the impact such an environment could have upon a young and precocious mind. A child often left alone and isolated..."

"I'm not immune to the atmosphere of the Grove," I said, "but I haven't observed any direct negative effect on Max. On the contrary, he seems to thoroughly enjoy living there. Which is totally understandable.

Many kids his age would envy him his situation. He's at the age when fantasy worlds are still an important part of the development of intellect, of personality."

I stopped myself from venturing into discourse on childhood development. Nor did I reveal to Chaves the feeling of empathy that had so quickly developed in me toward Max. Just as Sarah knew it would. I needn't have bothered holding back. Chaves's response made it clear that my bland words had conveyed my feelings.

"You care about the kid."

"That's my job."

Chaves shook his head and smiled a half smile.

"No," said Chaves, "that's your choice. Many teachers just teach. And many nannies just—whatever the word is. For you, I think, it's a vocation. Just as it was for Ms. Lewis."

What could I say? What do you say when a stranger reads you so well?

"When I made the fort/prison analogy," said Chaves after a few moments of silence, "I didn't mean it in a negative way. I agree with you. For some kids, living in a place like the Grove could be like living in some fictional school for wizards. Could be that's how it is for Max."

Chaves paused to pull a notebook and cheap ballpoint pen from the left breast pocket of his blazer. From the state of the pen's cap, I judged that Chaves had either a nervous habit or a house pet with a taste for plastic.

"Has Max told you about a room he calls the crow's nest?

Watching Chaves with his open pad and pen poised to record my answer served as a reminder that I was not on a date. To Chaves, I was a source of information. Perhaps even a possible suspect in some yet undefined crime.

"No, he hasn't" I replied. "But Sarah mentioned it."

"Hm," was Chaves's response as he scribbled something in his notebook. "Shouldn't be surprised. Ms. Lewis told me it was a couple of months before she was admitted into Max's inner sanctum."

Sarah told me that Max's room had been converted from a book storage space shortly after Sarah's arrival, when she had commented that it would make a fantastic master suite. Sarah's innocent observation had been readily latched onto by Max and he had presented his parents with the scheme straightaway.

"According to Sarah," I said, "Mr. Willoughby thought it was a great idea. Mrs. Willoughby thought it was a waste of money and inappropriately secluded for a child of Max's age. Mrs. Willoughby put the blame squarely on Sarah for suggesting the idea, though she deferred to her husband's decision to proceed with the project. It was the flashpoint for what would be a somewhat adversarial relationship between Sarah and Mrs. Willoughby."

Chaves pulled an ugly face and raked his right hand through his hair.

"I hate to speak ill of the dead, but people like Fabiola Willoughby have no business raising children."

"How did we get here?" I asked. "You were talking about forts and prisons, not parenting styles."

Chaves harrumphed and flashed a smile that dispelled my unease.

"Sorry," said Chaves. "It's just that in my line of work you see so many cases like this. Kids neglected by parents totally unequipped to take on the responsibility of parenting."

While I agreed with Chaves's sentiment, neither of us had known Fabiola Willoughby, and could hardly pass judgement. His opinions, like mine, had been formed by tabloid and television gossip and the common assumptions people make about wealthy, career-oriented parents.

Chaves was staring out at the river again, his face unreadable and his posture stiff.

"Can we get back to the fortress theme?" I asked.

"Sure," said Chaves, turning his head and shoulders toward me. "The crow's nest. According to Ms. Lewis, it was part of the original structure of the attic dormer—used as a hidey hole in years gone by. It was Max's idea to turn it into a sort of mini man cave. His little sanctuary. From what Sarah told me, it's barely large enough for a twin-sized futon and Max's telescope."

I smiled as I thought of Max studying the night sky and imagining himself a castaway on some mysterious island.

"Ms. Lewis said it was their secret. She felt he was old enough to need a special private space and what he did with it was his own business. Somehow, though, I think Ms. Lewis's ideas of what Max might do in his hideaway were a bit more prosaic than Max's."

"Not a man cave, then?"

"No," said Chaves. "A conning station."

*

SO IT WAS that Maximillian Willoughby had covertly observed the comings and goings and other activities of his parents and the members of the household staff.

"I think I need to have a discussion with Max about spying," I said.

"Not so fast," countered Chaves.

He turned to face me fully and moved closer, his left knee pressing against my thigh. Chaves's natural, musky scent was heady, and I wished that we were just sitting together enjoying a lovely afternoon—not talking about adolescent angst, toxic parents, and sudden, violent death.

"I told you that Ms. Lewis believed she was being stalked," said Chaves. "Well, it turns out she was."

"You mean Max."

Chaves smiled as he shook his head. "Not exactly. Max was watching the stalker. Sarah told me that he loved to watch sunsets and that the crow's nest was the best vantage point. And with his telescope, he could observe the subtle changes in colors."

I nodded understanding.

"It was at the same time of day that Ms. Lewis liked to take a stroll around the grounds and the lake, and Max almost always caught sight of her solitary figure. Only, for several weeks before the death of Mrs. Willoughby, her stroll was *not* solitary. Max didn't think much of it at first, but then he began to see a pattern of behavior he thought was weird. He became convinced that the other person was intentionally keeping her presence unknown from Ms. Lewis. 'Creeping' and 'sneaking' were the words Max used to describe her actions."

"*Her* actions?" I asked.

"Yes. Fabiola Willoughby."

I almost laughed. The image I conjured of Mrs. Willoughby creeping and sneaking, dressed in some sort of designer camo outfit was ridiculous.

"Why?"

"I have no idea," said Chaves. "But that's what he told the police officer who questioned him about his mother's behavior in the days leading up to her fall. Sure, he could be lying, for whatever reason. But even if he was, you can't get around the fact that Mrs. Willoughby kicked the bucket right after the supposed stalking stopped And, who knows, that expression might prove to be close to the truth in her case."

"You think she committed suicide?" According to what I'd read, Mrs. Willoughby had accidently fallen to her death from an upper window of the Grove under the influence of alcohol.

"It's possible. Not every suicide is thoughtful enough to leave an explanatory note. And her marriage was widely known to be an unhappy one. People close to the Willoughbys said that only the kid kept them together. Or maybe it *wasn't* suicide. Maybe Mr. Willoughby didn't feel like waiting until Max goes off to college, so he gave Mrs. W. a little push to speed things up."

"Are you serious?"

"I'm speculating. But I know a detective who worked the case. Nobody was satisfied with the coroner's conclusion. Accidental death is what you call it when there's no evidence of anything else. The whole thing is odd. And I don't trust odd. Max said that the stalking stopped the day before his mother's fall. Why? And why did it begin in the first place?"

I could come up with no suggestions, but Chaves's curiosity was infectious.

"How would you go about it?" I asked. Not being legally employed in his professional capacity, I doubted Chaves had a snowball's chance in hell of discovering anything.

"Well," said Chaves, looking away from me and down at his hands folded in his lap. "That brings us to why I approached you today," he continued. "When I saw you walking the same path that Ms. Lewis walked, I began to think that maybe you could help me."

"How?" I asked, though I had an inkling.

"Keep your ears and eyes open. Report to me if–"

"*Report* to you? Damn it, Chaves, I'm a teacher not a spy."

Chaves smiled and I was reminded of Victor's laid-back, friendly personality. His dark hair, his swarthy complexion. He was about the same age as Chaves…

"Why are you looking at me like that?" Chaves asked.

"Like what?"

"Like you're *examining* me."

"Sorry. I was thinking of Sarah's fiancée, Victor. You remind me of him."

"So, he's tall, dark, and handsome?"

"He's gorgeous."

Chaves smiled, accepting the compliment for which he had so blatantly fished.

"Well," I said, standing, "I guess my next stop is Walmart."

"Walmart?"

"Of course. If I'm going to be a spy, I need a disposable, prepaid cell phone. A burner. Didn't they teach you that in private dick school?"

"If you're going to be a *good* spy, the first thing you need is for no one to know you're spying—making the mythical untraceable cell phone irrelevant. Besides, you'll be observing, not spying."

"Ah, the beauty of semantics."

"Anyway, Neil, I'd rather meet you in person," said Chaves, rising and placing his right hand on my shoulder. "Whether or not you have intel to pass on. I did promise a tour of the Castillo, remember?"

"I'd like that," I replied. "Seeing you again, I mean. Castillo or no Castillo."

We walked in silence the short distance to the tiny public parking lot near the Lightner Museum.

"I'm free on Sundays and Thursdays," I offered, as we approached our cars—Chaves's VW Beatle and my loaner SUV from the Willoughby stable. "Officially," I qualified. "Mr. Willoughby allows me a fair amount of flexibility."

Chaves smiled over the roof of the car that seemed impossibly small for his stature.

"Flexibility's a good thing," he said.

I can't honestly say I saw a glint in his eyes, but the wink he gave me was encouraging.

"I studied yoga at an ashram," I replied.

Totally true. Even if I hadn't mastered the ability to cross my legs behind my head.

Chaves laughed as he folded himself into his vehicle. "I'll file that nugget away for future reference. So, say three o'clock Sunday? I'll meet you at the Castillo."

"Done deal."

Chapter Four

"IT'S SUNNY AND eighty degrees in LA," said Max sullenly.

I glanced up from the geometry test I was pretending to grade. "How very nice for the Angelenos."

Max gave me a crooked smile. "I can see from here that you've been on page two for the last ten minutes, Prof," said Max. "It took me only four to do the equations."

I pushed the test aside and slumped over my desk, my hands cupping my chin. "Why does rain have such a negative effect on people?" I asked.

We were into the third day of rain that was forecast to continue for several more. The wind was cold and the Grove—which I'd come to realize was decrepit under its gilded veneer—felt more like the House of Usher than a billionaire's folly. With Mr. Willoughby away on a business trip to Los Angles, Mrs. Hanson enjoying her day off and Rodrigo and Rosanie visiting a relative at a nursing home, the Grove seemed to grow and we two remaining inmates to shrink.

"Not everyone," replied Max. "Sarah loved the rain. She said the colors of a rainy day are subtle and beautiful."

"Yes," I agreed, remembering Sarah saying the same to me, once upon a time. "Sarah told me that too. I replied that if she'd grown up where I did, she might have felt differently."

Max closed his laptop, then mimicked my defeated posture.

"Why did you come here?" he asked.

Max had that adolescent knack for asking direct questions apropos of nothing which caught one off guard.

My answer was honest.

"Because Sarah asked me."

"Is that why you stayed?"

The question took me aback. "You didn't expect me to?"

"I heard Rosanie say to her dad that nobody in their right mind would want to work here after what happened to Fabiola and Sarah."

"Maybe I'm not in my right mind," I replied, which made Max laugh—as I had intended.

I'd begun to accept that my teacher-student relationship with Max was unique. At the outset, I had attempted a wholesale transfer of Allerton rules and methods to my new situation, but soon realized that if I wanted to give my best for Max, I needed to learn to bend and adapt. "What say you to wrapping things up for today?"

"Prof! It's only eleven thirty!"

Max's look of shock at my proposal to break my own rules was comical.

"We have only one life to live, Maximilian. I think we can save the drudge that is mathematics for a sunny day when perhaps it will not seem quite so tedious."

Max did a double air punch. "Yes!"

Then, his expression clouded, and he slumped once more.

"What's wrong?"

"I've got nothing else to do."

Max had a point. This was his usual day for skateboard practice—one of the few opportunities he had to interact with a group of people his own age.

"What about Lionel?" I asked, referring to the quiet, Korean-American boy who appeared to be Max's only close friend. Lionel was a frequent visitor to the Grove. He and Max would hole up for hours playing chess in Max's loft. Aside from his sessions with the skateboarding gang who met somewhere in Ponce de Leon Shores, Max rarely left the house. And when he did, Rodrigo was never far behind. I found it odd that Lionel always came to him, but—as far as I knew—Max never went to Lionel's house.

"He has the flu."

Well, chess was out of the question. I could play. Just. I was no match for a preteen grand master. I tried to think of something entertaining to while away the day but drew a blank. Television was verboten at the Grove and Max's internet access was strictly limited. While I had mixed feelings about sheltering young people from reality, I had to agree with Mr. Willoughby on these strictures. There was little on television worthy of an intelligent adult and hardly anything suitable for a twelve-year-old.

I suggested recreational reading. It was something both Max and I enjoyed, and we had yet to start on the adventure of the Count of Monte Cristo. Max surprised me by declining.

"Well, what then?" I asked. "Mahjong?"

I was joking, but Max took me seriously.

"You know how to play?"

I nodded and Max considered it for a moment.

"I read about it in an Agatha Christie book," said Max. "It sounded interesting."

"It is. Do you have a set?"

"No."

"So much for that."

"I've got a better idea," Max said, getting up from his desk and ambling over to mine. "Can you keep a secret, Prof?"

A question I've often regretted answering.

"It depends on the secret."

"It's nothing bad, I promise."

"Okay."

Max turned and practically ran to the door.

"Come on," Max said impatiently, as I tidied my desk and powered off my computer. "What about having only one life to live?"

Nothing is more embarrassing than having your words thrown back at you by a smart-ass kid. I laughed and gave in to Max's youthful enthusiasm.

"Right behind you."

I followed Max to the foyer where he retrieved a flashlight from a long rococo table surmounted by an enormous mirror. The mirror was quite old, and while its gold frame was in pristine condition, the glass itself had a grayish hue and produced a somewhat distorted reflection of the room. On a day such as this, with rain beating down, occasional flashes of lightning and bulbs in the central chandelier flickering, the effect was spooky.

"Are you expecting a blackout?" I asked, as Max tested the flashlight.

Max shrugged. "The lights go out sometimes when the weather's nasty. The wiring hasn't been updated since 1950. But Rodrigo showed me how to reset the breaker, so don't worry."

"All right, MacGyver. Where to now?"

"This way."

Thinking I'd guessed Max's secret and would soon find myself climbing the spiral staircase to his room, I was surprised when he set off down the hall in the opposite direction of the library. So much for getting a peek at the crow's nest.

As Max walked, he trailed his left hand along the wood-paneled wall. I was about to scold him for this when he turned to me and smiled.

"*Et voilà, mon professeur!*"

Max pressed his hand to the wall and a portion of it swung open silently.

A secret door!

Genuinely surprised and intrigued, I nearly uttered those words aloud. Instead, I rubbed my chin and said, "Interesting."

"Nobody knows about it but me," Max declared proudly.

I doubted that but had no desire to rain on Max's parade.

As I followed Max through the doorway, and it closed behind us, I understood the need for a flashlight. The door did not open into another room, but a pitch black, narrow corridor.

"Where does this lead?"

"Everywhere."

Max soon guided me down a flight of stairs which ended in another corridor. Max flashed the light ahead, and I was amazed at what I saw. All along the left wall were stairs that led up to other doors. I was reminded of the concealed alleys behind New York's Broadway theaters, by which actors and VIP audience members could slip away unnoticed.

"This is amazing," I said. "Is there a door to every room?"

"Yes. Except for the kitchen."

"Why?"

"Why what?"

"Why build this? What purpose did it serve?"

I saw the shadow of Max's shoulder shrug.

"Assignations?" he suggested. "Like in the Three Musketeers. Or Caligula."

"*Caligula??*"

I was beginning to have doubts about the efficacy of Willoughby's internet policing.

"Lionel has it. The R-rated version. Not the porno one. It isn't nearly as raunchy as he claimed."

The disappointment was clear in Max's voice, and I was glad of the gloom that hid my sympathetic smile.

Max mounted the third flight of stairs, and I followed.

"This is a secret room," Max whispered.

Of *course,* it was.

Then, I hesitated, my amusement and indulgence giving way to common sense.

"Max, if you're not meant to go in there then neither am I."

I was beginning to doubt my assumption that everyone else knew about the "secret" doors and the subfloor passage.

"I've been here hundreds of times," Max assured me. "I could probably pick the lock from the other side, but this way is more fun."

Pick the lock?

"Max, I don't think–"

"Please, Prof. You won't get into trouble. I promise."

I was already in trouble. I was becoming Max's friend. A potentially slippery slope for a teacher.

"All right. But only because it's our unofficial day off, got it?"

"Got it."

Truthfully, I was dying to know what was inside.

As we entered the room and Max switched on a small table lamp, I felt a shock of disappointment. Had I expected to find a sarcophagus? A mad old woman in a rocking chair? The twin that Max had joked about on my first day? A few cobwebs at the very least. What I found was a beautifully appointed room as scrupulously shined and polished as the rest of the Grove. The strong scent of roses drew my attention to the far right of the room, where a large arrangement of these flowers occupied a cloisonné vase which sat atop a gleaming grand piano. Slightly to the right of the piano stood a golden harp and next to that a harpsicord.

A music room.

"Horrible—I mean, *Mrs.* Hanson, keeps the roses fresh all the time," said Max. "Always white roses. She thinks I don't know, but I've seen her."

"Why?"

Max gave me another of his shrugs.

"I think my dad puts her up to it."

"I mean, why bother? Your father has made his feelings about music quite clear. So why keep a music room spic and span and filled with fresh flowers if no one uses it? Why keep it locked? For that matter, why have a music room at all?"

Max turned the beam of his flashlight to the opposite end of the room, to a spot above the fireplace mantle.

"Because of her," Max said, pointing to the object now bathed in the makeshift spotlight.

The portrait was breathtaking.

The painter had captured both the subject and her exquisite black evening gown with equal skill. If the artist was as honest as he was talented, the woman had been elegant and bewitchingly beautiful. Her olive complexion, raven hair and large, dark, almond-shaped eyes suggested Mediterranean or perhaps Middle Eastern heritage and the slight twist to her scarlet, full-lipped smile seemed to hint at a sarcastic sense of humor.

"Who is she?" I asked, though I could not shake the feeling of recognition. The diamante tiara nestled in her upswept mass of hair sparked a memory, but I could not say of what or whom. There was a strange, mirrorlike quality to the painting. I could see my own reflection in the glossy oil paint, but it was more than that. Then, I realized the background of the portrait was the music room.

"I don't know," replied Max. "Her name, I mean. But I *do* know that she's someone from my father's past. Before I came along, anyway."

"How so?"

"I overheard Rosanie and Rodrigo talking in the kitchen one day," said Max, in an offhand manner which indicated he felt no shame in the action.

Spying, lock-picking, eavesdropping. It seemed I had a regular Artful

Dodger on my hands.

"And?" I prodded. If I could not undo what Max had done, I might as well try and learn from it.

"They said stuff like 'Just can't let her go. Even after all this time'—Rodrigo—and 'I don't understand how she puts up with this nonsense. It's not healthy, papa.'"—Rosanie. There was more, but they kept moving around, so I couldn't catch most of it."

"When was this?"

"After they took me out of regular school. Just before Sarah came." Max glanced at his watch. "Speaking of Rosanie and her dad, we'd better go. They'll be back soon."

"Okay."

I was about to follow Max through the secret door when I noticed he'd forgotten to switch off the small table lamp. As I moved across the room to do so, I looked toward the piano. There was music on the rack.

I darted quickly to the instrument, holding my breath in anticipation.

You're crazy.

"Prof!"

"Just a sec, Max."

I wasn't crazy.

The score of *Samson et Delila* lay open to the aria I had heard on my first night at Jessamine Grove

*

"I CAN SEE how completely underwhelmed you were by the tour," said Chaves, looking at me askance as we made a leisurely circuit of the Castillo de San Marco. The sun was warm and the days of rain a memory.

"Sorry. I've obviously overrated my skill at feigning interest to be sociable."

"You mean, you actually have some?"

I wasn't sure how to take Chaves's remark since his poker face provided no clue how it was intended.

"A modicum," I replied. "When pressed."

"I'll press harder next time." A twitch of a smile came and went on Chaves's face. "Anyway, I wouldn't have believed you if you'd come out of there gushing about how captivating it was."

We walked in silence for a while, moving away from the fort proper and toward the wall that faced the river. Chaves leaned back against it, folding his arms across his chest as he gazed up at the impressive military structure with what I took to be admiration. I joined him, but failed to see anything other than a big, ugly fort covered with coquina.

"It's the history that fascinates me," Chaves said. "What it represents."

"War?"

"Not exactly. Colonialism. The special variety of the Conquistadors: rape and pillage with the blessing of Holy Mother Church. Of course, it's the British and US period that's touted here. Forget about all the indigenous people the Spanish massacred."

Having only met Chaves twice, I had no idea how to respond to this. Whatever I said could lead to either a mine field or an intellectual discussion. And I had my reasons for avoiding the exploration of this sensitive subject. Fortunately, Chaves was not the type to need prompting.

"I never thought much about it before I moved to Florida. I was raised as a gringo. My father was white, I went to schools that were mostly white. Assimilation was the norm back then. I walked the walked the walk, talked the talk. I passed, for the most part. But I could play the race card when it suited me. It was my claim to indigenous heritage, not my grades, that got me a college scholarship. Anyway, it wasn't until years later that I was forced to accept my Latino heritage, not just barter with it."

"Forced?"

"Maybe that's an exaggeration. But my *abuela* once warned me that I would always be living a lie until the day that I took pride in my *sangre*. That happened when I moved to Miami. Suddenly, I was living in this immense Latino ghetto. It was as much a culture shock for me as if I'd moved to South America. I felt like a fraud. Not Latino enough to fit in. I was born Dean Thomas, but by the time I joined the Miami police force I'd adopted my mother's maiden name. My dad was understanding, and I knew my *abuela* would have been proud of me."

"But you weren't proud of yourself."

Chaves nodded. "Very insightful, Professor Boehm."

"It's a skill one develops over years of teaching. But I don't understand what this has to do with Castillo de San Marcos."

"My history. My family's history. You see, when I did finally embrace my Mexican heritage—the language, the culture—I began to question just what ancestry, what 'culture' I was supposed to be proud of. Proud of the Spanish bastards who considered the native peoples heathen, sub-human, and disposable? Or proud of the native peoples who converted to Catholicism, kissed the ass of the Pope and the king of Spain and assimilated?"

"Many of your native ancestors fought well and died with honor. You can be proud of *that*."

"You took that line from *Star Trek*, didn't you?"

"Would you like me to repeat it in Klingon?"

Chaves laughed, and I was glad I'd hit the correct note. "I know you're right," he said. "But a little shame doesn't hurt now and then. It keeps you from getting complacent." Chaves turned around and looked out over the river. "So," he continued, "any progress with your investigation?"

I was relieved at Chaves's abrupt change of subject, having anticipated the standard "and what about you?" response to such a personal revelation.

"Well, if a ghostly pianist and a portrait of a beautiful mystery woman kept locked in a secret room count, then, yes." I reported the incidents to Chaves, and he responded with a disbelieving look.

"Are you kidding?"

"Do I have to do a pinky swear? The music was real. I'm sure of it. And now I think it was coming from that room, not from the antique piano. As to the portrait, I'm certain I've seen that woman—or at least her portrait—somewhere before."

"Willoughby's a collector. Maybe you saw it in a museum or a gallery before he acquired it."

"Maybe. But what do I do? Search the internet for a portrait of a woman in a black evening gown wearing a tiara?"

"You never know. You might get lucky. What does she look like, this mystery woman?"

I took a moment to reflect, searching for the right words to describe her.

"Voluptuous. Sinuous. Dangerously beautiful. And I got the impression of a wicked sense of humor."

Chaves chuckled. "All that from a painting?"

"The artist is—or was—a master. As to the woman's physiognomy, she has—"

"Masses of black, wavy hair, an ethnicity you can't quite put your finger on, striking eyes that have a look that's more 'on your knees, slave' than 'come hither'?"

"I thought you said you weren't psychic?"

"Your description was enough to confirm a suspicion. I believe the woman in that portrait is Alma Montresor. An opera singer."

The lightbulb went on.

"Of course! La Montresor. Not *an* opera singer, Chaves, a true diva."

"I know. My ex-wife was an opera lover. She'd never seen a big-time production, so as a birthday present, I took her to La Scala to see Montresor in *Madama Butterfly*."

"Wow! That was some birthday present."

Wait. Rewind. Ex-*wife?*

"I was in love at the time. Anyway, I gritted my teeth or nodded off through most of the show. But when Montresor sang, I was blown away. I had never heard such a beautiful voice in my life. And it wasn't just her voice. She was… I can't think of the word."

"Incandescent?"

"That's the word."

"You were lucky. I never had the chance to see her perform."

"I didn't become an opera fan," continued Chaves, "but I began to understand it—the power of it in the right hands. I cried when Montresor sang that song about waiting for Pinkerton to come back." He made a little harrumph. "Kind of like life imitating art in our case."

"What are you talking about?"

"Willoughby and Montresor. You didn't know?"

"Know what?"

"They were lovers. Or so the media reported. That's why I thought of her when you described the portrait. According to gossip, he was mad about her; proposed to her several times. Said he would divorce his wife. Alma always refused. Then, she went missing. Willoughby waited years for Alma to return."

"I think he's still waiting. He's made that room into a shrine."

I thought of Willoughby's prohibition of music study to his son and told Chaves about it.

"That makes no sense," said Chaves. "Wouldn't Willoughby be happy if his son took an interest?"

"Possibly," I replied, drawing the word out to convey my sense of doubt. "If Alma had died, perhaps Willoughby would have had the closure needed to move on, and he would have honored her memory in a healthy way, by celebrating her music—music in general. Instead, Alma simply vanished and was never heard from again. The trauma of that extended limbo must have affected Willoughby greatly. But what does any of this have to do with Sarah?"

"Maybe nothing. But in my experience, oddities like to hook up." Chaves held up his left hand and counted, starting with his thumb. "One: Willoughby's lover does a disappearing act. Two: Willoughby keeps a locked room preserved in her memory. Three: Willoughby prohibits his son from studying music, but someone plays the piano in said locked room. Four: Fabiola Willoughby falls to her death. Five: Willoughby keeps Max locked up like the Prisoner of Zenda."

"Max is not locked up," I said defensively. "And while your laundry list of oddities could be the makings of a Brazilian soap opera, I don't see how they all hook up.

Chaves sighed heavily. "Neither do I. Yet. Anything else you can tell me?"

"I'm afraid I'm not a very good spy."

"I'm not so sure about that. You've established yourself as a member of the household. That's the hardest part."

"So, now I can start poking and prying and betraying their trust?"

"I wouldn't put it quite that way, but yeah."

I felt glum and must have looked it because Chaves said, "You'll feel better after you've eaten."

"What do you have in mind?"

"Food."

"Clearly. Where? What type of cuisine?"

"My place. Steak *frite*."

"You're on, Chaves."

"Stop calling me Chaves. I'm Beto to my family and friends."

"Beto?"

"Short for Norberto, my middle name."

"Well, I'm Neil. I don't have a middle name, much less a diminutive."

"How about NeNe?"

"Do you want your face rearranged? I kind of like it the way it is."

Beto looked me up and down, assessing.

"What else did they teach you at that ashram?"

"Not the ashram. My dad. He was a featherweight boxer before he went into the antique business. I hated it at first. But I learned how to defend myself—and it's a great way to blow off steam and relieve tension."

"I can think of at least one better way," said Beto, "and you can't do it with a boxing glove on your hand."

"Says you."

*

BETO'S HOME WAS not far from the Grove. It sat at the end of a cul-de-sac in one of the older phases of Ponce de Leon shores. While unmistakably a community of tracked houses, most of the residents had made efforts to individualize their properties with unique paint colors and an abundance of shrubbery, flowers, and trees. Beto's house, however, stood out for its lack of curb appeal or character. With its artificial-looking lawn and model-home starkness, it looked about as welcoming as a budget motel.

"Cute little place, isn't it?" asked Beto, accurately reading my expression of dismay. "Just wait until you see the inside."

"I'm aquiver with anticipation."

The walls of the living room were painted bloodred and the furniture appeared to be antique—with velvet upholstery and fringed, embroidered shawls thrown here and there. A Victrola stood next to a rolled-arm chaise of deepest purple and a faded Persian rug covered most of the hardwood floor. A large rectangular mirror, which may have been genuine Art Nouveau, dominated the wall above the fireplace. The bay window facing the street was festooned with swaths of dark pane velvet and chiffon of an off-white color.

"If Stevie Nicks came twirling into the room, it wouldn't faze me," I said drily.

"Me neither. My parents shared a love of boho. I didn't have the heart to redecorate after they'd both died. And, well, it sort of grows on you."

"It reminds me of Sarah's rooms at Allerton. All you're missing are some African violets and a nephrolepsis exaltata."

"A *what?*"

"A Boston fern."

"Oh. Sounds better in Latin."

"Most things do."

"How about I take you to the kitchen and you choose the wine while I prep the steakus fritimus?"

I followed Beto the short distance to the kitchen, which was shockingly contemporary in comparison to what I'd seen of the house thus far.

"When I moved in here," said Beto, "I decided that I could live with the overall décor, but the kitchen and bathroom had to be fixed up."

"Fixed up" was an understatement. From the glossy white Italian designer cabinetry to the stainless-steel Swiss appliances and gleaming marble countertops and floor, Beto's kitchen was a well-to-do home chef's dream.

"It cost a fortune," continued Beto, putting my thoughts into words, "but I got the house for free, so I figured it balanced out."

"A practical philosophy," I said, as I observed the wine rack and refrigerator that occupied the base of a large island. "Shall we start with a white?"

"Sounds good. There's a baguette in the bread box and Manchego under the cheese dome."

"I haven't seen a bread box since I was a kid," I said, retrieving the baguette from its wooden case.

"The only remnant of the old kitchen I kept." said Beto. He opened the massive refrigerator and I marveled at the quantity and variety of its contents as well the precision of their arrangement.

"You're a serious chef," I said with admiration.

Beto shrugged. "It's another great way to relieve tension."

I chose the wine and retrieved the cheese while Beto broke the bread, tearing it with his hands. "Do you like the butt end?" he asked, holding up the tip of the loaf. "Or…"

"I can go either way," I replied, smiling, certain I had interpreted his double entendre correctly.

"Good to know," said Beto as I handed him the wedge of Spanish cheese. "I always like to get that one out of the way as soon as possible. Just in case…you know."

It was reassuring to my self-esteem that Beto considered "you know" a possibility, and I admired his practical approach.

"And you?"

"I share your bread preference," Beto replied. He proceeded to split the baguette pieces open and stuff them with slices of cheese and placed them each on small, olive-wood boards. Beto handed me my portion, then swore, smacking his forehead with the palm of his hand. "What a terrible host I am." Beto opened a drawer, removed a knife and fork, and handed them to me with a bow.

"You're not going to let it go, are you?" I handed back the knife and fork. "Bread is on my short list of foodstuffs that do not require utensils."

"Pizza?"

"That's a gray area. Beto nodded gravely. "It is, isn't it?"

I laughed along with Beto, and we each took a bite of baguette.

"Change of subject," he continued. "How are things going with the kid?"

"Well," I said. "Maybe too well."

Beto looked a question and tilted his head to one side, reminding me of Max.

"It's tricky," I said. "A teacher wants a student to respect him, not necessarily like him."

"I hated my teachers."

"Two sides of a coin, Beto. Too much of either can be a bad thing. Striking the balance is not easy."

I poured the wine into the glasses Beto handed me, then followed him into the adjoining family room that was sunken, in typical seventies style. The seventies' theme continued with a wicker chair suspended from the ceiling, a blue, pleather bean bag and a rust-colored velvet sectional sofa. I opted for the hanging chair; unsure if I could rise gracefully from the bean bag and shy of getting too cozy with Beto too soon.

"So, what's the problem?"

"I won't be around forever, Beto. It would be cruel to establish a close relationship with Max only to walk away at the end of my contract."

Beto seemed to consider this as we sipped our wine—a vintage Lacryma Christi—and munched on our bread and cheese. Eventually, Beto said, "Just how long is your contract, by the way?"

"Two years. With an open-ended renewal."

"Whoa."

"Unfortunately, this is one of the challenges of my profession. Even the end of a semester can be hard. Hard to say goodbye to those students with whom one has bonded and, sometimes, even harder with those with whom one has failed to connect."

"*One* has a tough job, methinks."

I smiled at Beto's gentle sarcasm. "It can be, but the rewards make it worthwhile." I took another drink of the excellent wine. "This is delicious, by the way."

"I'm glad you like it."

"Thank you for inviting me today. You're the only person I know in Saint Augustine outside the Willoughby household."

"What about the gorgeous Victor?"

"He moved back to Italy shortly after Sarah died."

"I see. Did Sarah have any friends in the area that she spoke to you about?"

"I don't recall anyone in particular," I replied, noting that Beto had subtly shifted to detective mode. "Didn't you ask her yourself?" I added, surprised. I also wondered why Beto seemed to know nothing about Victor. If Sarah had claimed she was being stalked, wouldn't her boyfriend have been a suspect?

"Yes. But it is possible that she may have told you and not me. There may have been someone she didn't think could possibly relate to her situation, so she subconsciously withheld the information from me. People do it all the time. We all tend to answer questions differently, depending on who's doing the asking."

"True."

Beto proceeded in the same vein for a while, asking questions about the Willoughby household—the answers to most of which he surely knew already.

"There's really nothing more I can tell you, Beto."

"I know. Just keep your eyes open."

"I will." I was beginning to wonder if, after all, there really was nothing to Sarah's amorphous suspicions. But Beto's conviction of something odd having occurred was infectious. An idea came to me. "Why don't I question Max? As you just said, people answer the same questions differently from different people. Maybe—"

"Absolutely not."

The forcefulness of Beto's reply surprised me.

"There's no need to be rude," I said. "I'm only trying to help."

"I'm sorry. That didn't come out right. I just think it's better if Max remains unaware that you have any knowledge of my involvement."

"I wasn't suggesting I interrogate him, Beto."

"I know. Again, I apologize. This is your area of expertise."

"Actually, I agree with you. What I meant was that I could ask Max questions that might lead to his opening up on his own."

"Leading questions?" Beto nodded. "You're a better detective than you think."

"I'm concerned more with Max's mental health than with what he might tell me. He's very tightly wound. I need to help him unwind carefully and gently. He's been through a lot."

"Thank you."

"For what?"

"For caring. The kid needs it."

Beto fetched more wine, and I took a moment to reconsider his involvement with Sarah and Max. It had seemed almost obsessive to me at the outset, but as I warmed to Beto, less so. Now, however, I was beginning to wonder if my first impression hadn't been the correct one.

"Do you know how to make french fries?" Beto asked, as he returned with the wine.

"Yes. I preheat the oven to 425 degrees, take a handful from the freezer and bake them for twenty to thirty minutes."

"Really? I took you for one of those insufferable people who know how to do everything. Like Martha Stewart."

"I appreciate the compliment. I do know how to make proper french fries—among other things—but I've rarely had the opportunity. I got to enjoy cooking again for the first time in years while I was in Florentina Bay."

"Florentina Bay?"

"Northern California. I grew up there. I went back for a time after leaving Allerton. It's a lovely place, but I couldn't see myself settling in again."

We finished our rustic appetizers, then Beto led me back to the kitchen and introduced me to his battery of pots and pans. After a tour of Beto's pantry we began to work together to the sound of his off-key humming.

As my potatoes cooked, Beto expertly pan-fried the steaks and prepared a bearnaise sauce. I opened a bottle of burgundy and we sat down next to one another at the island. Beto had cooked the T-bone perfectly and his bearnaise was silky smooth. I complimented him on his skill, he praised my crispy fries, and we ate with gusto.

"Where would you have gone if you hadn't taken the job at the Grove?" Beto asked as he made quick work of his steak and dipped his fries in the remainder of the bearnaise.

"I don't know. On the advice of a very good friend, I took time off just to be and think. Then, Sarah reached out to me about taking over her job. The timing was right."

"You believe in fate?"

I skewered a few fries, considered. "Yes. Some people can't reconcile fate or destiny to free will. But I think they are complimentary. Imagine you come home from work every day, walk the same path."

Beto nodded.

"Imagine someone else does the same thing—from a different car park or a different metro station—both of you heading to roughly the same point. If you never vary from your route, there is no chance that you could meet. But what if someday one of you changes that route, that routine, and your paths cross? Free will allowed you both the choice, but fate orchestrated the meeting."

"Too deep for me," said Beto, sawing at the bone of his steak. "Either something happens, or it doesn't. Doesn't matter how."

"I appreciate the elegant straightforwardness of your idea, but life is never that simple."

"Speaking from experience?"

I considered my answer and opted for honesty. "Yes. Fate is real and not always kind."

Beto chewed the last of his meat, sipped his wine. Then he looked at me askance and said, "Seems to me she's done pretty well by you."

"And by you," I countered.

"Meaning?" prodded Beto.

"By your admission, your early opportunities in life were afforded you because of your race and skin color as much as your merits. You and I aren't so different, Beto. I can't pretend that having wealthy parents, pale skin and blond hair haven't given me an advantage in the world. That's the way things are, unfortunately. But strange as it may seem, your experience mirrors mine."

Beto appeared to consider my words, then after a long drink of wine said, "So, what's your shame, Neil?"

"My *shame?*" My heart pounded as Beto probed as close to my subconscious as he had to the bone of his steak.

"Yeah. I saw recognition, understanding, in your eyes when I was talking about my ancestors back at the Castillo. You've embraced your whiteness, your privilege—probably after a lot of soul-searching and pragmatic consideration, if I read you correctly. And you're right. You and I aren't that much different in how we've used our race to our advantage. But I have a feeling there's something else with you, Neil."

"It's a dark family secret," I said, intentionally sounding sarcastic but speaking the truth.

"All right," said Beto. "I'll drop it. For now."

I smiled at Beto, inwardly thanking him for letting me off the hook so easily.

Beto polished off his wine and suggested opening another bottle. I demurred. The prospect of getting inebriated with Beto—and what it might lead to—was tempting, but I had to be responsible.

Always responsible.

I could have it engraved on my tombstone: *Neil Boehm. Always Responsible.*

"Espresso?"

"Yes, thanks."

Beto continued to speak to me from the kitchen as he fetched the percolator and set the coffee to brew.

"I told you I was married once. What about you? Married? Partnered? Divorced?"

"None of the above. It's tricky when you live on campus."

"Weren't you the headmaster? I thought those guys got a house."

"Usually just in fiction these days, though Allerton was an exception. I did have my own house for the last two years I was there, but it didn't come with a husband."

"Was there anyone before Allerton?"

"No one serious, really."

Beto pounced on my unintended qualifier.

"*Really?*"

"Okay. There was one guy when I was in art school in New York. My roommate."

"Art school? So what happened?"

"With art or the guy?"

"Both."

"Both were mistakes. I realized I was not meant to be an artist, so I dropped out of art school. My roommate wanted me to live in a menage of sorts with his girlfriend. I wanted him all to myself, so I walked away."

"A three-way, huh? I don't think I would have passed it up. Were they also art students?"

"No. Edward was lead singer and guitarist in a rock band. His girlfriend was a wealthy groupie."

"Sex, drugs, and rock and roll. Not at all what I expected of the young Professor Boehm. I was thinking poetry and punting in Central Park."

"It was more like cheap wine and cigarettes in Fort Green Park. Edward and I met again a few years later, but it didn't work out. What about you? You told me you were married. What happened?"

Beto served the espresso, and we sat once more at the island.

"Me," said Beto, answering my question after a few sips of java. "I messed up big time. She caught me with another guy."

"Oh my."

"The guy was her brother."

"Oh my, my, my!"

"One more 'oh my' and you're outta here, bro," said Beto, barely repressing a laugh.

"Sorry," I said. "Are you and she still…?"

"Friends? Hell no. If it had been a woman—and not a relative—things might have worked out. But I betrayed her in two ways that she could never understand or forgive. I can't blame her. I was an asshole. The kicker was that I really loved her. And then, she got… Never mind, you get the picture."

"Yes." We sipped in silence for a while, then I returned to the subject of Jessamine Grove. "What can you tell me about Fabiola Willoughby?" I asked. "I didn't get much from an internet search."

"You didn't check her and Willoughby out before you took the job?" Beto was incredulous and I could not blame him.

"I took Sarah at her word. If the Willoughbys were good enough for her, they were good enough for me. She never mentioned anything untoward."

"Well, you won't find anything *untoward* on the internet. Even though Mrs. Willoughby was a well-known television personality, her social media presence is nil. The dangers of the internet were among her hobby horses. She was known to speak out about the dangers of voluntarily, though unknowingly, giving away your privacy on the net and about criminal activity glamorized on TV and in pop music. She started out as a family court attorney (which is how her reality show got started), so I guess her opinions were well informed."

"That explains the absence of television at the Grove," I said. "And Max's internet access is strictly limited."

"What does he do for fun?"

"He skateboards with a group of neighborhood boys, reads, and plays chess with his friend Lionel."

"Well, we don't want him to be overstimulated, do we?" asked Beto archly.

I thought about that for a moment. "Overall, I think Max is happy. He's a natural loner—and that's a damned hard thing to be in this world. It's not encouraged. Hell, it's barely allowed. I believe his parents made the right decision when they withdrew him from school. Max is fortunate to have the freedom to choose his friends, activities, and ideas–not have them forced upon him by others. Some kids can thrive under peer pressure, others can break irreparably. I've seen the latter happen too often."

"He's a lucky boy."

"Mr. Willoughby genuinely cares," I allowed. "And that's rarer in parents than you might think."

"I wasn't talking about Ezra Willoughby," said Beto, resting his left hand on my shoulder. "Max is lucky because he has *you*."

Beto's words seemed informed with sincerity, his touch natural and assuring. Yet I recoiled from the intimacy. I'd had my share of sexual relationships and anonymous encounters over the years but had avoided romantic involvements. There had been none. Not in years. Not since Edward. Unlike as Beto was to Edward—dark versus light, muscular versus lithe, neat versus uncouth—there was something about Beto that kindled memories of my youthful, ill-fated love.

"Penny for them," murmured Beto as he topped up my espresso.

"Sorry. I zoned out. I'm tired, Beto. I'd best be going on my way. I've got Max's lessons to review for tomorrow. And I promised to take him to some lighthouse in the afternoon."

"*The* lighthouse," corrected Beto. "The Saint Augustine Lighthouse and Maritime Museum. Cool place."

Despite my pretended vagueness, I knew all about the lighthouse. From its website, I had learned the number of twisting steps up to the lantern room. I dreaded the outing. Like the winding staircase leading to Max's room, the thought of the steps of the lighthouse inspired unease, foreboding. It was irrational, I knew. Just like fear of arachnids or serpents. Or cats or dogs. I understood the psychology behind my phobia; the origin of it. Yet, that acknowledgment, that acceptance of truth served only to ameliorate the fear, not eradicate it.

"Max is really looking forward to it. He told me he'd been there before with his father but didn't really enjoy it because his father never stopped talking. It's easy to sympathize. Ezra Willoughby loves the sound of his own voice."

"He has a reputation as a blowhard."

"I wouldn't go that far. He is rather arrogant, but he's also intelligent and well-versed in many subjects."

"A man after your own heart?"

I gave Beto a mild fuck-you look. "I like him. But I can understand how a man like Ezra might be difficult to imagine as an ideal father figure. Of course, Max adores him."

"Of course?"

"The dynamic is classic, Beto. The more distant the parent, the more the child strives to please the parent. Often, the need to please manifests itself in hero worship. Max may make sarcastic comments about Ezra behind his back—actually, he does this with everyone and he's usually on target—but woe betide the fool who speaks unfavorably of Max's dad."

Beto nodded slowly. "It was kinda like that with my older brother and my father. Cam was always talking the old man up to his friends, but they were distant—even antagonistic—with each other at home. That is, when my father was around. There was Vietnam and then one-year tours of duty. I don't remember any of that. I was too little. In my memory, my father was always around, and he'd always come home with candy in his pockets. And he taught me how to cook." Beto's eyes began to glisten, the grief apparently still raw. "I was lucky to have known my father as a friend as well as a parent," he continued. "Same with my mother. Cam wasn't so lucky."

"They were estranged?"

"No. Cam died trying to be just like his father. Got blown up in Iran when he was only twenty. Operation Eagle Claw. A nasty irony, isn't it, to get killed in action without ever having done any fighting? He was just in the wrong chopper at the wrong time."

I could think of nothing to say that would not sound hackneyed, so instead of speaking, I reached out and touched Beto's cheek.

"What was that for?" said Beto.

"For all the things I don't know how to say."

"I like your language, Professor Boehm," said Beto, returning the gesture and tracing the line of my jaw; the pale stubble crackling as he did so. "Do you have time to give me a lesson?"

With Beto so close that I could smell the day's sweat wafting up from his shirt, it was difficult to say no, yet the timing didn't feel right. I liked Beto, and my attraction to him moved me to wonder if it wasn't time for me to make a go at a serious relationship. If there was a potential for this with Beto, I didn't want to sabotage it by moving too fast.

"Raincheck?"

Beto shrugged. "It rains a lot this time of year, so I shouldn't have long to wait."

Chapter Five

"KNOWING WHEN TO Leave." The melody of that song was on a loop in my head—just as it had been on that summer day in 1985. I lay staring at the ceiling, a book open but unread on my chest. I hadn't known all the lyrics of the song back then, and still don't, but the title had seemed to sum up my situation at the time very nicely. Recalling that music now reawakened memories like water rejuvenating a Rose of Jericho.

"Have you always known you're gay?"

Edward asked the question casually as he passed me the joint which I declined. I took a drag of my cigarette and then a gulp of wine as I tried to calm the thumping in my chest. We sat side by side on the floor, our backs against the side of his bed as we gazed at the first hints of dawn in the sky through the bay window of Edward's room. We were close enough to experience a shared field of body heat and the humid summer air ramped up the eroticism of the proximity. Now and then, Edward would brush my left leg with the fingers of his right hand. He did it then, as I hesitated with my answer.

"Yes," I finally said. "Have you always known you're straight?"

My heart went from thumping to pounding.

Edward laughed mid-toke and coughed a bit before he replied, "I don't know. I've been attracted to guys, but I've never, you know, done anything." He turned his body toward me and smiled. "Maybe I just never met the right guy."

It was a line. Of course, it was. It had to be.

But when Edward reached out to touch my hair, when Edward guided my head to his, and his mouth met mine, my doubts disappeared. There was nothing but Edward's smell, Edward's taste, the sensation of his warm hands on my body, his breath on my skin. I don't remember the pain I must have felt when Edward entered me. I remember the shock, the surrender. I lost myself in Edward's eyes and savored the musk of his scent and the tang of his perspiration as he fucked me to the edge of oblivion. Edward was mine. We were one.

"I love you, Edward," I murmured against his lips as he came. "I love you so much."

Edward did not return the declaration, nor did he do so in the letter written on a page torn from a spiral notebook that he pushed under my door the next day.

Edward told me, in his cramped but legible hand, how important I was in his life, how much he needed me, how much our relationship meant to him. He described the huge apartment on the northern tip of Manhattan with views of the Hudson and enough room for my own studio. The place was old, he said. Edgar Allen Poe had—supposedly—once crashed there. Edward knew that would appeal to me. Everything about the apartment appealed to me. Everything except the fact that it belonged to his girlfriend, Laura, inherited by her from a deceased great-aunt.

"I want you to come live with us…"

Should I have swallowed my pride and done what he'd asked? Should I have held on and fought for my man? When a second chance came five years later, should I have leapt at it? Would we still be together now, two aging hipsters with a small circle of eccentric friends and hearts full of joy?

"Why are you running away again?" Edward demanded.

We were drinking margaritas at a bar in Terminal 2 of JFK. My flight for San Francisco would soon be called.

Three weeks earlier, Edward had appeared unannounced at my miniscule Murray Hill walk-up with a suitcase, a guitar, and the smile that still made me weak in the knees. Surprise and joy at seeing him again after many years trumped my vestigial resentment and I found myself in his arms and us in my bed within an hour.

I remember the morning after, thinking how much older he looked: forty-four to my twenty-six, with gray-shot hair, frown or concentration lines around the mouth that I recollected as perpetually smiling and the frenetic energy of once-upon-a-time memories mellowed by maturity.

"So, what happened?" I asked, as I watched Edward roll a joint. I'd given up cigarettes and outgrown cheap wine, but Edward's old habit remained. "Where are you guys at now?" He knew I was referring to him and Laura. Names did not need to be spoken.

"Splitsville. She hooked up with some trust fund guy. Threw me out."

"Oh. So, you came here to crash and indulge in a belated makeup fuck? Well, now that both of your goals have been accomplished, you may leave." I rose from the bed and strode naked to the kitchen, proud of the gym-toned body that had replaced the skinny frame Edward had known before. "Coffee before you go?" I asked, boiling water for the french press.

"When did you become such a bitch?"

"Still two spoons of sugar and a dash of cream?" I said, ignoring Edward's jibe.

"Yeah."

After coffee, bagels, and another round of mattress polo, I finally said, "Things have changed, Edward. You've changed. I've changed. We can't go backwards."

"I loved you. I've never stopped loving you."

"You loved me so much that you let me walk away?"

"Let you? That was your choice. I wrote to you, Neil. You never answered."

"You always said the same thing. And Laura was always part of it. Do you have any idea how that made me feel? You were my first. I thought it was something special—something life changing. I believed it was. I still believe it was. For both of us. But you chose Laura. You chose convenience, history, and financial security over love. Do you have any idea how much you hurt me?"

"You're throwing it back in my face?"

"Yes." Part of me wanted to take back the word as soon as I'd uttered it. Another part felt years of suppressed anger finally find its outlet.

Now, we drank silently as I waited to board my flight. We had not discussed the past since that first night, both regretting our actions—then and now—but finding no way to reconcile them. Neither of us willing to own up to our responsibility.

"So," said Edward, echoing his words of eight years before on the day I'd walked away, "this is it? You're going? Again."

I knocked back the dregs of my cocktail. "Goodbye."

"Don't go. I can make it right, Neil. I screwed up, okay? You've been in my heart, always. Always."

"Leave it, Edward. It's over."

My flight was called.

I was shaking as I slung my messenger bag across my chest, my heart pounding with the adrenaline of a decision made for better or worse. Edward followed me silently to the gate. Then, as I joined the queue of boarding passengers, Edward said, "Fuck you."

His last words. They would haunt me for years.

It's said that you can never go back, that you shouldn't waste time thinking about what might have been. They say you shouldn't cry over spilled milk. But I did. And I had run from love many times since that day, hoping to avoid a repeat of my history with Edward. What you never know won't hurt you, right?

Tap, tap, tap.

The sound pulled me from my self-pity. I sat up quickly, my weathered copy of *All Things Bright and Beautiful* falling to the floor as I stood and began to walk toward the bathroom—certain the sound had come from the adjacent suite. Nocturnal noises from that room had awakened me on previous occasions, and I now made a vow to roust the vermin I was certain were the source.

Tap, tap, tap.

I stopped. Not mice. A rapping on my chamber door.

I glanced at my watch. 3:21 a.m.

Who the hell?

I opened the door.

Max stood before me, dressed in black silk pajamas topped with a matching jacquard silk robe. His small feet were wrapped in black velvet slippers with a gold crest on the vamp. Max's habitually unkempt mop of hair was swept into a neat man bun, taking the softness from his face, and lending it a mature severity. What had become of the disheveled skater boy?

"You clean up nicely," I said.

Max, in his turn, looked me up and down, taking in my wide feet in their multi-colored, cat-print socks, my ancient, paint-splattered sweatpants, and my weathered souvenir T-shirt from Madonna's *Confessions* tour.

"Who are you?" Max asked. "And what have you done with Prof?"

"Very funny."

"I couldn't sleep. And you told me you were noctambulous."

"I said that I stay up late, not that I sleepwalk. And you being here alone at this hour is totally inappropriate."

"Please, Prof. I need to talk to you."

Whether it was Max's sophisticated appearance or the clear sincerity of his words that tempted me to step aside and let him in, I can't say. Probably a combination of both. He had that same air of regal command I had noticed on our first meeting when I'd been summarily dismissed with a turn of his bony shoulders. But there was also a childlike supplication in his dark eyes. The combination was compelling. I could not have turned Max away any more than I could have left a stray cat to a cold, rainy night, or an innocent king to the guillotine.

"Come in."

I watched as Max took in my lodgings with curious glances at whatever view my body did not block: the fallen paperback, the bottle of whiskey and the half—consumed tumbler of the spirit, the atypically less-than-neat pile of papers on my desk. I tried not to think about the potentially disastrous circumstances I was putting myself in should someone discover us. Me, in my slovenly state with liquor on my breath, Max in his pajamas. Careers had been destroyed for less.

"Tell me about it," I said settling myself back on the sofa, and waving Max to a chair on the other side of the coffee table. Only as Max moved to sit, did I notice that he was holding something behind his back.

"I stole it," he said, setting the object down on the table. I immediately recognized it as one of Sarah's handcrafted journals. "At least, I think I did."

"You *think*?"

"Well"—said Max, pulling the sleeve of his robe, the guilty, childish gesture shattering his superficial image of maturity—"when he came for Sarah's stuff, he asked Mrs. Hanson especially about Sarah's diaries."

"He?"

"Mr. Adami. Sarah's boyfriend."

I nodded.

"Anyway, he asked Mrs. Hanson for the diaries. She didn't know about them, but I did."

"How?" I asked, apprehension clear in my inflection.

"Give me *some* credit, Prof. Sarah showed them to me. One day, I found her in the kitchen writing in one. When she closed it, I saw how beautiful the cover was. She told me that she made it by hand with all different pieces of magazine pages and wrapping paper and stuff stuck together with shellac. I asked Sarah if she would teach me, and she said yes. So, like, that's how I knew about them—where they were and everything. She showed me her collection." Max pointed in the direction of the bathroom. "She kept them in there, along with her supplies. In the junk room next door. Sarah said she liked to work there because the light was better and because there was interesting old stuff in there."

It was easy to imagine, knowing Sarah's love of the obscure and antique. I could see her in that room, surrounded by discarded furniture and bric-a-brac, working painstakingly on her handicraft.

"But that does not explain why you *think* you stole this," I said.

"Because, well, I think Sarah wanted me to have it. Or would have, if, like…you know…she hadn't…"

I nearly took Max to task for his repetitive use of "like, well, and you know," but his obvious distress stayed my professional instincts. Instead, I said, "Do you mean to say that she prepared it for you as a gift, but never had the chance to present you with it?"

"Not *exactly*." Max looked even more guilty and became even more fidgety, twisting the tie of his robe again and again. "I—I read some of it. I know I shouldn't have. And it was an accident, really."

"Oh, come now."

"It *was*. I swear! Sarah was painting the house—I mean painting a picture of the house—from the viewpoint of the pool enclosure. It's a great angle, really. It was Sarah's day off, but she didn't go to visit Mr. Adami that day. She just sat out by the pool, painting and writing in her diary. Anyway, the light was perfect. I asked Sarah if she would mind if I photographed her painting and writing. An artist observing an artist kind of thing. She thought it was a great idea."

I nodded encouragement, though Max, like Beto, needed little encouragement once he started.

"So, when I was developing the pictures, that's when it happened."

"When what happened?"

"When I saw what Sarah was writing in her journal, or diary, or whatever. I used the zoom to get some shots of her hands with the lawn in the background—the shadows of her hands on the page juxtaposed to the shadow of the sunlight on the lawn."

I was impressed with both Max's artistic concept and his unabashed enthusiasm. Perhaps photography would prove to be his métier.

"So, like, I kind of couldn't help but look at what Sarah had written. It was about me. I thought about it. In a diary, you sort of talk to yourself about what happens every day, or something, right?"

"Correct."

"Well, I figured if Sarah was writing about me and, um, probably everybody else at the Grove, then, well… I mean…"

"You thought you had the right to it after she died?"

Max nodded.

"Your logic is flawed, Maximilian."

"I know, Prof. I've thought about it a lot. And I haven't read any of it yet—except the little bit in the photo. But we worked on the cover together—Sarah and me—when Sarah was teaching me how do it. That's why I thought maybe she wanted me to have it. *Would* have wanted me to have it."

"Then, why have you brought it to me?" I knew the answer. It was evident in Max's pained expression—in the way he had placed the journal on the table cautiously, as if it might bite him.

"Passing the buck?" I suggested, as Max remained silent. "Give it to Prof. He'll know what to do and I can wash my hands of it. It will be someone else's responsibility. Am I warm?"

Max's lowered head seemed to speak his acceptance of my scenario. A few seconds later, a gentle sniveling backed up the gesture.

Oh shit.

I stood and crossed the room to where Max sat. Crouching on the floor beside him, I tapped one of his velvet-shod feet and he looked up, his face streaked with tears.

"Look, man," I said softly. "We all make mistakes. It took a certain amount of valor for you to come to me and tell me this. That counts for a lot. I'm not judging you." I thought about my next words and decided: *fuck it*. I blamed the whiskey. "I would have done the same thing."

"Really?"

"Yes. That does not make what you did right, but yes."

Max swiped the back of his left hand under his nose and snorted snot in the oddly endearing way only the young can pull off.

"Now what?" he asked.

I shrugged. "I keep the journal and come up with some story to tell Victor. Something like: 'Victor, you won't believe what I found in the room next to mine.'"

"You'd do that?"

"You've already implicated me, kiddo."

Max smiled. "Sorry."

I reached out and put my hand on Max's shoulder. "I'm not here just to teach you Latin. Whenever you need to talk about *whatever*, I'm here for you. Okay?"

"Thanks, Prof."

I stood up, straightening my Madonna T-shirt like Captain Picard tugging his uniform top.

"Now, off to bed young man. The lighthouse awaits anon."

Max mimicked my gesture, smoothing his robe and tightening its sash as he rose from the chair. Then, he surprised me by giving me a bear hug. I responded gingerly, feeling the bones of Max's back under my hands. I tried to recall if I had ever seen Ezra hug his child. No. I had not. Had Sarah ever held Max in her arms?

"All right," I said, gently disentangling myself. "Enough tears and confidences for one night. Get some sleep."

"Okay. See you tomorrow—I mean today, actually."

"Quite true. Go, already!"

Max smiled, ducked his head in acquiescence, then departed silently, closing my door with the utmost care.

I raked my hand through my textured crop of blond-gray hair—remembering when I used to have a mass of shaggy locks like Max. More than forty years, gone in the blink of an eye. Or so it now seemed. I had longed to be thirty-five (a magic number, for some reason) when I was Max's age. I had imagined myself grown up, independent, wealthy, a famous artist.

Reclining on the sofa, I turned my thoughts once more to the past—something I'd been doing frequently since leaving Allerton.

Although my parents did not actively discourage me, I was inclined to believe that neither of them considered being an artist a real job unless you were the next Rembrandt. So, if I maintained high marks in school, and I chose to spend my free time painting, that was fine with my parents. I could imagine one or both observing that at least I wasn't into drugs or promiscuity.

With a mediocre talent in which someone on the admissions board saw promise, I managed to squeak into a good art college. Lack of a true gift, boredom and depression got me on probation by the end of the first year. The second year didn't last past the spring semester.

"There's a place for dilettantism, Neil," said the department head, "but that place is not here. You have potential, but you lack ambition. Look, you excel in all your non-art courses. I suggest you reconsider your career path before your GPA is irreparably damaged."

I had been told. And I was not delusional enough to argue. Life as an artist was as much of a pipe dream as was life with Edward. So, coinciding as they did, I left both dreams behind. With a good recommendation from my English professor, I transferred to a small but respectable university where I earned my bachelor's and master's degree in my native language, then moved abroad for graduate school in Spain where I acquired additional advanced degrees in Spanish, Latin, and ancient history.

"So, what do you do with all these degrees, Dr. Boehm?" My mother had asked upon attending my graduation from the University of Barcelona. "Teach?" The sarcastic tone of her words was betrayed by a subsequent smile and kiss.

I saw my mother off at the airport, on her journey back to California and her lucrative career of persuading people to buy things that they did not need and could not afford. But I could not begrudge her success. We were different people. Fortunately, we'd acknowledged these differences and remained close until she, too, passed away.

In my youth, "Jakob's Gems" was a landmark in Florentina Bay. Not because of the antiques and curios of sometimes dubious provenance offered for sale therein, but because the building which housed my father's business had been a whorehouse during the California Gold Rush and a schoolhouse during the Spanish colonial period. Today, the building is home to a real estate agency and a halal market. *Tempora mutantur.*

I could walk from my house to my father's shop and from my father's shop to the small Catholic school where I acquired my love of learning for learning's sake. My parents were nonpracticing Lutherans, and they considered the parochial school only a slight step above the local public school.

But I came to appreciate their choice—even if I had to endure the taunts of the ignorant bullies among my classmates. In a small town populated by the descendants of Spanish, Mexican, Portuguese, and Irish Catholic families who had lived there for decades, if not centuries, I—a Protestant and son of a postwar German immigrant—was an irresistible target.

The day I came home with a swastika worked with a magic marker into the canvas of my bookbag was a turning point.

"Why is Papa so angry?" I asked my grandfather, as we shared a peanut butter and jelly sandwich. Upon seeing the vandalism, my father had cursed in the German he rarely spoke, dumped the contents of my bag on the dining room table, and tossed the bookbag into the fireplace. "I didn't do anything wrong."

"Neither did your father do anything wrong, *mein Junge*. That's why he's so upset."

I did not understand, but I nodded as if I did and Opa smiled and patted my shoulder, then returned to his knitting.

What I did understand was that my life at school changed after that day. I was not only bullied, I was shunned. Alone, afraid, and unhappy during recess, I found solace in the library. Sister Benedicta—the librarian—allowed me free access to her domain, encouraging my love of reading and teaching me that solitude could be a good thing. She also taught me about art, literature, and thinking "outside the box." Most importantly, for the life ahead that I never imagined back then, I learned the power and importance of mentoring, of connecting to the young and yearning.

Sister Benedicta was a character. An ex-hippie, she mingled with the local artist colony as well as with the surfers. She was admired for both the watercolors she sold on the boardwalk during the summer and the sage advice she gave to the youth of the town who were not so much younger than she. Sister Benedicta was cool. I flourished in the shade of her coolness and by the time I was in my early teens, found myself part of a group of misfits who called themselves "the Benedictites."

Memories of good times.

I've kept a little picture of Sister Benedicta in my wallet since I was an adolescent. In it, she's standing on the boardwalk, next to her easel, her smile bright, her veil flapping in the breeze. When anyone has asked me who she is, I've told them that she was my best friend.

My father and grandfather were another story altogether. And though my thoughts had naturally turned to them, it was not a story I wished to revisit that night. But it came, nonetheless.

I recall what I considered the oddity of my grandfather: a handsome, athletically built man in his late sixties, sitting on a feminine-looking settee wearing a red cable-knit cardigan and khaki pants, clicking away at his needles as he and I watched reruns of *Dark Shadows*. In my memories, the weather mimics the rainy gloom of most of the program's episodes, and I suppose these memories are accurate since, even in summer, the temperature in our northern California seaside town rarely climbed beyond the upper seventies, days of rain equaled those of sunshine, and the waves of the Pacific crashed against our craggy coastline just like those in the fictional New England town of Collinsport.

If I were to say I remember my grandfather as clearly as the weather or the episodes of the gothic soap opera, it would be a lie. I remember his face, his seemingly unchanging Mr. Rogers wardrobe, and the crisp scent of his aftershave. And I can recall the timber of his baritone voice; tinged with the vestiges of a German accent. But of the man himself—his thoughts, his feelings, his likes and dislikes, his dreams, his nightmares—I knew nothing then, thus remember nothing now. He was simply *Opa*—Grandfather—a figure to be respected, a kindly elderly man who made sweaters and scarves, pottered around the garden, and watched *Dark Shadows* with me when I came home from school.

Opa died when I was eleven. I remember his sparsely attended funeral and what I considered the appropriate rain and darkness that accompanied it—just like our companiable hours spent in front of the television. I cried. Not just for the old man, but because I saw a bleak future of empty afternoons ahead for me—alone in the house with only the sounds of the breaking waves for company.

My parents were appropriately somber throughout the service, and received condolences with murmured words of appreciation, my mother pulling off a closeup worthy melancholy smile when confronted with mourners offering what they believed to be humorous anecdotes about her late father-in-law. Later, in the foyer of our home, my mother removed her gloves and said to my father, "Thank God, it's finally over."

From the tone of my mother's voice and the slow, considering nod with which my father responded to her words, I knew she had not been referring to the funeral. It would be several years before I understood the hopeful look on my mother's face or my father's uncharacteristic silence; before I discovered that "it" was not over—the worst of *it* was yet to come.

*

I POURED A finger of whiskey and brought myself back to the present by contemplating Sarah's journal. Its glossy, multi-colored cover beckoned. From the moment Max had given it to me, I'd known that I would read it—

or at least glance through it—which is why I'd been reluctant to chastise Max too severely. I had told him the absolute truth: had I been in his place, I, too, would have withheld the journal from Victor. Had Sarah intended it as a gift to Max? Possibly. A thoughtful gesture such as that was in keeping with Sarah's personality. Of course, there was only one way to know for certain.

I reached for the book, looking it over front and back. It was larger than Sarah's usual journals and tied with a leather cord, rather than Sarah's customary ribbon. A masculine touch? Max had said he'd helped Sarah create it. I tugged gently at the cord. *Quaeso, dona mihi remissionem…*

Max was proven correct in his assumption. The flyleaf held a dedication to him from Sarah. As I flipped through the pages, avoiding the temptation to read rather than observe, I discovered that the book was more of a keepsake than a diary; some pages were headed with the year, month and day of the week and were filled with Sarah's observations in her neat, enviably legible hand. Others contained pasted photographs or pressed flowers. There were recipes, sketches, and miniature watercolors of places she had visited with Max. An unfinished portrait of Max toward the back of the book was a poignant reminder that the journal was unfinished—Sarah's gift left incomplete by her sudden death.

There were some items paper clipped to the inside of the back cover. With mixed feelings of guilt and curiosity, I pried them loose: a pair of old-fashioned theater tickets from a local production of *Godspell*, a magazine article about chess, and a candid snapshot of Max and Lionel playing the game. The last two items were articles printed from the internet. The first was from a legal journal addressing the different types of adoption and various Florida state regulations. Had Sarah been doing research to better understand Max's particular situation; perhaps discreetly looking into the history of the Willoughby's adoption of Max to better understand the family dynamic? That made sense. I found the second article particularly intriguing. I sat up straighter and reached for my whiskey as I began to read the story:

US Reporter

November 21

"Must See TV in the New Fall Season"

NTN announced last week that it has renewed its flagship true crime series *Intrigues and Ambiguities* for a record-breaking twelfth season. A series that delves into unsolved crimes, mysterious disasters, and conspiracy theories, IA—as the show is fondly known by millions of viewers—has never been shy of venturing into the truly unknown and supernatural, presenting stories of closed-case investigations, ghost-hunters, and ancient alien theorists with equal gravitas. The new season of IA promises to honor its history and move boldly forward with its first episode titled "Flight of a Songbird," a speculative documentary about opera diva Alma Montresor. Produced, written, and directed by celebrated historian and filmmaker Anders Wilson, "Songbird" is set to premier on January twenty-first, kicking off a season of multi-episode documentaries which reexamine and attempt to solve cases of both famous and everyday people who have gone missing with no apparent or satisfactory explanation.

In an interview with U.S. Reporter, Wilson explained his choice of subject for the first installment of the series.

"The vanishing of Alma Montresor has always fascinated me. Look, you've got this incredibly talented, beautiful woman, rumored to have been struck down by debilitating illness or an unwanted pregnancy, eulogized as if she were dead by colleagues and fans when no one—I mean, no one—knew for a fact that she had indeed passed away. For me, this has always been a classic case of a planned exit—whether it was suicide or carefully executed withdrawal from the world. After Alma Montresor's *'departure' I could* not help but think of JFK Junior's words about his mother's death: 'She did it her way.' If—as John Kennedy's words seem to hint—Jackie took her own life, did Alma Montresor follow the same path? Or did she choose to disappear into a life of anonymity, unable to cope with the inevitability of a future when she would no longer possess the beauty and voice that brought her fame? Then, again, one must ask: Is there an alternative? Yes. The alternative is murder..."

Chapter Six

I TRIED TO think of the classic Hitchcock film *Spellbound* or—better yet—Mel Brooks's mash-up parody *High Anxiety* to keep my mind off the memories the lighthouse staircase triggered. Visual triggers. The lighthouse should have been a walk in the park after the small wrought iron ingress of Max's domain that reminded me so much of the one in my father's shop. The black twisting stairs that led up to the storeroom, the single bulb with a chain…

"Prof? Are you okay?" Max hurried down the stairs as he saw me close my eyes and grip the railing.

"I'm fine," I lied as Max came to my side. "Go on ahead," I said. "I'll catch up."

Disappointment was writ plainly on Max's face, though his words were cheerful and encouraging. Shit. I could *not* let the kid down.

"How about we go up together?" asked Max.

Max reached out, took my hand, and smiled. "Teamwork, right?"

"Right. Thank you, Maximillian."

Being humbled takes one's mind off things. The kindness of a twelve-year-old boy and the surprising strength of his grip were enough to close the door to the attic of Jakob's Gems and shake off the remembered trauma.

"I can't imagine living here," I said as we reached the top.

"In some lighthouses, people do. Or, at least, they used to," said Max as we stepped onto the balcony surrounding the lantern room. "Here, they lived in the lightkeeper's house. That's where the museum is now. Didn't you even *look* at the brochure?"

The view was spectacular. A cloudless sky of pale cerulean sheltered the length and breadth of Anastasia Island and the Atlantic Ocean on one side and Matanzas Bay on the other glittered under the intense sunlight. I looked on, impressed, as Max wielded his vintage Hasselblad camera with the confidence of a professional.

"Now, you, Prof," said Max, turning his camera away from the vistas and toward me.

I demurred. Max insisted. I leaned against the railing.

"All right. I'm ready for my closeup.

Click. Click. Click. Click.

"Enough already," I said putting up my hands in mock supplication. "My turn."

I waved Max over, and he stood beside me while I took a few snaps at arm's length from my phone. The last, with both of us smiling and Max's head on my shoulder, was one I would come to cherish.

I glanced at my watch. "Hungry?" I asked.

"Yeah."

"There's a place here. Probably glorified junk food, but–"

"Yes!"

"So much for twisting your arm. And I've got a surprise for you afterward."

"Junk food *and* a surprise? I'm scoring today, Prof."

"You deserve it. You've been working like a Trojan these last weeks."

Max humped his camera onto his shoulder and looked at me with a scrunched-up face.

"How, exactly, did the Trojans work, Prof?"

"Industriously, one presumes. The war, the horse, and all that."

Max laughed. *"Seriously."*

"Seriously, Max, I'm quite proud of you."

Max's face beamed like a lighthouse beacon.

"Race you down!" Max exclaimed, pushing through the door of the stairway.

I followed in his happy wake, apologizing to fellow tourists as I did so.

"Slow down, Max," I called. "I'm old."

"Yeah. Right. Come on, Prof. Junk food awaits anon!"

*

WHILE I SAVORED my juicy, grilled beef burger—grass fed and raised with gentle loving care before it was slaughtered, of course, since they had to justify the exorbitant price somehow—and counted the calories of each delectable Cajun home fry, Max devoured his forbidden fruit with gusto and washed it down with a large cola. Max looked on, fascinated, as I neatly sliced and skewered each bite of meat, greens, and tomato.

"I've never seen anyone eat a burger like that," said Max.

"Ambiguity, Max," I replied. "You should say: I've never seen anyone eat a burger that way. Otherwise, you mean that you've never seen anyone eat a burger that looks like this one."

"Right. Noted".

I smiled indulgently and turned my plate so that the uneaten half of my burger faced Max.

"Go on," I said. "You haven't licked your lips and drooled, but you may as well have. Anyway, I'm full."

Max grinned and transferred the half burger to his plate. Then he reached for my paper cup of fries.

"Touch the spuds and you're a dead man," I said.

Max stopped, mid-reach. "You said you're full."

"There's always room for another fry, right?" I said, as I dispensed the lion's share of the potatoes onto Max's plate.

"Thanks, Prof."

As Max munched, I turned my attention to the camera that lay on the table. "Where did you study photography?"

Max gulped and wiped his mouth politely with his napkin.

"School. It was that or Home Ec. I mean, seriously, was there a choice?"

"I wasn't so lucky in my own choice," I said. "I sewed my index finger and gave half the class food poisoning."

Max snorted a laugh as he sucked the last of his cola through a straw. "For real?"

I showed Max the faint trace of the scar.

"Fu—sorry. I mean, wow."

"I believe I uttered the first interjection when the needle pierced my finger," I said. "Points to you for refraining." I gave Max the rest of the fries. "Finish these. Then it's time for the surprise."

Just for a moment, as Max wolfed down the fries and I called over the waiter to settle our bill, I entertained a fantasy of parenthood. Wasn't this how dads bonded with their sons? Special "guys only" days? At least, that's how it was in the movies and on TV. I could hardly rely on personal experience. Tending the till in my father's shop while he got drunk was not bonding.

You could be my son, I thought as I watched Max, happy and glowing with life. *My grandson, even.*

But Max was not my son, nor had any of the other young men I'd taught and mentored over the years been my son. I pushed down rising melancholy and clung to Max's infectious joie de vivre, hoping that my surprise would be a success. We collected our belongings, and I led the way to the Lightkeeper's House.

"We saw the museum already," said Max, clearly crestfallen. "That's not a surprise."

"Oh, ye of little faith." I grabbed Max's hand and pulled him along to the side of the building, to the entrance marked employees only. The maritime museum was one of only a handful of places in the US where the ancient profession of the shipwright was still practiced and taught. Although models were always on display to the public, and truncated demonstrations of the craft were given to tourists during perpetually sold-out presentations, the actual practice of shipbuilding was done behind closed doors by a small group of masters and their apprentices. I knew nothing of this until Beto brought me up to speed. And it was Beto's "inside man" among the shipwrights—an ex-con with a woodworker's gift, named Gaspar—who helped me arrange for a private lesson for Max.

"That was awesome, Prof!" said Max two hours later as we left the museum with an invitation to return whenever we wanted. "Can we really come back again?"

"Gaspar said so," I replied.

"People *say* stuff all the time, Prof. That's not the same as meaning it."

I felt a little knife stab to my heart. Not just because Max was too young to be so cynical, but because he was right.

"I know," I said, squeezing his shoulder. "But Gaspar seems like a pretty cool guy, so I think we can trust him."

"Well," said Max, "I trust *you*. I guess that's enough."

"Thank you."

If I'd ever considered leaving, giving up on my new life, my new career—giving up on Max—his last words sealed my fate.

"Knowing When to Leave."

Had anyone written a song called "Knowing When to Stay"?

Chapter Seven

IT WAS A skateboarding afternoon, and I felt an unwarranted and unwelcome twinge of jealousy as I watched Max depart with Rodrigo.

But I want to go too!

Recognition of the childish sound of my inner voice helped to dampen the insidious emotion. I reminded myself that Max's outings with his bodyguard were an established tradition and that my morning field trip with Max was just one enjoyable day out of the ordinary.

Get a grip, Boehm. You're a responsible professional. And you're paid help. You are not part of Max's family.

True. Yet Sarah's words encouraged me to think otherwise.

"I don't want to leave Max without knowing that there is someone there for him. Someone to advocate for him. Someone to care for him."

"Later, Prof."

I shelved my mixed emotions and returned Max's smile and

valediction.

"Later, Max."

The front door closed, and I was alone.

Well, not really. Rosanie and Nessa were somewhere about, though I had not seen either woman since breakfast.

I adjourned to my room, where I decided I would have another look at Sarah's journal and the articles she'd collected, and perhaps do some research into the enigma that was Alma Montresor.

Picking up Sarah's book, I recalled Max telling me that Sarah had used the adjoining storeroom as a workspace. With belated curiosity, I made my way through the bathroom to the connecting door. It was locked.

Well, why shouldn't it be? I was annoyed rather than surprised. Yet, Sarah had apparently had free access. Why didn't I?

I retreated to my room, opened my door, and called down the short stairway.

"Rosanie? Nessa?"

It seemed ridiculous to send a text or call on the smartphone provided by Willoughby when we were all in the house. Besides, I had let the battery run down.

I was about to repeat my holler when Rosanie appeared at the bottom of the stairs.

"Yes, Neil?"

Rosanie had finally stopped calling me Mr. Neil when I'd commented that it made me sound like a hairdresser, but her attitude toward me, though friendly, continued to be somewhat formally respectful of my position. It seemed that, to Rosanie, I was Upstairs, and she was Downstairs. As now we literally were.

"Hello, Rosanie. Sorry to bother you, but I wanted to have a look into the room adjoining mine. It was open the day I arrived, but it's locked now. I understand Sarah used it as a workroom.

"Oh. I'm sorry. Of course…if you…um… Just a minute. I have to…" Rosanie twisted her hands in the pockets of her apron and looked down at the floor like a guilty child.

"Yes?"

"I'll go up and open it now."

Rosanie retreated.

What the heck?

I trotted back up the stairs and entered the bathroom just as Rosanie opened the connecting door, a ring of skeleton keys in one hand.

"Mr. Boehm…Neil, there's something I need to tell you. I should have told you before, I just–"

Rosanie's words halted as she followed my gaze over her right shoulder. Atop a stack of packing boxes sat the largest housecat I had ever encountered. Its short coat was of a black and tuxedo pattern, and its droopy-lidded green eyes stared at me with apparent bored annoyance.

I smiled at Rosanie. "It looks as if we've interrupted someone's afternoon nap."

"Please don't tell anyone, Neil. Especially *him*."

"Him?"

"Mr. Willoughby. He *hates* cats. If he finds out about Lulu, he'll kill me. Then he'll fire me."

"My dear," I said, stepping into the room, "if Mr. Willoughby did the former, the latter would hardly be necessary."

Rosanie flashed a puzzled look, then laughed. "You know what I mean. Mr. Willoughby would go ballistic if he found out we were secretly keeping a cat in his house."

"Then why do you?" I asked as I approached Lulu. "You're a big girl, aren't you?" I said addressing the animal.

"Boy. Lulu's a boy."

"A non-binary feline?"

"No. Not that I would know," replied Rosanie, as if she thought I was being serious. "When Sarah first brought him in, Nessa said, 'By God, that is one lulu of a pussy!', so we called him Lulu. It's because of Sarah that we kept him on…after."

"I see. Who are 'we'? Just you and Mrs. Hanson?"

"At first it was. I mean, Nessa and I helped Sarah keep him secret. It was only supposed to be until Sarah found him a permanent home. But then, Sarah died and…well, we just couldn't give Lulu away. He's like a living reminder, you know?" Rosanie was close to tears, and I nodded my understanding, afraid I'd go the same route if I spoke. "Anyway, we had to tell my dad at some point. He was furious, of course. And rightly so. But he gave in, eventually. He loves animals. Then we agreed that we had to let Max in on the secret. He promised he'd never tell his parents, and he's been as good as his word."

"I'm not a snitch," I said, approaching the cat and caressing him under his chin. He was a handsome, tranquil fellow. "But on your heads be it, if Mr. Willoughby finds out."

"Thanks, Neil. Just be sure to keep the door locked when you're out and Mr. Willoughby is home. I must have been careless on your first day. This room leads directly down to the kitchen. It was the cook's apartment back in the day. Or so my dad says. Makes sense, right?" Rosanie held up the ring of keys. "We keep an extra one in the pantry behind the flour. With a purple rubber band around it. The key, not the flour. Purple for pussy."

"Got it."

"Well, then," said Rosanie, fumbling her hands in her pockets once more, "I guess I'll get back to work." She turned toward the door and then back again. Rosanie opened her mouth, closed it, opened it. Finally, she said "Neil?"

"Yes?"

"Did you ever meet him?"

"Who?"

"The dark, handsome man."

"Testing your clairvoyant skills? As a matter of fact, I did."

"I knew it!"

I laughed. "Do you really think you have the gift?"

"I—I used to think so. Until I read for Sarah. I got it all wrong. If I'd been better, I could have prevented… I mean, she could have avoided…"

"Rosanie, even if you do have a true psychic gift, you can't be right all the time. You can't foresee every possible permutation of future events. Certainly, you could not prevent something like a stroke."

"But I was so *sure*. I sensed so much anger…a *person* wishing Sarah harm, wishing her dead. Not illness."

"Have you considered that you may have been right, after all? Perhaps someone *did* wish Sarah ill, and the stroke was a horrible coincidence."

"I never thought of it that way. But if I *was* right… I don't want to believe that anyone in this house could hate Sarah so much." Rosanie picked up Lulu and cradled him like a baby. "And people can harm other people with their thoughts. Don't you think? I mean, like voodoo and stuff."

This was treacherous ground, but I did in fact agree with Rosanie.

"I do," I said, taking the plunge. "But the object of those thoughts needs to be susceptible, suggestible, for it to do harm."

"Miss Sarah was a very sensitive person, Neil. Maybe…"

"Yes, she was. But she also suffered from atrial fibrillation. In this case, I believe a natural cause of death is more likely than a supernatural one."

"I suppose you're right," Rosanie admitted reluctantly. Lulu began to squirm and Rosanie quickly set him down before his claws could do any damage to her uniform. She pulled a small lint brush from her apron and began to whisk away the cat hairs. "Anyway, Sarah's gone. And wishing and second-guessing won't bring her back. Still, it worries me when I remember that reading."

"Worries you?"

"Yes, Neil. Don't you see? Even if Sarah's death was natural, it doesn't change what I saw in the cards. What I felt. Understand? If I was right, then nature did someone a big favor. And that someone is still out there… Someone evil."

*

ALONE WITH LULU, I tried to shake off the chill left by Rosanie's words. It seemed inappropriate to contemplate the potential for darkness in the human soul in such a sunny, cozy room. The sunshine was supplied by an eyebrow dormer window and a skylight, the coziness by shelves stocked with an abundance of quirky oddments including a large, articulated stuffed bear dressed in a pink, flower-patterned onesie, an ancient sewing machine, a hookah, a collection of clockwork mice, skeins of wool, plastic-covered newspapers, and a variety of books. Boxes were stacked neatly—and not so neatly—around the room as well as on the shelves, and in the center of the room was an old-fashioned hobby horse that had seen better days. Under the window were a Danish Modern table and chair—Sarah's workspace, I assumed.

As I moved toward the desk, my attention was caught by a glimpse of cobalt blue in my peripheral vision. I turned to face the object and found myself looking at a large, glass candle vase. I recognized the make immediately by its golden flower embossment. French and exorbitantly expensive, this brand of scented candle had been one of Sarah's few frivolous indulgences. With a feeling of nostalgia, I plucked the candle from the shelf, and in doing so, noticed a folded piece of paper with my initial written on it taped to the bottom. I dislodged the note and read:

> <u>Darling</u>,
>
> I know you love these little treasures as dearly as I do, but you're too cheap to buy them.
>
> Do enjoy this one.
>
> I could not <u>bear</u> to leave you totally in the dark.
>
> Sara

A quick riffling of the drawers turned up a box of fireplace matches, and the room was soon filled with the delicate scent of the Ayesha variety of hydrangea.

I sat at the desk and imagined Sarah there. How had she come to inhabit this room? Had it been before or after the arrival of Lulu? Looking around at the boxes, books, and newspapers, I wondered if Sarah's curiosity had overcome her sense of propriety, and she had indulged in a bit of the poking and prying that I had been tasked to carry out. Putting aside my own misgivings, I set first upon the open boxes on the shelves. No great sin in that. They were already open.

At first, what I discovered was entertaining, if not enlightening: family photos dating back to the nineteen twenties, a copy of *LIFE* magazine from 1968 with a cover photo of the Grove and a corresponding article about the late Harrison Willoughby. I was drawn to plastic-wrapped newspapers with headlines that captured the historically significant events of the time in which they had been printed: the assassinations of JFK, MLK, RFK; the Apollo moon landing.

The Willoughby family's collecting mania seemed to have petered out sometime in the early seventies. I imagined that either there was no news they felt warranted preserving, or their lives got in the way of collecting. I placed my bet on the latter. Further perusal of the shelves, however, proved me wrong. I found many more contemporary newspapers with headlines concerning the lives and deaths of prominent public figures over the last thirty years or so. Curious, I picked them up to take to the desk for closer inspection. As I did so, I nearly dropped them. At the bottom of the stack, in a clear plastic envelope with a hook and loop closure, was a copy of an opera magazine with a cover photo of Alma Montresor. I added it to the top of my collection and sat down at the desk.

Putting the newspapers to one side, I examined the magazine cover. Montresor reclined on a white leather chaise wearing white jeans and a smock-like white blouse. Though elaborately made up, she wore no jewelry and no shoes and lay with her right arm on a bolster and her right hand resting in the mass of her loose dark curls. The tableau was at once studied and casual and could have been captioned "Diva Relaxing at Home." Instead, "Remembering Alma" was printed at the bottom of the cover. I opened the magazine and read a tribute to the singer written by the musical director of the Metropolitan Opera. In it, the director praised Montresor's exceptional talent, her beauty, her professionalism. Worded like a send-off speech for a retirement party, it made no allusions to the singer's unexplained disappearance.

The entire issue was dedicated to Alma Montresor: articles about her unique voice, her most celebrated roles, her status as a fashion icon, her successful foray into classical crossover recordings—which had irked purists but had drawn millions to opera for the first time. Little was said of her personal life, but I was soon reminded that a picture can indeed be worth a thousand words.

The photo was taken at the Met's New Year's Eve gala. Standing at the foot of the opera house's central staircase were—from left to right— Fabiola Willoughby, Alma Montresor, and Ezra Willoughby. Fabiola wore a white, Grecian-style gown and her blonde hair was styled in a suitably curly updo. Fabiola's left hand rested on Montresor's shoulder, and her face was turned toward the singer, but her gaze was clearly focused on her husband, who had his right arm wrapped tightly around Montresor's wasp-thin waist. The diva was magnificent in the same glittering black concoction she wore in the portrait hanging in the music room. Smiling, her head thrown back slightly, she looked as if she'd been captured on the cusp of a burst of laughter. Ezra Willoughby, handsome and distinguished in his perfectly tailored tuxedo, seemed to share in the joke—his smile warm and genuine.

Fabiola's expression, however, was hard, her smile frosty.

A hammering of rain on the skylight pulled me abruptly from my study, and the room was plunged into almost instantaneous gloom. Still unaccustomed to the sudden afternoon storms that were common to Florida, I cursed under my breath. In New England, storms brewed—announcing their advent for hours, if not days, with increasing brooding darkness and humidity. In Florida, they came in a rush—like celestial incontinence.

Fumbling as my eyes adjusted to the darkness, I switched on the Tiffany floor lamp next to the desk. No sooner had I done so than the bulb flickered, fizzed, and died.

I looked toward the bathroom. No light shone through from my adjoining suite.

Fabulous.

I made to get up and find my way in the darkness to Rosanie or Nessa but checked myself. Max had said power outages were a common occurrence during foul weather. I'd look like a first-class ninny running to the women in a panic. A massive roll of thunder that could be felt, as well as heard, passed over and I shuddered. Lulu, who had been sprawled on the floor near my feet, clambered into my lap, the nails of his back paws poking my thighs under his considerable weight.

"It's just thunder," I said to the cat. "Angels are bowling in heaven." After a bit of head bunting, the creature settled into a crescent on my lap and seemed to doze. I pulled the candle closer and returned my attention to the magazine.

Regarding the tableau of Fabiola, Montresor, and Ezra, I thought of the classic love triangle: Ezra Willoughby's arm wrapped possessively around the waist of his lover, his wife looking on with barely contained jealousy and rage. Of course, that was all in my mind—my interpretation of the image. It might just have easily been that Fabiola was bored, Montresor was acting; hamming it up for the photographer, and Ezra was the diva's happily willing stooge.

Beto had said that rumors of an affair between the two had been fodder for the press. Maybe that was all it had been. A publicity stunt to fan the flames of Montresor's reputation as a femme fatale. Montresor and Ezra may have been nothing more than friends. Would Fabiola have played along with such a charade? Perhaps. She was a television personality, after all. She knew the score, as they say. But her expression in this picture told me otherwise. She was not bored; she was pissed off.

I read the photo's caption: *Alma Montresor's Last Public Appearance.*

So, this laughing, beautiful, virtuosically talented woman—admired by both peers and fans alike—had decided to simply walk away from it all and vanish into obscurity. Why? The article I had found in Sarah's journal quoted Anders Wilson as saying the consensus had been that Montresor had fallen ill or pregnant and that one or both of those conditions had led to the end of her career. The interviews and editorials that accompanied the many photos throughout the magazine seemed to support this theory. There were reports of missed rehearsals, emotional outbursts, physical weakness—all behaviors at odds with the focused, consummate professional all had known.

A friendly rival had observed of Montresor shortly before her disappearance: "She was nervous, agitated, short-tempered during rehearsals. All the 'diva' stereotypes. But that wasn't Alma. No. Alma could be a real bitch off-stage, but she was truly a joy to work with. It was amazing to see her transformation into character. It was something truly magical. Have you seen that clip of Callas singing Habanera in recital? The intro is fantastic. An entire—I don't know—three minutes of just watching Callas *become* Carmen…grow into the music, into the character. It was like that with Alma."

I found the comparison to Callas interesting. The tragedies of Callas's personal life had led to the destruction of her voice—her late-in-life attempts at a reclamation of her glory days had been disastrous and embarrassing. Many years would pass after Callas's death before her genius was embraced by new generations of opera lovers—her personal failures and misfortunes forgiven if not forgotten as her singular voice, musicality, and acting ability became her legacy. But Callas had died. If Montresor chose to withdraw at the height of her powers and popularity, it was a different story.

Or was it?

Anders Wilson's words haunted me there in that dark room—silent save for the thrum, boom, and spark of the storm: "*Did she simply choose to disappear, unable to cope with the reality that one day she would no longer possess the voice and beauty that brought her fame and wealth and seek a life of anonymity? One must ask: Is there an alternative?*"

Closing the magazine, I fell into contemplation of Alma Montresor. Her voice was clear in my mind: heartbreakingly emotional, visceral, one with the music of whichever composer's work she interpreted. No. *Channeled.* Even in recording, her living presence could be felt. A vocal muse for musical geniuses long since dead, preserved forever. What did it take to become a Callas or a Montresor? Above all else, I thought, it was love of the craft. Love of the music. Dedication to the principle of bel canto.

I looked at the last public photo of Montresor: brimming with life, exuberance, happiness. A star at the zenith of her career. Did someone like that commit suicide?

I thought not.

Would someone like that retire? Become a recluse?

Again, I thought not.

The rain pelted, the lightning crackled, the thunder rolled, and I thought. I wondered. I began to doze off.

Then an intense beam of light snapped me out of my reverie. I turned my head toward the source of the light and saw nothing but a long, black shadowy figure behind the bright shaft. The figure advanced into the room as the rain again turned to pounding hail.

"Having a good rummage?"

Nessa Hanson asked the question as she moved her hurricane lamp about the room. Advancing to the desk, she cast the light upon me, her face a strikingly, frighteningly beautiful moon of sharp planes and crevices against the surrounding darkness. Nessa's facial scar, almost unnoticeable in daylight, stood out clear and cruel. She glanced at the magazine and then back at me. "I see you've discovered our secret," she said.

"Your secret?"

"Yes. The twenty-five pounds of cat snoozing in your lap." Nessa laughed, lowering the lamp, and as the pool of light engulfed us both, the fearful mask disappeared to be replaced by the kindly face I'd come to know. "I brought you one," she added, handing me a second lamp. "Wasn't sure if Sarah had left one in your room."

"Thanks. There may be one, but I haven't looked. I should have after Max warned me about the power outages."

"Humph. Unfortunately, only Max and Rollo understand the damned wiring in this place. So, we'll have to rough it until they get back." She glanced up at the skylight. "Which shouldn't be long now. This doesn't look like one of those flash showers. Max will have to forgo skateboarding to-day."

"Well, I'll trust in your experience." Though I knew Nessa had been at the Grove for more than ten years, I'd never inquired about what came before. "Have you always lived in Florida?"

"No. But long enough."

Was Nessa's answer intentionally evasive, or did she think I was only referring to her apparent knowledge of the weather? Aside from the deceased husband Nessa had mentioned on my first day, I knew nothing of her life beyond the Grove. Belatedly, I realized that I was at a singular disadvantage. All the inmates at the Grove knew something about me through friendship or acquaintance with Sarah, yet I knew next to nothing about them. I never exchanged more than polite greetings with Rodrigo. Rosanie talked a lot, but never about anything personal—aside from today's confidences about her psychic visions—and Nessa, though the friendliest of the three, kept her conversation general. I had learned at a young age the value of keeping one's council regarding one's personal life, so I couldn't hold the same behavior against anyone. Still, it felt as if the Grove staff had made some sort of pact of silence against me.

You're imagining things.

"Don't worry about the secret," I said, dropping the subject of Nessa's past. "As I told Rosanie, I'm not a snitch. And I think I can tolerate his company."

Lulu pushed his head against my leg as if to thank me for my words, and Nessa said, "It doesn't appear as if he'll settle for tolerance." She peered at the cat with her head tilted to one side. "I wonder if somehow he knows that you were Sarah's friend?"

"That sounds like a question Rosanie would ask," I said.

"It does, doesn't it? But cats *are* strange creatures. I always wonder what they're thinking about. And then they have that way of looking at you as if they're reading *your* thoughts."

"You're fond of them?"

"No. I mean, I don't dislike them. And I'm not afraid of them, like Ez—er—Mr. Willoughby."

"According to Rosanie," I said, shelving Nessa's near, and surprising, slip into familiar address of her employer for future consideration, "Mr. Willoughby *hates* them. She didn't say he is afraid of them."

"Isn't it all the same thing?"

"Hate and fear? No. Though people often hate things they fear."

"Or that they love," added Nessa in an undertone. Before I could pursue that line of thought, Nessa changed the subject. "Well, then," she continued in her usual, hearty tone, "I'll leave you to it."

"Thanks again for the lamp."

"No worries." Nessa flashed a smile and was on her way.

I returned to my perusal of the opera magazine but found nothing more of any particular interest. Nothing that might have provided a clue to Alma Montresor's disappearance. I glanced through a few more old newspapers then returned them and the magazine to where I'd found them. A further rummage of the boxes would have to wait until a day without rain or blackouts.

Back in my room, I reexamined the articles tucked into Sarah's keepsake. The story about the proposed television biopic drew my attention. *Intrigues and Ambiguities* had been a popular show—a favorite of both students and faculty at Allerton. I'd watched many episodes with Sarah over the years. I did not recall one about Alma Montresor.

When the power returned as unexpectedly as it had gone, I opened my laptop and began to do a bit of research. A query of *Flight of a Songbird* took me almost immediately to an article about the program—and its cancellation. The show was scrapped just before filming was set to begin. Disagreements over casting and a lawsuit filed by the Montresor family put an end to the production.

Montresor's family. I'd never heard anything about them. Like many celebrities, Alma Montresor had carefully crafted her origin story, so that she seemed to have been born in an opera house. La Montresor was a diva. She had no need of family, only adoring fans. But, of course, there had to be family—distant, dead, estranged, jailed, whatever. Somewhere, there were relatives.

Further reading rewarded me with an answer. It was Alma's grandmother, one VL Montresor, who had brought a suit of defamation against Anders Wilson and the production company.

What kind of name was VL?

Luckily, the name was highlighted in blue, and a click took me to a page dedicated to the woman. Virgilia Louise Montresor, a successful writer of period romance novels, was born in New Orleans in 1920 and died in the same city in 2016. She had two children, Virgil Carl, and Anna Constanza, and two grandchildren, Agnes Clothilde and Alma Ramola.

Good grief. What names!

I searched for Agnes Clothilde Montresor and came up with nothing. Agnes Clothilde apparently shunned the press, the internet, and social media. Her sister Alma, however, had no aversion to publicity. Tabloids had a particular fondness for the singer. Many of the articles concerned the size and/or genuineness of her bosom or the extent and cost of her wardrobe and jewelry. Others linked her to any number of famous men—eligible or otherwise—from Hollywood royalty to the real thing. A photo of Montresor in a rather cozy pose with a Middle Eastern prince preceded an article that hinted at trouble in paradise for the young man's principal wife. More articles followed the same pattern: married men rumored to be the object of Alma Montresor's vamping. She was portrayed as an irresistible seductress, a siren, a new age Mata Hari. Though she appeared to have embraced the image with gusto, there was little evidence that she lived the life it represented.

For the most part, Alma Montresor's relationship with the media had been a game that profited both sides. Only in reference to her involvement with Ezra Willoughby did this relationship show signs of strain. The media bit into the putative affair with ferocious tenacity and would not let it go. The alleged scandal was covered by every outlet from supermarket checkout rags to the *Wall Street Journal.* The game was no longer profitable for Alma Montresor, and she made direct and unequivocal statements to the press. She and Willoughby had met through a mutual acquaintance—an entertainment attorney who'd been a college classmate of Fabiola Willoughby—and moved in overlapping social circles, as both she and Willoughby were art collectors and shared many of the same tastes. They were good friends. End of story. There had been no marriage proposals, and there had never been any question of Willoughby divorcing his wife, who was also a dear friend.

But the rumors persisted. Unwisely, I thought, Willoughby and Montresor made a point of publicly distancing themselves from one another— which only led to the belief among the scandal mongers that the rumors had indeed been true.

Then there were more stories of Montresor missing rehearsals, of fainting on stage, of uncharacteristic irritability. As I scanned the internet articles, I saw that each corroborated the words of Montresor's colleague quoted in the opera magazine I'd found in the storeroom. In the last few months before her disappearance, Alma Montresor had been under emotional and physical strain. I scrolled further, and a *Daily Mail* headline jumped out. "Baby Maybe?" was accompanied by an unflattering image of Montresor captured on the streets of Paris wearing a black smock and leggings with her right hand pressed to her stomach. The ensuing article referred to the pose as a "protective gesture" and suggested that perhaps the diva's voluminous top was concealing a baby bump.

Was it possible?

I read a few more articles, then closed my computer, my eyes tired from the strain of reading by hurricane lamp. I lay down on the sofa and considered what I had learned.

It was shortly after the flurry of rumors and inuendo about a possible pregnancy that Montresor vanished, leaving her attorneys, agent, and financial advisors to deal with the fallout. The press had hounded Montresor's sister—her only living close relation—for comment but had been met with resolute refusal to speak of the matter. In the words of Agnes Clothilde Montresor, "What my sister does with her own life is her own fucking business." Although I agreed with the sentiment, my curiosity was piqued, and I was left as unsatisfied with Agnes Clothilde's answer as the press must have been.

Had Ezra Willoughby really been Alma Montresor's lover? Had pregnancy been the cause of Montresor's uncharacteristic behaviors?

These questions nagged as I rooted around on the sofa, trying to find a comfortable spot for a late-afternoon snooze. As I settled on my left side, I looked across to my desk and to Sarah's book which lay next to my laptop. The folded articles jutted out in a haphazard way, and my neat-leaning temperament did not allow me to leave them in that state. I hauled myself up and set to restoring order to the papers. As I did so, my attention was caught by the article on adoption laws in Florida. I'd ignored it before, but now read it through with attention. One passage was highlighted.

"A closed adoption," the article stated, "is the most common form of adoption in the state of Florida. In a closed adoption, neither party has any knowledge of the other, and all records are sealed. The adopting family receives nonidentifying health and other background information."

This surprised me. In my experience as a teacher, the open adoption model had been the norm—particularly in cases in which there was a distinct cultural or racial disparity between the child and his adoptive parents. The Willoughbys had been a high-profile couple. Surely, I thought, recalling the heated public debates certain celebrities had stirred by adopting foreign children, any irregularities or oddities in the adoption process would have been leapt upon by the media.

The disappearance of Alma Montresor roughly coincided with the Willoughby's adoption of Max. I wondered if Sarah, as I was beginning to do, had pieced together a possible narrative in which Alma Montresor gave birth to Ezra Willoughby's child who was then adopted by Mr. and Mrs. Willoughby. Had Montresor's alleged extramarital affair with Ezra Willoughby and the resulting pregnancy been traumatic enough to cause her to withdraw from the world?

Chapter Eight

RISING AT DAWN every day, I took advantage of my access to the Grove's spectacular pool. Relaxing on a chaise after doing my laps, it was easy to conjure images of lavish parties, flowing champagne, drug use, and debauchery back in the prewar heyday of the Grove. Hollywood Babylon meets Saint Augustine. I was lost in thoughts of glamorous starlets with long cigarette holders and beautiful male prostitutes with their own lengthy attributes, when my fantasies were interrupted by the sounds of the diving board being flexed and a subsequent splash.

I observed Ezra Willoughby's precise strokes, graceful dolphin kicks and crisp turnarounds. My admiration trebled when he finally emerged from the water, his powerful, hirsute physique even more impressive than what I had imagined lay beneath his finely tailored clothing.

"The best all-around workout," Willoughby declared as he strode toward me, toweling off. "But you obviously know that already," he added as he approached my chair, looking over my supine body in a way that I found both uncomfortable and arousing. "You've got the classic swimmer's build. I'm more like a sea cow."

Sea bull, more like, I thought, taking in the outline of his privates encased in immodest white swim briefs.

"You swim like a professional, sir," I said.

Ezra Willoughby laughed.

"Since we're both practically naked, I think we can dispense with formalities. Please, call me Ezra."

"You swim like a professional, Ezra," I corrected, thinking we were long overdue for the dismissal of formalities and glad of the step forward.

"Fact is," continued Ezra as he lay on the chaise next to mine, "I never knew how to swim until I met Fabiola. We took our honeymoon on San Andres and Fabiola was hell-bent on scuba diving. I just smiled and said that it sounded fantastic. I was too embarrassed to admit I couldn't swim—much less I was terrified of diving. Of course, I couldn't bluff my way out. I had to fess up, eventually. Fabiola took it in stride and became my personal trainer. She was like a mermaid…so at home in the water. She told me I really didn't need to learn anything—that being one with the water, with the ocean, was buried in the subconscious of every human being. I think she was right. She was right about a lot of things."

Ezra Willoughby surprised me by relating something so personal. Perhaps he'd just been waiting for the right moment. He surprised me even more with his next words, as they hit very close to home.

"Those were the good days, Neil. I've decided to remember just the good days. Do you think that's right? Or even possible?"

I recalled my opa and our afternoons of television and knitting. I remembered working in my father's antique shop when I was a bit older, my father's distracted kindness, my mother's sarcastic humor, singing, and piano playing. The good things, before everything went wrong.

"Sometimes," I replied, "It's necessary."

Ezra looked at me sharply, a slight frown giving away the age that his body hid so well. Did he suspect something of the trauma that I'd not revealed? He seemed poised to ask me to elaborate, but apparently changed his mind and turned his gaze toward the house.

"I didn't come here just to swim," said Ezra. "I saw you from my bedroom." He pointed to French windows opening to a small balcony in a tower overlooking the adjacent garden. My thoughts went to Fabiola Willoughby and, as if reading them, Ezra added, "No. It didn't happen there. Fabiola fell from a balcony in the turret directly over Max's bedroom."

"Jesus, did he…?"

"Thank the Lord, no. Max didn't see anything. He was with Rosanie in the kitchen when it happened." Ezra brushed his hand over his head and sighed before adding, "I wasn't here. I had dinner out with a colleague after a meeting of the historical society. If I'd been here… Could I have prevented it? Could I have changed anything?"

"It was an accident, Ezra. You can't blame yourself." It was a standard what to-say-to-a-grieving-spouse response, but Ezra seemed to accept it gratefully.

"I know," he said softly. "Everyone says that, but I don't think the what-if in the back of my mind will ever go away. I'm sure you've heard or read the rumors that my wife took her own life?" I nodded, though I'd only heard it through Beto. "That's nonsense. Anyone who knew her well would agree. But if people believe it…well, in some ways its better than the truth. And I think Fabiola would appreciate the drama of it, the tragedy…as perceived by her multitude of fans.”

“What *is* the truth?”

“My wife’s death *was* a tragic accident. Fabiola was what’s called a high-functioning alcoholic. She never got *drunk*. She didn’t binge and act out. She was successful, amazingly fit in most every way. Yet, she was almost always high. I don’t know how she did it; how she could drink just enough to keep the buzz she needed without losing control. But she could quit cold turkey when she had to. Fabiola rarely drank when she was taping. Her image was too important to her.”

“I can understand,” I said. “My father was like that. Even though it seemed to me when I was a kid that all adults drank like fish, it was different for my father. Today, some people might call it self-medicating.”

“Cancer?”

“No. Nothing physical.”

“Oh. I’m sorry.”

My father had not been mentally ill—his sickness had been emotional—but allowing Ezra to assume as much was easier than explaining to him that my father drank to keep the demons at bay. Demons that would take his life and forever change mine.

“I came down,” continued Ezra, “because I want to tell you how much I appreciate what you’re doing for my son. I’ve never seen Max this engaged in his schoolwork—and it’s more than that. Max was telling me about your lighthouse field trip the other day. It was the first time I’ve seen him smile since Sarah passed away.”

Since Sarah *passed away. Not his mother. Interesting.*

Given Ezra's willingness to confide in me, I considered asking him about Max's relationship with his late wife but decided that the right moment had passed. I thanked him for his praise, and we both turned our attention to the sky and to our own thoughts.

*

"I MADE EXTRA, so you can give some to your dad." I said, pulling a pan of blueberry and walnut muffins from the oven. Today was technically Rosanie's day on the rotation, but she never objected when I took over.

"Thanks. *Papi's* become a recluse since Mrs. Willoughby passed away. I hope you haven't been thinking he avoids you because you're gay or something."

"Does he? Or something?"

"They look delicious!" said Rosanie, eying the tray of hot muffins covetously, as I set them on the cooling rack. I smiled as I prized one of the little cakes carefully from its cup, placed it on a dainty plate, cleaved it, topped it with a pat of butter and presented it to Rosanie. "Gracias. Nessa never lets me eat anything straight from the oven."

"It's bad for your stomach. But you haven't answered my question, so I'm hoping the rule breaking will loosen your tongue and nothing else."

"Sorry," said Rosanie, hesitating as she reached for the steaming muffin. "That *is* an old wives' tale, right? That eating hot baked goods makes you sick?" I shrugged. Rosanie put down her hand. "Papi's old-fashioned," she continued as I poured coffee. "Not homophobic. He thinks you're doing "women's work." Plus, there's Max."

"I don't follow."

"He's jealous, Neil. Papi and Mrs. Willoughby were tight, so he assumed this role of a sort of guardian over Max—like he was standing in for Mr. Willoughby when Mr. Willoughby wasn't, like, around. You know? Sarah was a woman, so it was, like, a different dynamic with her than it is with you."

Like, I understood perfectly.

"That's a very astute observation," I said, settling myself across the butcher block from Rosanie. "I wonder if you could help me with something else in the observation line. Max and his mother. What was their relationship like? Max rarely speaks of her. The most he's ever told me is that he hated her. But kids his age often say that without truly meaning it."

Rosanie nodded and made a pouty face as she considered my words. She took a large bite of muffin and a gulp of coffee before replying.

"*Dios me perdone,* Neil, but Fabiola was a total bitch. And the worst kind. The kind who thinks she's a saint."

I sipped my coffee, instinct telling me that this was something Rosanie had kept bottled up for a very long time and that to interrupt or prod would be a mistake.

"I'm sure you've met people like her," Rosanie continued, "dealing with all those parents and families back at Allerton. In *novellas,* they always say things like: 'How could you? After everything I've done for you!' The kind of people who only do things for others when it's to their own advantage and get all upset when someone they helped isn't grateful enough. They're always right. Always. And they think the sun shines out of their— well, you get the idea."

A toxic narcissist.

Mommy Dearest.

"I see. And Max took the brunt of this behavior?"

Rosanie laughed.

"Oh, no. Max was one of only two people in this house she couldn't twist around her little finger to one degree or another. I mean, she could be so…so… What's that word? Not *believable*. Something more subtle…"

"Plausible?"

"That's it. Plausible. Anyway, Max tolerated her, but he saw through her, if you know what I mean. Kids are always good at that."

"Yes," I agreed, knowing from my own experience that this was not always true. Opa had gone to his grave leaving me with the impression that he was nothing but a kindly, rather quiet man who liked knitting and gardening. Children don't always see the truth. "You said two people were immune to Mrs. Willoughby," I continued. "Were you the other?"

"I wish. No, it was Miss—it was Sarah. She had Mrs. Willoughby's number from day one. That's why they didn't get along. You see, it was Mrs. Willoughby's idea to hire a tutor. Mr. Willoughby wanted to send Max to some institute in France. In this case, I think Mrs. Willoughby was right— but I don't think she got exactly what she expected."

No. People like Fabiola Willoughby expected unquestioning compliance and constant praise and gratitude. Sarah had questioned everything and had given praise and offered gratitude only where they were deserved.

"It's terrible to say that it was funny, sometimes, the way they argued over stuff," continued Rosanie, "But it *was*. Sarah was always so calm and cool. And the calmer and the cooler Sarah was, the more Mrs. Willoughby would rant and rave. To give Mrs. Willoughby her due, I have to say that it wasn't exactly fair that Mr. Willoughby always took Sarah's side. I can see how Mrs. Willoughby could have taken that in the wrong way. I mean, Sarah was beautiful and kind and Mr. Willoughby—" Rosanie stopped, pressed her lips together and looked down at her muffin. "I'm talking too much. Papi says I have a motor mouth and he's right."

Intrigued but respectful of Rosanie's reticence, I returned to something she had mentioned in a previous conversation. "If I remember correctly, you told me your parents worked for Mrs. Willoughby before her marriage to Mr. Willoughby?"

"Yes," said Rosanie, visibly relieved that I had not pursued the subject of Sarah's relationship with Ezra. "She was living in Miami then—where she filmed her TV show. My mom was her stylist, and my dad was her driver. That's how they met. Weird the way things work, right? Mrs. Willoughby brought them together and Mrs. Willoughby drove them apart."

I raised an eyebrow at this, making the typical assumption, but Rosanie was as quick to read my thoughts as she was to counter them.

"Oh, it wasn't like *that*. I mean, Papi didn't have an affair with her or anything. I mean…"

"A sin of thought rather than deed?" I prompted.

Rosanie laughed. "You sound like Papi. He says stuff like that."

I wondered if Rodrigo's involvement with Fabiola had been as chaste as Rosanie believed or if her parents had presented their daughter with a fairy tale version of something more sordid, and the adult Rosanie had held on to that lie to protect the image of her beloved papi.

The portrait that Rosanie painted of her late employer was far from flattering. And though it was certainly biased, it squared with Sarah's impression and Beto's speculation. Adding in Max's confession of loathing, I concluded that I was lucky not to have met Fabiola Willoughby in the flesh.

*

"BY THE WAY," I said to Max as I closed my laptop, signaling the end of our afternoon session, "I know all about the Great Secret."

"The *Great Secret*?"

"Lulu."

"Oh."

"You guys must find a home for him. He can't live his life cooped up in that storeroom."

"He gets out. When Dad's not here. Which is always."

I was glad that Max had brought up the subject of his father's prolonged absences. Max had appeared tired and distracted of late, and I wondered if this was the cause.

"I understand it's hard for him to be here," continued Max, displaying his precocious maturity. "I mean now…since Fabiola and Sarah…you know. I mean…it's his way of dealing with things."

"That's very insightful, Max. And how are *you* dealing with things?

Max rubbed his hand back and forth over his hair, a gesture reminiscent of Ezra. "Okay, I guess. I miss Sarah a lot."

I was about to utter the comforting pearl of wisdom that time heals everything but, knowing the fallaciousness of the aphorism, I refrained. Instead, I opened the top drawer of my desk and withdrew Sarah's diary.

"Maybe this will help," I said, holding the volume out toward Max. He came forward, a perplexed look on his face.

"I thought you were going to give it to Mr. Adami."

"I changed my mind. It's dedicated to you. Sarah created it for you."

It came then. The flood of pent-up grief, of anger, of love. Max took the diary and clutched it to his narrow chest, emitting a keening sound somewhere between a sob and a wail. Then, he began to cry in earnest, leaning over my desk like a marionette whose strings had been severed.

"I'm sorry," he said, gulping for air.

"Sorry for what?"

"For crying. For acting like a baby."

"Expressing one's emotions appropriately is nothing to be sorry for," I said. "And it's not being a baby. It's being a man."

"My dad says only sissy's cry."

I gave you more credit than that, Ezra!

"Do you think I'm a sissy?" I asked.

"No."

I rose from my chair and went to Max. I hugged him close as I said, "My first night here, I cried. I cried thinking about Sarah and all the years we spent together at Allerton. I cried for the things I should have said but didn't. I cried because I felt alone and afraid. And the crying helped. It made me feel better. Don't ever feel ashamed to cry, Max. When that happens, you stop being human." Belatedly realizing what I'd implied about Ezra, I added, "Your father meant well. It's just an old-fashioned way of thinking. My dad told me the same thing." He had not, but I *had* learned from him the efficacy of white lies.

Max held Sarah's journal to his chest, and I held Max to mine. Sarah was there with us at that moment, I was certain.

Thank you, my friend. Thank you for bringing Max into my life.

Chapter Nine

Convent of the Sacred Heart

Florentina Bay, California

August 10, 2015

My Dear Neil,

Your mother confessed to me before she died.

How's that for being direct? Well, you know me better than anyone, I believe, and I am sure you will not take offense. You might, however, wonder what prompted Eve to confide in me after all these years. Answer: death. Deathbed confessions may sound cliché, but they happen all the time. Especially with Catholics when a priest is hovering and ready to play stand-in for God and forgive all their sins. Of course, your mother wasn't Catholic or the least bit religious. In her case, it was more of a desire for closure.

My first reaction was anger. Anger not with Eve—who's years of silence were her own punishment and who was undeserving of more—but with you, my friend. How could you not have trusted me with your secret, I wondered? Upon reflection, the anger gave way to understanding when I admitted to myself that I would have behaved no differently had I been you. After all, I did not tell you everything about my life before the Church. And it never serves the greater good to be judgmental. Now, my heart goes out to you—as it always has and always will—my sweet boy.

Yes, you will always be a boy to me. My boy. The child I could have had but chose not to bring into the world— at once a reminder of my sin and an affirmation of God's mercy and love.

There you have it. Sister Bendedicta's Confession. I blame your mother for setting me the example.

You're smiling through tears, I know. Just as it should be.

I love you dearly, Neil. Never forget that your life is your own; that your world is what you make it. Haven't you already proven this? I am proud of you, and I pray that everything your mother told me has not marked you forever—that you have learned to let go of a past and of sins that are not yours.

We'll talk more at Christmas.

Benedicta

I kept the letter from Benedicta in its original envelope, tucked between the pages of *The Wind in The Willows*. Fitting, I thought, as the book had been a gift from my mother.

Eve

For many years I had thought of my mother by her given name. It began on the day of my grandfather's funeral. At the time, I turned against her—interpreting her apparent joy at my grandfather's passing as cruel. I imagined, in a flash of understanding, that she had hated her father-in-law. But my understanding of the reason for her feelings or the duration of them was beyond the scope of a child. I suppose choosing not to think of her as "Mother" was a way to distance myself from the woman I felt I no longer knew or trusted.

I remembered the day she'd come to me as I sat on the beach, trying to paint and be somewhere else other than in the here and now. Somewhere my grandfather hadn't been evil, and my father hadn't drunk himself to irreversible despair and death.

I almost didn't recognize my mother—striding toward me dressed in worn jeans and a white T-shirt, her pale blonde hair pulled back in a simple ponytail. So different from the woman in high heels, power suit and the big, blown-out coiffure to which I'd grown accustomed. She sat down next to me and tried to explain why she'd withheld the truth from me and why she had decided to reveal it. I pretended not to listen. I did not want to know.

Only later in my life did I realize how the death of my grandfather liberated my mother, though it failed to do the same for my father. After many years of resentment and coolness on my part I came to appreciate how much my mother loved me and how her secretiveness and denials had been her way of expressing that love. She had colluded in her husband's and father-in-law's deceptions for my sake—hoping to shield me and provide a life for me that was clean, untainted.

Had the relationship between Max and his mother been similar? Had some secret in Fabiola Willoughby's life prevented her from being as close to her son as she might have wished? I saw Fabiola only as she had been seen by others and Max had seen his mother through the eyes of a child. Neither of us would ever know or understand the whole woman.

I had gained little understanding of what caused the unspecified *something* that Sarah had mentioned in our last conversation. But something did permeate the atmosphere of the Grove. Oddness, to paraphrase Beto. If only I could have spoken to Sarah at length. If only she could have shared with me her impressions and feelings. Then again, perhaps she had—if inadvertently.

I returned *The Wind in The Willows* to the fireplace mantle. Rereading Benedicta's letter did more than spark fond memories and make me reconsider the character of Fabiola Willoughby and her relationship with her son. It also sparked an idea.

*

AS I LAY the items I had removed from Sarah's journal on her desk, I felt a twinge of guilt. Certainly, the articles could not have been meant for Max—but what about the theater tickets? Had Sarah broken the no-music rule and bundled Max off to a secret entertainment? Sarah had been impulsive but not reckless. Or had Victor been her companion? If that was the case, then why had she kept the tickets in Max's journal? My private stash of letters had been keys that solved the final mysteries of my childhood. I now wondered if Sarah's articles and the theater tickets—like my letters—were keys to something.

Lighting the perfumed candle, I recalled what Max had said about holding back his journal when Victor had come to collect Sarah's things. He would have to have done that *before* Victor arrived. I never thought to ask Max where exactly he had discovered the book. If Sarah had been in the process of completing the work, it would likely have been on or in her desk. Sarah had died suddenly. What else might she have left undone and undiscovered. I looked to where she had placed the candle, certain I would discover it.

Did you also intend to leave the articles and the tickets for me, Sarah? Was there anything else?

I examined the tickets more closely. The performance had taken place in October of the previous year at the Ponce de Leon Playhouse in Old Saint Augustine. The price of admission seemed high for a local theater, and I wondered how they justified it. I retrieved my laptop from my room and looked up Ponce de Leon Playhouse. It had been established in the 1970s by a well-known, retired Broadway actor and his life partner: a retired producer and director. PLP—as it came to be known—was well-endowed by public donations and various grants, including a sizable one from Fabiola Willoughby who had also served on the theater's board of directors.

Further reading revealed that the production of *Godspell* had been one of the highlights of the fall season. I was not particularly fond of the musical loosely based on the *Gospel of Matthew*, but I knew it well. Indeed, Allerton's theater department had mounted the show three times during my tenure. I turned my attention to a review of the PLP production:

> Saint Augustine's PLP has once again done a time warp to the 1970s, following up the season's less-than-stellar premier of *A Little Night Music* with a refreshing new production of *Godspell*. The ensemble of talented young performers gives the somewhat dated material a needed facelift and lends each character a degree of natural individuality often lacking in other productions.
>
> This outing is also notable for the return of Nessa Hanson—this time in the director's chair. Readers may remember Ms. Hanson's star turn as Carlotta Campion in PLP's well-received Follies of last season...

Interesting. But what—if anything—did it signify? Fabiola Willoughby had been a benefactress of the local theater company of which Nessa Hanson was a member. Nothing sinister about that. It looked good on Fabiola's resume. And if she'd had anything to do with giving Nessa entrée to the company, that fit nicely with Rosanie's assessment of Fabiola's personality. My discovery also gave me a peek into the private world of Mrs. Hanson. I tried to imagine her on stage, singing and dancing, but could not. I did, however, wonder if I had unmasked the phantom pianist.

I searched Sarah's desk thoroughly for envelopes labeled, "To be

Opened Only Upon My Death," notes taped to the undersides of drawers, and the classic hidden compartment containing a letter written in cypher, but I found only a few paper clips and a broken correction-tape dispenser. I was being ridiculous. Time to call it quits.

*

I FELT OVERDRESSED with my fresco wool suit, silk tie, and straw fedora. Although my family had not been regular churchgoers, we put on our Sunday best when we attended services. The crowd at St. Barnabas Episcopal Church tended more toward business casual—a few elderly gentlemen elevating the button-down and chinos look with a sport coat and their female contemporaries clad in muted floral frocks topped with cardigans.

St. Barnabas, just off the plaza in Old Saint Augustine, was small and suitably quaint for a parish established in the early nineteenth century. The stained-glass windows were beautiful and the grounds immaculate, the interior rich with original woodwork and smelling comfortingly of oil soap and incense. Sarah had mentioned the church only briefly in our conversations, but I knew she had attended Sunday mass regularly. Had Sarah made friends here? Had she also made enemies?

A conspicuous newcomer, I sat at the back of the church. Fortunately, I had sometimes accompanied Sarah to mass—for the music as much as the companionship. So with the knowledge I'd gleaned of the Episcopal liturgy, I managed to navigate the service without any embarrassing fumbles.

Mother Anne, the vicar of St. Barnabas, was willowy and middle-aged with graying, wavy red hair and seemed to radiate warmth and kindliness suited to her title. It was her I'd come to meet. If Sarah had been involved in church activities, Mother Anne would know with whom she'd interacted.

At the end of mass, I waited patiently as the priest engaged in conversation with her parishioners as they exited the church. When the last had gone, I approached Mother Anne and introduced myself.

"What a wonderful surprise!" Mother Anne took my hand and squeezed tightly. "Sarah spoke of you often and warmly. Welcome, Neil." I was invited to coffee in the rectory garden and accepted with pleasure.

In mufti, the priest appeared shorter than in ceremonial garb, and at proximity looked younger than I'd first imagined. Freckles dotted her fair cheeks and her green eyes sparkled though the lenses of her granny glasses.

"I was hoping you'd come," said Mother Anne as she poured coffee into dainty cups that were rimmed with gold and painted with flowers. "I've been wondering how Max is doing."

"Max?"

"Yes. He always came along with Sarah to the early mass. It warmed my heart to see him take such an interest—all thing considered."

"All things?"

"Well, his father used to be a regular until his second marriage. All the Willoughby family were members of the congregation—since the beginning of time, it seems. Now, Mr. Willoughby and Max are the only Willoughbys left. Max was baptized here, and I've always hoped it was a sign that the tradition would continue. There's something special in a parish where families are in it for generations." Mother Anne passed me a plate of oatmeal cookies and added, "But that's just me. My father was a priest, and I grew up in the Church. I'm unashamedly prejudiced."

"I know what you mean about generational parishes," I said.

"Delicious cookies, by the way."

"Thanks. *How* do you know?"

"I know," I said, "because I attended a Catholic school in just such a parish when I was a kid. Some families had children in multiple grades. And they were the 'special' kids. The nuns seemed to think there was something saintly about their mothers popping out good little Catholics on a regular basis."

Mother Anne snorted a good-natured laugh that made me smile and relax in the comfortable wicker chair. "I take it you were not one of the *special* kids," she said.

"No. I was one of the few non-Catholic students. We were always subtly reminded of how lucky we were to be allowed to attend. It was hard sometimes, but it was a good thing in the end. It gave me the experience I would need to understand my students; to make a connection. So many young people feel shut out, cut off."

Mother Anne nodded over her coffee cup. "I didn't make them," she said.

"I beg your pardon?"

"The cookies. I was tempted to take credit for them but, as George Washington is supposed to have said, I cannot tell a lie. My son's the chef in the family. His carnitas are to die for." She took a sip of coffee. "Sorry. I've gone off topic. It's PSD. Post Sermon Disorder. I spend a week working on it as if I were submitting to the Booker Prize committee, and once it's done, I'm totally discombobulated." Another sip of coffee. "And, yes, many of them do."

"Boys like Max?" I asked, just managing to follow her thread.

"I wouldn't say that. Max is amazingly self-centered—in the most positive interpretation of the term. I don't imagine he cares much what his peers think, or that he's not popular. Sarah told me he was taken out of school because of bullying. I don't get it, really. I can see why he might have been bullied, but I don't see him as the type to put up with it. For all his bashfulness, I suspect he's got a hidden kick-ass streak."

"You suspect correctly. I've experienced the kick. Apparently, he gets it honestly from his adoptive parents."

"From *one*, certainly."

"Fabiola Willoughby?"

Mother Anne sighed and looked away. "It doesn't behoove me to be uncharitable," she said, addressing a rhododendron. "Did you ever watch *Dragnet*?" she added, turning back to me. I nodded, remembering watching reruns of the show when I was little. "Good," continued Mother Anne. "The story you are about to hear is true, only the names have been changed to protect the innocent. Once upon a time, Lupita Smith, a popular Latina television personality, married a wealthy philanthropist named Oscar Jones. Mr. and Mrs. Jones, unable or unwilling to conceive their own child, adopted a boy who they named Sam. Although she was Catholic, Lupita agreed to have Sam baptized in the Episcopal church, as was the tradition of centuries in her husband's family.

"It started off well, as bad things sometimes do. Lupita, with her outward charm and beauty, was welcomed warmly into her husband's parish. She attended services regularly with her husband and child and soon became involved in church activities. Unfortunately, Lupita was not content to be involved; she wanted to be in charge. As you can imagine that sort of attitude did not sit well with the existing parish doyennes—particularly since Lupita declined to renounce her Catholic faith."

"They booted her?" I ventured, easily envisioning the internecine battle.

Mother Anne gave me a side-eye and smiled. "That was the version of the doyennes. Lupita's version was that *she* walked out on *them*. Strutted, more likely. Either way, it was the end of the honeymoon."

I topped up our coffee and ate another cookie. "What of Ezra and Max?" I asked, discarding the pretense of a fictional family.

"Mr. Willoughby attended Sunday service with Max on and off for a few years, but they eventually dropped off the radar. I did not see Max again until he started coming with Sarah. He's grown into such a handsome boy. And he has the most beautiful singing voice."

I nearly choked on my cookie. "He *sings?*"

"People tend to, in church."

"Of course. It's only…"

"That music is forbidden at the Grove?"

I was gobsmacked.

"Sarah told me all about it," continued Mother Anne. "It was Sarah's opinion that the rule applied only to the Grove and did not preclude her from exposing Max to music at other venues."

"*Godspell,*" I murmured.

"What?"

"Nothing. Sorry for interrupting."

"Well, it was a lovely interlude while it lasted—a gift from our Lord to hear Max's voice raised in His praise. Our choirmaster believes Max has the makings of a great countertenor."

Opera.

I nursed my coffee, considering my next words. "I wonder if Max inherited his talent from his biological parents. At Allerton, I often found that artistically inclined children came from families with a lineage of artists." That wasn't really the case, but I thought it sounded good.

"Interesting," said Mother Anne. She sat up straighter in her chair, her beautifully manicured hands draped over the armrests. "And laughably transparent. What you're fishing for is my opinion on whether Alma Montresor was Max's mother."

"Yes."

"I have no idea. I was aware of the gossip, of course. But I never met the woman; never saw her in Mr. Willoughby's company—though I knew *of* her. She was once a frequent guest at the Grove, according to the papers. One year, the church suffered serious hurricane damage. The Willoughby Charitable Trust donated funds to cover the replacement of several stained-glass windows and Ms. Montresor's personal contribution paid for the replacement of the organ. I assumed that Ms. Montresor had heard of our plight through her philanthropic connections with Mr. Willoughby."

Nicely said and completely reasonable. I decided to change the subject.

"Did Sarah have any close friends in the church?" I asked, trying to sound casual and missing the mark entirely. I may as well have whipped out a pad and pencil.

"None that I'm aware of. She sought me out when she brought Max to mass the first time, and we had a good talk—and several thereafter. But I think she avoided getting too involved with the community, as she only planned to be here temporarily."

Mother Anne offered more coffee and cookies, both of which I politely refused. "Thank you for your hospitality, Mother," I said, as she took my hands in hers in farewell. "I'm glad to have met you."

Mother Anne returned the sentiment and added, "May the Lord be with you in your search."

"My search?"

"Your search for the truth. It's understandable that you seek it—just as Sarah did. But I would be remiss in my pastoral responsibility if I did not advise you that what is true and what is for the best are not always the same thing."

"You're preaching to the choir, Mother," I said.

"What do you mean?"

"A story for another day," I added, echoing Nessa Hanson. "Thank you for your advice."

Mother Anne smiled and embraced me. "Until another day, then. Make it soon, Neil."

*

AS I ENTERED the library the next morning, Max pulled up his left shirt-sleeve and made an eloquent gesture of glancing at an imaginary watch. He tapped his wrist for emphasis.

"I apologize for my lateness," I said, feeling every bit the guilty pupil as I sat at my desk. "It was unavoidable."

Max gave up his stern-teacher look and smiled. "You missed a button," he said, pointing at the protruding fabric. "And your hair is sticking up." I buttoned the button and passed my hand over my head. My hair was still damp and sticky with mousse. "The other side, Prof."

"Thank you, Maximillian," I said, feeling the small stray lock and pressing it into place. "Now, let's—" I stopped speaking as I looked down at the surface of my desk. Lying atop my computer was a heavy-looking envelope with my name and title written in elegant calligraphy.

"Don't just stare at it," said Max. "Open it."

I retrieved my letter opener from the top drawer and carefully slit the envelope. I unfolded the watermarked stationary and read,

You are cordially invited to a private viewing of the Maximillian Willoughby Collection.

Location: The crow's nest

Time: At your leisure

Yes! I nearly did a Max-style air punch.

"I am honored," I said. "Thank you, Max. And as I've already screwed up our schedule for today, I hereby declare myself officially at my leisure. With your dad's blessing."

"My dad?"

"Yes. He challenged me to a relay race this morning. Hence my tardiness."

Max chuckled. "Don't tell me. You ended in a tie."

"How do you know?"

"I can't believe you fell for it. He'll clean the bottom of the pool with you next time. My dad never loses."

"Don't bet on it. Shall we proceed to the exhibition?"

"Walk this way," said Max. I followed him, mimicking his ungraceful gait with exaggerated parody. "Sarah was right about you, Prof."

"In what way?"

"You really *are* silly."

The crow's nest was a pleasant surprise. What I'd imagined as a make-shift, cobweb-ridden retreat strewn with dirty socks and underwear was a cozy aery. A denim-upholstered futon-cum-sofa, draped with a brown faux-fur throw, occupied one wall. The opposite wall was mostly windows—large and louvered—affording an enviable vista for a professional-looking telescope and tripod. The central wall of the cathedral-shaped ceiling featured a small, exquisite Kahlo work.

"You're a big fan of Frida," I said, as I ducked my head under the doorway and took in the room.

"She was a genius, Prof. I mean, everything she did came from *inside*, not from the world that everyone else knew and accepted. You know what she said? She said, 'People have called me a surrealist, but I'm not. I've never painted dreams. I've painted my own reality.' How lit is that?"

"I like Kahlo too," I said. "But I'm here to see the Max Willoughby Collection."

Max dropped to his hands and knees and began to pull sketches, photographs, and watercolors from beneath the futon.

"These are the best ones," he said. "I mean, what I think are the best ones."

I sat on the floor next to Max as I surveyed his work. The watercolors were good, the sketches promising. The photographs were beautiful.

"I think you know where your *visual* artistic talents lay," I said, passing Max one of the pictures he'd taken from the lighthouse.

"Thanks, Prof," Max blushed, raking his hair away from his face. "I'm really proud of that one. I like drawing and painting but—well, I mean, I just can't put what I see on paper. You know what I mean? I *see* with the camera."

"'I am a camera,'" I said.

"Where's that from?" asked Max, sensing the quotation marks.

"Christopher Isherwood. From *Goodbye to Berlin.* "'I am a camera with its shutter open, quite passive, recording, not thinking.'"

"Wow. That's it. That's *it*, Prof!"

"Isherwood's story was the basis for the musical *Cabaret*," I added, wishing I'd kept my mouth shut. I was not prepared to explore the sexual and political themes of either work. Fortunately, Max went in a different and more rewarding direction.

"Sarah took me to see a musical once," Max said. "It was about the Bible and Sarah had to explain everything to me, but I really liked the music."

Thank you, Max, for the opening.

"What did your father have to say about that?"

"He sort of didn't know. Sarah said something about the spirit of the law versus the letter of the law. Sarah told my dad it was a church-related event, and since it was on Sunday afternoon and had to do with Jesus, she figured it really was church-related in a way."

"One of these days, you and I need to have a talk about the concept of the end justifying the means," I said. "Was your father aware that you went to church with Sarah?" I added in a less censorious tone.

"How did you know? Sarah told you?"

"I knew that Sarah was a regular churchgoer, and I knew the reason why. As you must since you accompanied her."

"For the music," said Max, a bit of defiance creeping into his voice. "Sarah said she really wasn't a believer, but she liked to sing, and she said they had good music and a cool lady priest. My dad knew. He wasn't crazy about the music part, but he said he could not deny me a 'Christian educa-tion.'" Max smiled broadly and added, "I think Sarah tricked him into it. I mean her not being a believer and all."

"And your mother?" I asked.

Max shrugged. "She was happy to get me out of the house. Or happy for me to get out of the house. I'm not sure which." It was an observation that was both sad and funny. I chose to laugh. "But how did you know if Sarah didn't tell you?" Max added.

"I saw Mother Anne yesterday," I said. "She asked after you. She misses you. More precisely, she misses your beautiful singing voice." Max's face lit up at this.

"I thought she would have forgotten me by now," he said.

"Why? Have you forgotten her?"

"Well, that's all over, anyway. My dad only goes to church at Christ-mas and Easter—sometimes."

"What about me?" I asked. "I'm not Episcopalian, but—"

"You'd go with me?"

"If you had let me complete my sentence, you would have heard me say that I would be happy to accompany you. Surely, your father can't object as his agreement with Sarah set the precedent."

"Awesome! Thanks, Prof."

"You're welcome."

"Prof?"

"Yes?"

"Sarah told me that you taught music before."

"I taught music *appreciation*."

"Oh. But you can read it and stuff, right?"

"Yes," I said, not liking where I thought Max's line of questioning was headed. "But your father made it quite clear to me that the subject is prohibited from your curriculum. I'm sorry, Max."

Max screwed his face into a mask of childish petulance. "It's not fair!" he said, grabbing up his artwork and throwing it in the air like confetti, breathing heavily with pent-up frustration; then he dropped onto the futon, burying his face in the pillow.

I moved to Max's telescope and took in the view from the window in front of which it stood. Immediately below was the walkway that led to the pool pavilion off to the right. Ahead was the swath of green through which Sarah had made her daily walk. From this distance, the vegetation lacked the heavy, disorienting effect it had had on me as I moved within it. The paths were clear, delineated. Perspective was everything.

"You're lucky to have this room," I said, my voice quiet, talking to myself as much as to Max. "Your own space away from everything and everyone. Many young men your age are not so lucky. They share their room with a sibling or siblings. Some families share just one room. Even at Allerton, boys from the wealthiest families shared dorm rooms."

I heard Max stir and could sense that he was looking at me, his attention caught, but I did not turn around.

"Lionel shares his room with his little brother," said Max. "That's why he always comes here. It sucks at Lionel's house. It's noisy and his grandmother is always cooking. We can't play chess or, you know, do stuff."

I smiled to myself, knowing quite well the kind of "stuff" healthy twelve-year-old boys got up to. And I was satisfied the mystery of why Max never visited Lionel was solved.

"Did you share your room when you were a kid?" Max asked.

"No. It was just me." I had not meant for the statement to sound self-pitying, but Max interpreted it that way.

"I'm sorry, Prof. For acting like a spoiled brat and for…well, for you being lonely, back in the day."

Max's keen perception impressed me. "I didn't say that I was lonely, but you're right; I was." I turned to face Max, who was now sitting on the edge of the futon, his hair sticking up like a caricature of Albert Einstein. "Until I met someone who showed me the difference between being alone and being lonely and how to appreciate the gift of solitude. Some of us never learn—or learn too late—and we spend our lives searching for other people to make us happy, to love us. While all the time happiness and love are there inside us."

"That's deep, Prof."

I sat down next to Max. "But I think you understand."

"Kind of."

Laying a hand on Max's shoulder, I asked, "When you said, 'It's not fair,' you weren't referring only to your father's music prohibition, were you?"

Max bit his lower lip and shook his head. Then, he turned and faced me. "Why did God take Sarah away?"

It was a question I wished I could have answered. And Max knew that I could not, but he asked it because he had to. I reached out my hand and Max met me halfway, returning the gesture. I pulled him gently into a hug. "I understood about her leaving," Max mumbled against my shoulder. "I mean, she was in love with Mr. Adami and everything. But her dying isn't right. It isn't—"

"I know, my friend," I said. "It isn't fair."

I allowed myself to cry along with Max, feeling safe with him as I'd not felt with another person in many years. Eventually, we disengaged, wiping our eyes. I gestured toward the strewn artwork. "How about we straighten up the mess you made, and then you can show me how to work that telescope?"

As we separated the photographs, sketches, and paintings into individual piles, Max asked, "Who were they?"

I looked questioningly at Max over a very good sketch of Sarah seated at her desk in the workroom.

"Who?"

"Whoever it was who taught you about being alone and all that."

"Her name was Benedicta. Sister Benedicta."

"A *nun?*"

"What? A nun can't be a friend?"

"I guess so," Max allowed. "I just never thought about it. I've never met a real nun. I mean, I've never met a nun in person. Did she wear one of those weird outfits, like in the movies?"

"It's called a habit. And, yes, she did."

"Tell me about her, Prof."

As we organized Max's artwork, and Max explained the workings of his telescope, I turned back my mental clock once again and relived a part of my childhood for my young friend.

Sacred Heart School

Florentina Bay, California

1976

"I asked you a question, Neily!" Steve Soto shouted as he knocked my books

from my arms.

I remained silent, fighting back the urge to weep from anger and embarrassment.

"He carries his books like a girl," Steve sniggered, looking over his shoulder at his group of loyal hangers-on, all of whom laughed on cue. If Steve Soto thought something was funny, it was funny. "Were you going to meet your boyfriend?" More sycophantic laughter. "Who is he, Neily? Huh? Father Gay-doza?" The laughter was less enthusiastic this time. Apparently, there were lines that even the great Soto crossed on his own. Father Mendoza was a popular new priest in the diocese who was young, handsome, and rumored (inaccurately) to have a predilection for boys.

I took the slight lull in support of Soto to find my voice. "Leave me alone," I said. The worst thing you can say to a bully.

Soto grabbed me by my shirt collar. "I asked you a question, faggot! Answer me. What's you're fucking middle name?"

"I don't have one."

"Bullshit. Everyone's got a fucking middle name, right guys?" Enthusiastic agreement rose from the gang of boys. I refused to speak more, and Soto smiled nastily at his admirers. "I bet I know what it is. It's Andsuckmydick. Get it? Neil and suck my dick!"

The hysterical glee, back slapping, and congratulatory comments this pronouncement brought about gave me my opening and I took it, swiftly gathering up my books and fleeing the boy's bathroom like The Flash. My heart was still pounding when I gained the assembly quad, but a quick glance over my shoulder told me I was not being pursued. Soto and his cronies had had their fun with me for the day.

I contemplated returning to my classroom for the remainder of the long midday recess but reconsidered as I realized I would be an easy target there—alone and unsupervised.

The library.

Even Soto and his followers maintained a modicum of self-censoring within its environs—as if they somehow understood that their childish humor and cruel goading could not stand up to the strength of the written word of scientists, historians, novelists, and playwrights. Nor could their budding macho swagger find free expression under the supervision of Sister Benedicta—the librarian who ruled her domain with imperious sangfroid.

"Welcome, Neil," said Sister Benedicta, putting aside her copy of the San Francisco Chronicle. "I'm happy to see you, but why aren't you outside enjoying this lovely day?" She took in my flushed face, my disheveled uniform shirt and sweater, my breath that was still short and slightly panting. She looked out the window toward the quad with a speculative expression and then back at me. "Maybe it's not such a lovely day for everyone, eh?"

How did she know? Did everyone know? Was it common knowledge that I was a friendless, pathetic faggot?

"I…I just wanted some time by myself," I said with as much dignity as I could muster. "Away from… I mean…"

Sister Benedicta nodded. "You're seeking sanctuary. The doors of the basilica are always open, you know," she said, referring to the church to which the small school was attached.

"I know, Sister. But the church doesn't have books."

"Good point. Then you've come to the right place." She raised her head proudly and moved her right arm with a sweeping gesture, as if indicating the collection of the great library of Alexandria. "As always, seek and ye shall find."

"Thank you, Sister."

I made my way to the back corner of the small main room, where books on world history, Greek and Roman mythology, and other books that did not fit, in size or subject, anywhere else were kept. By consequence of its offerings, this area was rarely visited—

which suited me just fine. I had recently discovered Martin Gardener's The Annotated Alice stuck between two volumes on the British monarchy and decided that I would pick up where I left off on my last visit. Though there was much political and social commentary beyond the understanding of a sixth-grade student, the book's concept fascinated me, and I found the quirky illustrations both compelling and repellant. It was not the Disney version of Lewis Carroll's work that I was familiar with, and I considered that a good thing.

"It doesn't belong here."

I looked up from the crouched position in which I was reading to find Sister Benedicta looking down at me from what seemed an impossible height—as if she'd eaten one side or the other of the caterpillar's magic mushroom.

"What, Sister?" I said, stupidly. She could only have been referring to the book.

"It was a very kind donation to our library, but I'm afraid it's not suitable for the young children's section. It's a lovely addition, and I don't want grubby little hands all over it."

"I'm sorry," I said, closing the book.

"For what?"

"I don't know," I said. "It's a habit, I guess."

"Then break it. You've got a lifetime ahead of you and you will do things that you will genuinely regret, so don't squander your apologies. I didn't say your hands were grubby, did I?"

"No, Sister."

Sister Benedicta smiled as she perched on the edge of a nearby study desk. Her voluminous habit made her figure something of a mystery, but her face, surrounded by wimple and veil, was kind and pretty. "So, who was it?" she asked, cocking her head toward the closed library door.

"Soto," I said.

"I worry about that boy," said Sister Benedicta softly, as if Soto were the victim, not the bully. Noting my silent incredulity, she continued. "I don't believe he was born that way, Neil. He was made that way. We all have a cross to bear. Remember that. Boys like Steven Soto often bear one of the heaviest of all."

With that, Sister Benedicta returned to the reception desk and left me to read and think. It would be more than a year before I understood the specific meaning of her words—when Soto's father was jailed for domestic abuse. I never forgave Soto for the way he'd treated me, but I understood why he'd done it. It was the moment in my life when I began to understand the meaning of sympathy.

I extracted the photo of Benedicta from my wallet and handed it to Max.

"She was an artist too?" Max asked, as if the idea of a nun doing anything besides praying and teaching was beyond his comprehension.

"Why not? Some of the most gifted and important artists, writers, and philosophers in history were nuns. We haven't yet arrived at the Middle Ages in your studies, but when we do, I will introduce you to Hildegard of Bingen—among others."

"I'll settle for Benedicta of Florentina Bay," said Max, handing back the photo. "You didn't finish your story. What happened with that ass—er—joker, Soto."

"Benedicta was right. Soto was messed up because he was abused by his father. If it hadn't been me, it would have been someone else upon whom Soto vented his anger and frustration—there were lots of others, I'm sure. Domestic violence and abuse are behaviors and patterns of thought that are transferred from the abuser to the abused. I didn't understand that then, of course."

"Did your parents take you out of school, like me?" Max asked.

"My father taught me how to box, and my mother told me to kick Soto in the balls."

"Seriously? Did you?"

"I did learn how to box, but I did not do any damage to Steve Soto's testicles." Max laughed and I felt encouraged to pursue the subject of Max's own experience with bullying. "What about you?" I asked. "Who was your Soto?"

Max gave me one of his eloquent shrugs. "I don't know. A bunch of guys." Max proceeded to recap the lens of his telescope and cover the device with a custom-made, black velvet sheath. I took this as a nonverbal signal that the conversation was closed, so I was surprised when Max added, "It wasn't because I'm gay. I mean, they all think I am—because of Lionel, because, like, he *is* gay. Everyone thinks I'm his boyfriend. Lionel kissed me once, and it was nice, but I didn't feel anything…you know…*down there*."

I resisted laughing at Max's sweet innocence, instead giving my own Max-like shrug. "I didn't kiss anyone until I was in college," I confessed. "We all discover ourselves and our sexual and romantic desires in our own time. Don't rush. And never let anyone rush you."

"Thanks, Prof. When I told my dad, he left a copy of the *Sports Illustrated* swimsuit issue in the top drawer of my desk."

I did laugh, then, along with Max. "I'm sure he meant well. So, what was the bullying about?"

"The usual. Because of Lionel. Because I'm skinny. Because I kind of look like a girl. It wasn't *so* bad, really. I mean, I could deal with it. It wasn't until this kid named Emer Kelly came to the school the year before last that everything changed."

"Your Soto?"

"Big time, Prof. She was a total know-it-all. Stuck-up, obnoxious, nasty. Always bragging about her rich family in Ireland and stuff—and saying that I was a faggot and that I'd burn in hell. Anyway, the problems started at tryouts for the glee club. They passed me over 'cause I couldn't read music—even though I could sing better than everyone else. I'm not bragging, Prof, it's true. So, anyway, Emer started being super snarky and whispering and giggling about me with her posse behind my back. Then, I got a nickname: the Bastard of the Opera. I didn't get it. I didn't understand why they thought it was so funny. I told my dad; he told Fabiola...and I was out of school."

Before Miss Emer got more specific and the shit hit the fan.

"I still don't get it," said Max, sitting on the windowsill and hunching forward.

"Sit up straight," I said for what felt like the umpteenth time in my acquaintance with Max. He did so, and I continued. "You mean the nickname?"

"Yeah—I mean, yes. It was so lame. Just because I like opera. All *Emer* could do was yell some stupid song from *Frozen*."

On the one hand, I was relieved that Max was still in the dark about his father's alleged affair with Alma Montresor; on the other, I wondered how long he could remain so and if it were even healthy. It seemed as if everyone in the world knew except Max. Ezra could not shield him forever.

"Emer was the last straw, I guess," continued Max. "My dad and Fabiola said my school sucked, anyway. That's when my dad decided to send me to that place in France. Have you been to France?"

"Yes. Several times."

"Me, too. I really liked it. And I was excited about going to live there. But Fabiola ruined everything. She talked my dad into getting a tutor instead."

I thought your dad never lost.

"Gee, thanks," I said.

"You know what I mean, Prof. She ruined everything *then*. It's different now."

Had Max been older, I would have taken his self-satisfied tone as an indication of callousness. Instead, I interpreted it as youthful honesty. Max had disliked Fabiola and had likely competed with her for his father's affections. Now, she was gone, and Max was the de facto castellan of Jessamine Grove. Ezra had fallen out of love with Fabiola—had lived in an adversarial relationship with her for many years. Now, she was gone, and Ezra had his devoted son at his side.

"My dad never loses."

Perhaps Max was right.

Chapter Ten

IF I COULD not hoodwink Ezra with Sarah's skill, I could build on my predecessor's foundation without actively disobeying Ezra's antimusic injunction. Sarah had been correct in her reasoning that the letter of Ezra's law specified no music in Max's curriculum—thereby intimating that music was verboten *at the Grove* but not necessarily elsewhere. Max had tried out for the glee club, after all. Could it have been that—not the bullying—that had been the final straw for his parents?

Recalling Ezra's response when I complimented him on his possession of the Bechstein piano, I wondered if painful memories associated with classical music were what led to Ezra's prohibition.

"A lucky find, I thought. But a bad investment, in the end."

The note of sadness in Ezra's voice and the faraway look in his eyes as he had uttered those words had seemed incongruous to me at the time. In a different context, one that I was able to imagine since then, they made sense. Perhaps Ezra had not been referring to the instrument itself but to the woman who might have inspired its purchase.

I met Beto the next day and floated my theory.

"Isn't that a bit of a leap?" was Beto's response. We were meandering through the eccentric collection of antiques, collectibles, and junk in the Villa Zorayda Museum. "Look," he continued, pointing to a case full of photographs. "Says here that this place was a nightclub back in Harrison Willoughby's day."

Styled after the Alhambra palace in Granada, the villa was built as a private home in the nineteenth century and had been a restaurant and a speakeasy before being converted to a museum in 1933. The museum had never been on Beto's radar but had piqued my interest because of its architectural and historic relation to the Grove.

I pointed at a photo of a distinguished-looking gentleman with a flapper on each arm. "And there is the man himself," I said.

"Really?"

"Yes. I saw a similar photo in one of the albums I found in the storeroom."

"Doesn't look anything like Ezra Willoughby," Beto said.

"Ezra's mother was Spanish. Didn't you know that?"

"No. I'm more interested in the living Willoughbys."

"Which brings us back to my leap."

"It does?"

"If Alma Montresor was indeed Ezra's lover, there is the possibility that she was also Max's birth mother. You've seen Max. He bears a certain likeness to Ezra—and he certainly has some Hispanic or Mediterranean ancestry. And I've just discovered something else." I now had Beto's full attention. He turned away from the case and regarded me with exaggerat-edly raised eyebrows. "Max has a beautiful singing voice."

"How did you make this discovery? The kid sang for you?"

"No. A little bird told me."

"Oh, come off it."

"Sorry. I went to mass at the church Sarah used to visit and I spoke to the vicar. She told me that Sarah brought Max with her so they could enjoy the music together. According to Mother Anne, the choirmaster be-lieves Max's voice has operatic potential."

"Aha."

"Aha?"

"As much as I want to find an explanation for all my oddities," said Beto, "I'm beginning to wonder if I'm clutching at straws. There may have been a perfectly reasonable explanation for Fabiola Willoughby's 'stalking' of Sarah Lewis—we only have an imaginative boy as a witness, remem-ber—and Fabiola's death probably *was* an accident. You're doing the same thing, Neil. I can almost buy that Willoughby keeps an old piano as a re-minder of a past relationship that went sour, but just because Max has a great voice doesn't mean that his mother was an opera singer."

"It's a bit late to backpedal, Beto. You're the one who got me into this."

"I know. I know." Beto glanced at his watch. "Come on," he said, touching my arm, "Let's shelve this for now. We still have to see the Sacred Cat Rug." I made a face that I thought conveyed incredulity. Beto took it for aversion. "You have something against cats?"

"Not at all. I neglected to tell you that I'm now part of the Great Pussy Conspiracy."

"Huh?"

I gave Beto the rundown on Lulu.

"Poor bastard." Beto rubbed his index finger over the salt and pepper stubble of his upper lip. "So, he needs a home…"

"Yes. And the longer he stays at the Grove, the less likely it is that the gang is going to make much effort to find one. They've collectively adopted him, but when Ezra finds out—and it's just a matter of time before he does—the jig will be up, and he'll probably end up in a shelter. Lulu, not Ezra."

"After John died, I promised myself that he would be the last," said Beto as we approached the room that held the supposedly ancient rug. "He was with me for almost ten years."

For a moment, I thought Beto was speaking of a departed lover. Then I recalled his well-chewed pen cap.

"You had a cat named *John?*"

"A handsome Havana Brown. Died in his sleep of old age. A blessing, really, that I didn't have to have him euthanized. That would have been horrible." The love and regret in Beto's voice was manifest, and the soft spot I was developing for him for him grew.

"You'd consider adopting Lulu?"

"Consider? No. I've already made up my mind. I'll take him. How old is he?"

"I don't know. Sarah must have taken him to a vet before he took up residence. I'm sure someone has the paperwork. If they make vermillion rubber bands, it shouldn't be hard to find."

"Vermillion rubber bands??"

"You know," I said, mimicking Rosanie, "V" for vet." I explained about the storeroom key and Beto made a guffaw that resounded in the sparsely populated museum.

"You're working in a nuthouse, Professor Boehm. Don't let them rub off on you."

We soon stood before the strange Egyptian rug woven entirely of cat hair. While Beto read the history of the rug, my eye was caught by an early twentieth century photo of a pool party at the Hotel Alcazar, now the Lightner Museum. My thoughts drifted to my first poolside encounter with Ezra and what he had revealed to me about Fabiola. Maybe Beto was right. When Beto had finished reading, I said, "I was thinking of what you said about Mrs. Willoughby's death probably being an accident after all. Something Ezra told me about his wife might bear that out." I repeated what Ezra had said about Fabiola's alcoholism and was surprised at Beto's reaction.

"Why the hell would he tell you that?"

"I suppose he needed to confide in someone. It's probably something he's kept to himself for years."

"No. I mean why would he lie to you? Fabiola Willoughby was not an alcoholic—high functioning or otherwise."

"How do you—"

"The autopsy, Neil. If Fabiola had a drinking problem, it would have appeared in the medical examiner's report. She *had* been drinking at the time of the fall, but according to the ME, Fabiola Willoughby was a healthy, exceptionally fit woman. Willoughby is playing you. The question is: what's his game?"

*

Alleluia! Sing to Jesus!
His the scepter, His the throne;
Alleluia! His the triumph,
His the victory alone!
Hark! The songs of peaceful Zion
Thunder like a mighty flood:
"Jesus out of every nation
Has redeemed us by His blood.

I knew the hymn, but I had never heard it performed as a solo with violin accompaniment. The bell-like clarity of Max's voice and his delicate phrasing lent a brightness and freshness to the old song that had always struck me as sounding like a funeral dirge. I was moved by the combination of sweetness and power Max projected, and I was not the only one. The elderly woman seated to my right was smiling serenely and dabbing tears from her cheeks with a lacey handkerchief.

Sharing space in my heart with the pleasure derived from hearing Max sing was a feeling of anger toward Ezra Willoughby. How could he be so selfish? Max did not just sing well; he had a talent that deserved to be encouraged and nurtured. That Ezra could deny this talent and forbid its expression in his home was unconscionable. How could he love his child, yet allow the bitter memories of a past relationship to prevent him from experiencing the joy of hearing his child sing?

As we filed out of the church at the end of the service, I wrapped a congratulatory arm around Max's shoulder and praised his singing. As Max responded with shy denials and self-criticism, the old lady with the handkerchief approached us.

"Oh, Mr. Willoughby," she said as she peered at me myopically through extremely thick eyeglass lenses, "you must be so proud of your son!" She turned to Max. "You sing beautifully, young man."

"I'm —" I began to correct my mistaken identity, but Max cut me off.

"Thank you, Mrs. Simmonds. That's really nice of you to say."

"God bless you both," said Mrs. Simmonds, then made a stately, though somewhat shaky, exit with the assistance of her cane.

"Sorry," said Max, as we watched the old woman depart. "Mrs. Simmonds is nearly blind. I didn't want to embarrass her."

"She must be," I said, deciding to laugh off the potentially awkward moment, "if she could mistake me for your father."

Max looked up at me and smiled, his head tilted quizzically. "I'm not so sure about that," he said.

Before I could respond, we were joined by the choirmaster. Adam Ballas was a short, dark, stocky man of perhaps thirty-five or forty years with a buzz cut who looked to me more like a soccer coach than a church musician. Maybe he was both.

"Pleased to meet you, Mr. Boehm," he said offering a firm, two-handed shake. "Excellent work, today, Max," he added, beaming at his protégée.

"Thank you, Mr. Ballas."

Ballas clapped Max on the shoulder, then turned his attention back to me. "I've spoken with Mother Anne about your proposal. We can discuss it in the vestry if you like."

"Certainly." I made to follow Ballas, but Max hung back with a questioning look on his face.

"You, too, Max," said Ballas.

We gathered at the end of a long table which, Ballas explained, was used for parish council meetings, and I could not help but imagine Fabiola Willoughby seated there engaged in a tug-of-war with the council aristocracy.

"Coffee or tea?" asked our host. We both declined and Ballas got down to business. "Max, your tutor came up with a plan for your music education and Mother Anne has approved it." Max's eyes widened in surprise, but he remained silent. "Since you lack the…er…proper facilities at your home, Mother Anne has agreed to allow you to have private lessons here at the church. Mr. Boehm will instruct you in the fundamentals of the language of music and I will continue to serve as your vocal coach."

"I can't… I mean, I'm not…" Max said, finding his voice. He looked at me, bewildered.

"Leave that to me," I said, reaching out and squeezing his hand, knowing that he was referring to his father. "Unfortunately, for this to work out, you'll have to give up one skateboarding afternoon a week."

"What about Rollo?" Max asked, practically.

"I'll have a talk with him," I said. "I'm sure he'll agree (I was not) as he can come along to watch your back."

Max glanced from me to Ballas and back. "For real?"

"For real, Max."

*

RODRIGO VELEZ WAS a short, youthful looking man of early middle age with a deceptively slim physique. In his workday wardrobe of black suit and tie he appeared thin—almost delicate, but in his off-duty attire of snug polo and chinos, there was no mistaking that he was all sinew, bone, and muscle.

"Featherweight?" I asked, as I poured tea for Rodrigo.

"When I was in my early twenties, yes," he said. "How did you know? Rosanie?"

"No. It was an educated guess. My father was a boxer before he went into the antique business. I trained with him when I was a boy."

"*Gracias*," said Rodrigo, nodding over his mug of tea. I'd invited Rodrigo to visit me in my sitting room and was pleasantly surprised that he accepted. "I must apologize for my rudeness toward you. I had a talk with Rosanie—or, I should say, Rosanie talked at me—and she succeeded in making me feel ashamed of myself."

I took a sip of tea. "There's no need to apologize. I can appreciate that you're still in mourning for the late Mrs. Willoughby. Then there's Ms. Lewis's death. And now, me. A lot to deal with in a matter of months."

Rodrigo took a shortbread cookie I'd baked from the plate I passed to him, dunked, and munched. "Excellent. Maybe you can teach my daughter how to cook," he said with a smile. "Nessa has tried for years with little success."

"Rosanie is still finding her way in life," I said. "Who knows where her true talents may lie." I thought it best not to mention card reading and psychic phenomena. "Like Max in some ways."

Rodrigo looked at his tea mug with a frown. "I promised Fabiola I would look after him," he said softly. "But now… First Miss Sarah and then you. I-I don't mean anything against you, or Miss Sarah. It's just…"

"You feel redundant."

Rodrigo looked up sharply.

"Yes."

We ate and drank in silence for a few moments.

"Rosanie is not my only child," said Rodrigo, breaking the quietude with this surprising statement. "When I first met Fabiola, I had a daughter—my first born—Evelyn. My wife, Linda, and I were not happy together. Our marriage was 'on the rocks' as they say. Evelyn wasn't… My wife didn't want a baby—not then. But she saw the pregnancy through; for me and because of her Catholic faith. Evelyn was such a beautiful girl. I thought things would change between Linda and me after she was born. They should have. They would have, I'm sure, if Evelyn had been normal." Rodrigo took a deep breath and a long drink of tea before continuing. "She was born with Jarcho-Levin Syndrome."

I said nothing. I'd heard of the disease that caused bone malformation, and I knew that 'I'm sorry' could not possibly be adequate. Eventually, Rodrigo continued.

"Fabiola was wonderful," said Rodrigo. "I'd only been working for her for a few months, but she treated me like she had known me for years… She cared, you understand? We needed money for Evelyn's care, and Fabiola was there for us. Paid the bills. No strings attached."

No strings except eternal fealty.

"Then Evelyn died," said Rodrigo, his voice barely audible. "She was only eight months old. The doctors had prepared us for it—or tried to. How can a parent be prepared for the death of their child? Linda was devastated. So was I. But Linda turned her anger and frustration on Fabiola. Short of blaming Fabiola for Evelyn's death, Linda accused her of not doing enough…of making promises she could never keep, of using Evelyn as a pawn to keep us in her debt. I told Linda she was being ungrateful, and Fabiola was only motivated by Christian charity and friendship."

You walked right into her web, Rodrigo. You could defend yourself in the ring, but you were no match for Fabiola Saens Willoughby.

"In the end," continued Rodrigo, "We agreed to disagree. Then, Rosanie came. I thought it could be a new beginning. But Linda never warmed to her. I think she came too soon…before Linda was ready. Anyway, Fabiola took an interest in Rosanie, wanted to be a mentor, a female role model, I guess you could say. I appreciated her interest, her willingness to help financially. Linda saw the devil. And that was it. The end. Fabiola was a good woman, but Linda refused to see it. We got divorced. I got custody of Rosanie. When Fabiola married Mr. Willoughby, we moved here. Made our home here."

"Why are you telling me all this?" I asked, thrown for a loop by this outpouring of personal history from a man with whom I'd exchanged only professional pleasantries over the past months.

"Because of Max," Rodrigo said. "When Max came, I saw a way to repay Fabiola for all her kindness and generosity to me and my family. Mr. Willoughby has always been distant with Max. So was Fabiola, if I'm fair. They loved him; Mr. Willoughby loves him. But Max needed more, *sabes?* I thought, if I could take care of Max, look out for him, I could repay the debt I owed Fabiola. But with Miss Sarah and now you—as you say, I feel redundant. My dear friend, Fabiola, is gone. And Max doesn't need me anymore."

"That isn't true," I said. "You're an important part of Max's life. You've cared for him since he was a baby. You are part of his family, Rodrigo. You, Rosanie, Nessa. Max needs you now more than ever. I didn't come here to replace you. I came here to help you—to help Max, to do what's best for Max. Just as you've always done."

A tear fell from Rodrigo's left eye, and he swept it away with a thumb.

"Forgive me," he said, "for being such a *pendejo*."

"*Amar a alguien no es ser pendejo,*" I replied, code-switching to Spanish.

Rodrigo gave me a critical look and said, "*Tienes razón, profesor. Creo que no soy el único que lo ama.*"

Unwilling to voice commitment to the emotion, I looked down and busied myself with refreshing our tea. When I glanced up at Rodrigo, he was smiling.

"I'm glad," said Rodrigo. "Sarah told me you are a good man. She was right." He took a sip from his mug. "And you know how to make a decent pot of tea. Extra points."

"Thank you. I'm going to need them."

"Why?"

I explained my plan for Max's music education. When I'd finished, Rodrigo leaned back in his chair, crossed his arms over his chest and gave me a stern look.

"So," he said, "You're asking me to lie to Mr. Willoughby."

"Well…"

Rodrigo smiled. "Miss Sarah was much better at this sort of thing than you are," he said. "She could have sold a titless cow to a dairy farmer. But you don't need to persuade me. I think it's a good idea. I've never understood Mr. Willoughby's obsession, anyway."

"Obsession?"

"Yes. With that woman. Alma Montresor. How he's allowed her memory to corrupt his life and his relationship with his son."

"I understand that Mr. Willoughby and Ms. Montresor were close."

"You know about the rumors, I see. Don't believe them, Neil. Mr. Willoughby was devoted to Fabiola. You see, he wasn't in *love* with Alma

Montresor. He was in thrall to her. Somehow, Fabiola understood this and tolerated it. But after Alma disappeared, Mr. Willoughby changed. He shut himself off, I guess you'd say. That's when things started to go bad between him and Fabiola. He'd spend hours alone in the music room—just him and that horrible portrait of Alma."

I nearly asked Rodrigo why he found the portrait horrible, forgetting that I was not meant to know about it. "What music room? What portrait?" I asked instead.

Rodrigo gave me a funny look, as though he knew I was being disingenuous. "It's kept locked now. Has been for years. But Mr. Willoughby makes certain that fresh white roses are always on the piano and that horrible portrait is dusted."

"Why is the portrait horrible?" I finally asked. "Do you mean it's a bad likeness?"

"No. It's a perfect likeness. Maybe too perfect." Rodrigo looked earnestly at me, and his voice dropped a notch or two in volume and tenor as he continued, "That painting is…*escalofriante, entiendes?* Like the old stories about portraits with eyes that follow you. Or like the opposite of Oscar Wilde's *Picture of Dorian Gray*. Alma Montresor has been gone for years, but that painting lives on, eternally beautiful, waiting to entrance some innocent with its wicked gaze and seductive smile."

"I take it you disliked Alma Montresor?"

Rodrigo put up his hands in a disavowing gesture. "I did not know her intimately, Neil. Who am I to judge? But I did not trust her face. I met her in Miami at a museum fundraiser organized by Fabiola. She was beautiful. Undeniably, she was beautiful. But it was a false beauty. A glittering image. '*And the woman was arrayed in purple and scarlet color, and decked with gold and precious stones and pearls, having a golden cup in her hand full of abominations and the filthiness of her fornication.'"*

"Revelations, 17:4," I said, recognizing the Bible quotation. "Isn't that a bit much?"

"It was my impression, Neil. That is all. Though I think I was proved right in the end. I believe the artist who painted her portrait shared my impression. That is why I call the picture horrible."

I swirled the dregs of my tea and saw the painting of Alma Montresor in my mind; recalled the magazine photographs I'd seen of the diva. I had to admit that Rodrigo had a point regarding the artifice of Montresor's appearance—if not the quality of her soul. But she was an actress, after all.

"Do you know who painted this *horrible'* portrait?" I asked. "Who was the man whom you believe knew her so well?"

Rodrigo laughed, and I was taken aback by his response. "That's what you immediately think, isn't it?" he demanded. "What any man would think—*machistas* as we all are. Straight, gay or whatever. But, no, it was a woman who painted that portrait of Alma. Her sister, Agnes Clotilde Montresor."

Chapter Eleven

I'D TAKEN TO using Sarah's workroom as my office, finding the simple desk more functional than the rolltop in my room and the imprint of Sarah's spirit comforting and cheerful—even though most of the time I spent there afforded little use of the better natural light. Like Charles Shultz's "Pigpen" and his ever-present miasma of filth, rain clouds seemed to accompany me on every visit to that room.

On the last day of Lulu's residency, I sat at the desk reading a forwarded letter from an acquaintance from New York whom I'd not seen or corresponded with in years. The occasion prompting the missive was the arrival of his first grandchild. Apparently, the event had caused him to reflect on the passing of time and moved him to reach out to old friends.

Initially, I was touched. As I read on, I realized it was essentially a form letter he'd probably sent to everyone from his university days and all the people he knew in his present life. It was not a word processing document, but it may as well have been. I was reminded of the mother of a schoolmate from my childhood—Vera McMillian—who sent a typewritten holiday letter every December to anyone she knew even slightly, detailing the events in her family's life over the course of the year. I smiled, remembering how my mother would read them aloud at the dinner table, her voice dripping with sarcasm in a perfect imitation of Mrs. McMillian's voice.

I threw the letter from New York in the garbage.

Despite my cynical state of mind—or perhaps because of it—my thoughts turned to the little note Sarah had attached to the hydrangea candle. Something genuine and thoughtful. I pulled open the center drawer of the desk, retrieved it and read it once more.

> 'Darling,
>
> I know you love these little treasures as dearly as I do,
> but you're too cheap to buy them.
>
> Do enjoy this one.
>
> I could not bear to leave you totally in the dark.'
>
> Sarah

When I'd first read the note, I'd smiled, believing Sarah's stilted language and words underlined for emphasis referred to our old habit of speaking to each other in exaggerated British accents when we were sharing a silly moment; calling each other Nigel and Cynthia.

Now, I wondered…

<u>Darling</u>. <u>Bear</u>.

I looked toward the articulated stuffed animal in the flowered onesie and heard Sarah's and my voices having an imaginary exchange.

"Oh, Nigel! Isn't he the most darling bear?"

"I say, Cynthia old thing, you've got topping good taste, eh what?"

I laughed as I removed the bear from the shelf, wondering what secret joke or message Sarah had been trying to convey. Was this the elusive clue I'd been searching for?

I examined the toy closely. It was exquisitely crafted and certainly vintage, though the onesie was clearly a modern addition. I removed the garment and looked at the denuded bear. The center stitch along its spine appeared to have been resewn on several occasions and the latest repair had been rather crude.

If it *was* a repair.

I took the toy into the bathroom and proceeded to cut the stitch with nail scissors and remove tufts of ancient stuffing. Inside was a pale blue envelope addressed to me.

Clever girl, Cynthia.

I returned the bear to his resting place—vowing to restitch him when I had a chance—then sat down once more at Sarah's desk and began to read her letter.

*

Dear Neil,

I wonder how long it took you to find this. If it was more than a few weeks, I've already broken down and called you to tell you where it is. Otherwise, read on and we can compare notes when I get back from my honeymoon. Honeymoon! They should come up with a different name for it when you're over fifty and you've been having sex with your fiancée for thirteen years.

Where should I start? You know the beginning (departure from Allerton) and the end (marriage, honeymoon, et al) so I guess the middle is appropriate: those few months when I was deciding if I should stay on at the Grove, you were 'finding yourself' in California, and we rarely spoke to each other.

It would be an exaggeration to say that when I arrived at Jessamine Grove, I immediately experienced a sense of impending doom. That did not happen until after Rosanie read the Tarot for me. It was downright creepy. But I'm getting ahead of myself. What I did feel almost from the moment of my arrival was wrongness. Not wrongness in the moral sense (that, too, would come later), but…well, you know how you can just tell when someone has gone through your stuff or moved a chair ever so slightly or rearranged the books on a shelf, even if they were in no special order to begin with? Like the time your housekeeper accidentally washed your cashmere sweaters in hot water and shrank them, remember? She brazened it out, pressing and folding them neatly and putting them in their accustomed drawer. But you knew as soon as you opened that drawer—before you inspected the sweaters—something was wrong.

Do you get my drift? Probably not. I'm not explaining myself very well. Okay, here's another analogy: funhouse mirrors. They're meant to be silly and entertaining, but they always gave me the willies when I was a kid. I mean, what if the distorted image reflected was real and the way you saw yourself was the illusion? Sorry for going all Twilight Zone on you, but that's as close as I can get to my first impression of the Grove. Wrongness. Something—everything—just slightly skewed. Odd, as Detective Chaves would say. Have you met him yet? You will, I'm sure.

Dean Chaves is a man on a mission to prove that Fabiola Willoughby's death was not an accident. Given that there is no way in hell a woman like Mrs. Willoughby would have taken her own life (trust me on this) that leaves one alternative: the elephant in the room that everyone is pretending not to see. Everyone except Chaves. In fact, he gave up his job for it. He was the detective in charge of the investigation into Fabiola's death. When the case was closed with a verdict of accidental death, Chaves resigned. He's convinced that Ezra used his money and social position to influence the outcome of the case, and that is certainly possible. But Ezra wasn't here when Fabiola died, so he can't be considered a suspect if, indeed, his wife's death was not accidental. Thus, four suspects remain. I exclude myself, though the thought of doing away with Fabiola Willoughby did occasionally cross my mind. I'd like to give her the benefit of the doubt and just say that I never understood her, but that would be hypocritical in the extreme. I understood Fabiola quite well.

You know, the woman stalked me. I kid you not. She followed me everywhere—at a distance like a big-game hunter. It would have been funny if it hadn't seemed so creepy. One day, shortly before Fabiola died, Ezra joined me on my daily walk around the lake. Just as we were making our way back to the Grove, Fabiola sprang out of nowhere and made all kinds of inaccurate and inappropriate accusations about my relationship with her husband. Ezra, ever the gentleman, rose to my defense—which just made matters worse, of course. I guess that's when I finally decided to call it quits.

Sorry for the rant. I was supposed to be telling you about Chaves.

Anyway, I think his real motivation is Max. He sees himself as a sort of champion—a hero who can save the prince from his evil, corrupt father and free him from his imprisonment in the tower that is Willoughby Grove. That's nonsense, of course. Ezra may be corrupt (I like him, so I hope not), but he's not evil and he loves his son. But I believe that's how Beto perceives the situation. I've advised him to let it go, to accept that Fabiola's death was an accident. Otherwise, he could be setting himself on the path to a possible truth he may not be willing to accept.

I read the remainder of Sarah's letter with half a mind. It was Max's voice, not Sarah's, that spoke in my head.

"Fabiola was not my real mother. I don't care that she's dead. I hated her."

Max must have spoken those or similar words to Sarah, but they'd had a different impact upon her than they'd had upon me. Sarah had known Fabiola Willoughby. She had experience of the relationship between mother and son. Her perspective was entirely different from mine. Perspective, again. Like the view from Max's crow's nest nor the reflections in the mirrors of Sarah's fun house. But I recoiled from considering the horrible possibility that Sarah's words suggested.

No one appeared to mourn the death of Fabiola Willoughby—not even Ezra, who chose to remember the woman he'd married years ago, not the woman who died—and life went on as before at Jessamine Grove.

Let the past go. Forget about Fabiola Willoughby and the ghost of Alma Montresor. What matters here and now is Max.

Not a season or a year went by that I did not—if only for a moment—wonder what my life would have been like if I'd never discovered the truth that my parents had conspired to hide. What would Max's future hold if the truth of his adoptive mother's death—whatever it was—was revealed? If the truth behind the mystery of Alma Montresor was brought to light?

I returned to my room and tucked Sarah's letter next to those of Benedicta and my mother inside *The Wind in the Willows*. My only close friends, united in death between the covers of the book given to me by the mother I'd taken too long to love. I allowed myself a momentary fantasy that the three women were in heaven looking down at me. What would they see? What would they say?

Stupid. I shook off the idea. There was no heaven. There was no God. I would never see Sarah, Benedicta, or my mother again. There was no replay button in life.

My thoughts drifted to my father. If ever there were a man who deserved a replay button, it was he.

*

IT HAD BEEN an uncommonly sunny day, and I'd walked home quickly after school, ready to change into a T-shirt and board shorts, looking forward to an afternoon of watching Benedicta paint while I stuffed myself with popcorn and hotdogs, or hanging out on the beach playing *Dungeons and Dragons* with my small clique of classmates.

Passing my father's shop, I looked in through the window and felt a twinge of guilt. The shop was occupied by four customers—a crowd by Jakob's Gems standards—and my father was nowhere in sight. Probably passed out on his sofa in the backroom, I thought disloyally as I entered, shoved my bookbag under the counter, and put on my "friendly assistant" face along with my work smock. I thought hopefully that maybe I'd sell something.

The first three customers were lookie-loos—the ones who demanded to see endless items, hemmed and hawed as if they were making the purchase of their lives, then walked away with nothing, always promising to 'think about it.'

The last customer was different. Mrs. Johns. I'd served her before. She knew her stuff and took her time before zeroing in on a set of Occupied Japan cups and saucers. They were good, but we had better ones stored in the attic, waiting for someone just like her, a real collector. I started to feel less depressed about my stint of unexpected labor.

"These are lovely, Neil," she said, holding one of the cups up to the light, the delicate material pearlescent.

"If you like those, ma'am," I said, "I think we have an even nicer set up in the storeroom. Would you like me to check for you?"

Mrs. Johns smiled, recognizing a bait and switch when she heard it, but knowing that my father really did keep the special stuff hidden away.

"Thank you," she said.

I returned Mrs. Johns's smile and took off for the attic, grabbing the key from the hook in the hall as I went.

Afterward, Mrs. Johns said she would never forget my scream.

I don't remember screaming.

What I do remember—and will never forget—is the glow of the old-fashioned lightbulb at the top of the winding stairway, the smell of piss, and my father's body hanging from a makeshift noose.

*

"THAT'S GREAT, NEIL," said Nessa as she poured a late morning coffee for the two of us. "Rosanie will be pleased it's someone Sarah knew."

I told Nessa about Beto's decision to adopt the Grove's secret mascot, fashioning Beto as a friend from Sarah's church whom I'd recently met. As comfortable as I'd become in the company of Nessa, I'd yet to feel familiar enough with her to offer confidences about a potential love interest.

"Beto's cat of many years recently passed away," I said, sounding like an animal rescue volunteer. "I'm sure this will be a good fit for both of them."

"Beto? Like the guy who ran for president?"

"Yes. Beto Chaves." Nessa paled, her scar becoming momentarily more prominent. Her coffee mug trembled slightly in her hand, and she leaned heavily against the counter. "Are you all right, Nessa?"

"Fine. The name caught me by surprise, that's all. Chaves was the last name of one of the detectives who interviewed us after Mrs. Willoughby's accident. Hearing it again rakes everything up, you know? Even though it's a common enough name. And the guy's first name was Dean, not Beto. I'm just being silly."

The other shoe dropped. I'd been so preoccupied with one aspect of Sarah's letter, that something else she'd said had failed to sink in. Until now.

I gulped the rest of my coffee. "Sorry to rush, Nessa, but I've got a cat to deliver. Thanks for the coffee."

Back in my room, I reread the letter, fury building.

The lying bastard!

*

"HERE'S YOUR CAT," I said, standing on the threshold of Beto's house and passing him the pet carrier, "Enjoy." I turned away and began to walk back to my car.

"What's wrong with you, Neil? Aren't you even going to come in? I've got—"

"I don't give a damn what you've got," I yelled over my shoulder. "Keep it."

"What's wrong with you, man?"

I paused, my hand on the door handle of the SUV, then looked over the hood toward Beto. "What's wrong with *me*? Tell me something, *Commander* Chaves, are you a pathological liar, or was this a one-off? Private dick, my ass. You probably lied about that too."

"Neil, I can explain."

"Please. As good as you are at inventing stories, I would have thought you could come up with something better than that line. You say Ezra Willoughby is playing me. He's not the only one."

"Come inside, and I'll tell you everything."

Just go. Leave. Forget him. It worked before; it will work now.

Lulu wailed piteously from the confines of his carrier.

"Look, Neil," said Chaves, "whatever you think about me, you can't just walk away on the cat. Can you?" Lulu wailed even louder, as if on cue. "He needs some transition time."

"Transition time? You just made that up."

"You said I was good at inventing things."

I hesitated, and I knew Beto knew I never had any intention of leaving.

"I'm only staying for the cat. Understood?"

"Understood."

Beto was right about Lulu. He refused to leave his carrier when I brought him into the house and gave me a deadly stare when I attempted to coax him out.

"Leave him be," said Beto, moving Lulu to a corner of the kitchen and placing water and a small bowl of catnip treats close to the open cage. "Once he sees that you're comfortable with me, he'll come out and explore."

"I'm *not* comfortable with you," I said. "So, you'll have to come up with a different plan."

Beto ignored me, turned to the wine refrigerator, and removed a bottle from within. "You know where the glasses are," he said as he applied the corkscrew.

"It's barely eleven thirty," I said.

"And? Pretend its Sunday and we're having brunch."

I retrieved two glasses and Beto poured.

"All right," I said after two sips. "Explain away."

"Look, I didn't *intend* to lie to you. It was an inspired fabrication. When I first saw you walking along Snake Lake, I planned on being totally up-front with you about my involvement with Sarah and the Willoughbys. I figured you probably knew already, anyway. But when it became obvious to me you had no idea who I was, and Sarah had not discussed me with you —" Beto stopped talking and looked toward the oven. "Just a minute," he said, turning away, "I need to take out my shepherd's pie."

Wine and shepherd's pie. This was not going as planned. "It smells delicious," I found myself saying. The delicate aroma of herbs, potatoes, and lamb, which I'd tried to ignore since my arrival, was enticing.

"Thanks." Beto placed the dish on a cooling rack, then padded back to me.

Beto was barefoot, his clingy gray joggers left little to the imagination and his black tank top revealed a smooth, powerful torso. There was no evidence of six-pack abs, but his solid build had a natural sexiness that I found as difficult to ignore as the scent of the meat pie.

"Where was I?" Beto asked.

"Inspired fabrication."

"Ah, yes. Well, by the time we arrived at the restaurant I realized how totally clueless you were—"

"Charming."

"How clueless you were about Fabiola's death and the police investigation into it. I decided that your lack of knowledge could be an advantage. If I'd told you everything up-front, you might have turned down my proposition—just like Ms. Lewis did. Plus, I had no idea how good of an actor you were. I didn't want you to give yourself away. And I really am a private investigator now. Did you think I forged an ID.? Come on."

Beto's words held the ring of truth. Then, again, he could have been a consummate liar with impressive culinary skills and big muscles who knew how to work his assets. "And the stalking"? I asked.

"That was true," Beto replied, confirming what Sarah had told me. "Though Ms. Lewis did not seek me out to investigate it. It came up during my partner's interview with Max—just as I described to you. Then, in my initial interview with your friend, I told her that someone had observed Mrs. Willoughby, following her on several occasions. She denied any knowledge of it, but her denial was far from convincing. Later—after the inquest and my resignation, I approached Ms. Lewis and suggested the same arrangement I proposed to you. She refused. She told me that if I really wanted to help Max, I should let things be."

I poured more wine and said, "You know what she meant, don't you? You must. You were part of the investigative team. If Fabiola Willoughby was murdered and her husband's alibi is valid, that leaves only four people—excluding Sarah—who could have committed the crime."

"I know," said Beto, his voice soft, his delivery terse.

"And of those four people, there is one who hated her enough to do it."

I felt disloyal, treacherous, but Sarah had planted the seed of doubt in my mind, and Max's own words could be interpreted as damning.

I don't care that she's dead. I hated her.

Fabiola ruined everything… It's different now.

"Don't go there, man," said Beto as if he'd heard my thoughts. "There is no way it was the kid. *No way.*"

"I don't want to entertain the possibility either, Beto, but if Fabiola was murdered, the possibility is unavoidable."

"She *could* have killed herself. It *could* have been an accident."

I recalled something else Max had said on my first day at Jessamine Grove, as I'd hesitated at the foot of the stairway to his bedroom.

"Did you know that Fabiola Willoughby was afraid of heights?" I asked. Beto shook his head, but I saw understanding dawn in his eyes. "If she intended to kill herself," I continued, "she would hardly have chosen the highest balcony in the house to jump from. Nor would she have been there at all unless she was with someone whom she trusted—someone with whom she felt safe. Think about it, Beto."

"How do you know that Fabiola was afraid of heights?"

"Max told me."

Beto turned away from me and buried his face in his hands. It took me a moment to realize that he was crying. I set down my glass and put my hand on his shoulder.

"What is it, Beto?' I asked. "What the hell is going on?"

Beto turned around and I looked into his eyes, seeing fear and desperation.

"It can't be the kid," he said again, his voice a choked whisper. "It *can't* be."

"Why?"

"Because Max is my son."

*

THE PIE WAS history, and we were making inroads on our second bottle of wine when Beto finally confided in me about his past. His version of it, at least. When you discover that someone has lied to you once, you tend to take everything said subsequently with a grain of salt. That was the mindset in which I endeavored to put myself. But the comfort food, alcohol, and my attraction to Beto whittled away at my reservations.

"I told you about Lisette, my ex-wife," said Beto, slicing a wedge of the brie cheese that served as our dessert and handing it to me on a crispy, savory cracker. "And about our divorce."

"Yes, but you didn't tell me her name."

"Lisette. And her brother was Camillo. Anyway, now you know their names. Like I told you, I loved Lisette. But that wasn't enough. I should have known that from the beginning. I was too young and stupid not to let my penis do my thinking. I wasn't ready for marriage. For commitment. But

I went along with it—everything: church wedding, house paid for by the in-laws, expectations of heirs to the family name. My parents were happy, her parents were happy…" Beto shrugged and reached for his empty glass. I refilled it. "So," continued Beto, "we were the golden couple. Lisette was fantastic. The first year was perfect. Then, I started to lose interest. Physical interest. I mean, we still did it and it was great—at least Lisette said it was. But for me… I needed something else. The something else that I could never admit to needing. It tore me up inside, Neil. I don't know how else to say it, to describe it.

"Anyway, after the…er…incident with Camillo, Lisette called it quits. Could I blame her? It was bad enough that I cheated on her. But with a man? Her own brother? I didn't even try to defend myself, make excuses. I knew it was hopeless. If Lisette hadn't told her parents, if it had just been between us, maybe it would have worked out differently. I don't know. Two months later we were divorced, and I was a pariah. Camillo too. Disowned by his family. I'd damaged two lives—three, if you include me—four, if you include the baby.

"I didn't know about the kid until after the divorce." Beto sipped his wine gingerly, as if realizing he'd already had too much. "The first time I heard about the baby was when I was notified by the court."

"I don't understand."

"In Florida, putting a baby up for adoption can be like selling a co-op. The mother owns the shares (the baby), and she has the right to sell them—as long as the board (the father) does not exercise his right of first refusal. I thought about it and thought about it, but by the time I finally decided to exercise my right to claim custody, it was too late. The statutory period had expired. I was angry with myself at first, but eventually decided that Lisette was probably right after all. I was a single cop. How could I manage a baby?"

I thought about the article on adoption that Sarah had saved. "Did you tell any of this to Sarah?"

"No. Why?"

"Just curious." By Beto's standard, I was not lying. I *was* curious. Why had Sarah kept that article? Had she believed Alma Montresor to be Max's biological mother? Or had she somehow become suspicious of Beto's paternity? "When did you find out about Max?" I asked. "How did you discover who adopted him and where he was?"

"By chance," replied Beto. "At least the opportunity came by chance. I don't know if you read about the case, but about three years ago a Miami police investigation uncovered an illegal baby selling racket that was led by a well-known pastor and his wife. The orphanage they ran was legitimate, but these two had their own side business that raked in a fortune by promising to smooth or fast track the adoption process. And they weren't too scrupulous about where the babies came from. I didn't work the case, but I knew the officers involved, and I followed it closely, for obvious reasons. Up until then, I'd managed to put my ex-wife and the baby I never knew on a shelf in the back of my mind. I'd wanted to forget and move on. But this case got to me big time. What if my kid had been one of those babies?

"Anyway, I called in a favor. Someone I knew who could access the adoption records. I told him I just wanted to know that the kid was okay. That everything had been done legally. Of course, he knew what I really wanted. The guy worked as a hacker for my division. Unofficially, of course. Long story short, that's how I found out that I had a son and that he was now Maximillian Willoughby."

"And that's why you moved to Saint Augustine," I said. "Did your parents really live here, or was that more inspired fabrication?"

"They did. Remember, I asked you if you believed in fate? Well, I didn't until then. And you're right. Fate can be a bitch. My parents had no clue that they had a grandchild and he was living just a few miles away from them. I *had* to come here."

I understood why Beto had done what he did. I could imagine the regret that must have haunted him since the day he'd given up the right to his child by inaction. What I could not understand was what he intended to do now. I asked him.

"I don't know," he replied. "I never had a plan. I just wanted to be near Max. To see him. Do I want him to know me? Of course, I do, even if I realize that's selfishness on my part. Max has my blood, but he's not my son. Ezra Willoughby is his father, and I can't change that. But if there's something going on at the Grove, if Max is in danger, I can't just sit back and do nothing."

Could Max be in danger? I recalled Rosanie's conviction that someone had wished Sarah ill. Someone evil who'd been done a favor by Mother Nature. Had that same someone taken advantage of Mrs. Willoughby's drunken state and pushed her to her death? If so, Beto could be right.

"Take Max out of the equation, for now," I said. "Where does that leave us? When you investigate a murder where do you start?"

"Motive and opportunity. Look, Neil, I've been over this hundreds of times in my head. Everyone had the opportunity. Their alibis mean nothing because there were no outside witnesses. You've lived with these people long enough. Tell me, would they lie to protect one of their own?"

"Probably. Mrs. Willoughby was hardly well-liked. And they are all loyal to Ezra. Speaking of Ezra, isn't the spouse always the first suspect?"

"Absolutely. Statistics don't lie. And his alibi is just as shaky as the others."

"I thought he was at a meeting of some kind. And dinner with a colleague. There should have been plenty of witnesses."

"There were. Thirty at the meeting."

"And the dinner?"

"They dined at the colleague's home, which is only a few minutes' drive from the Grove. They dined alone."

"Domestic staff?"

"None."

"Cozy."

"Your mind immediately goes there, doesn't it?

"Well, Ezra Willoughby is famous for being a lady's man."

"That's just it," continued Beto. "The colleague was female. But I didn't tell you that. You assumed it was a woman because of Willoughby's reputation. And you assumed a romantic context. But in all fairness to Willoughby and his lady friend, there is no reason to make that assumption. Going over this again makes me question if Willoughby and Montresor weren't exactly what they claimed to be: nothing more than good friends. Or else the Willoughbys had an open marriage."

"I think you may be right." I related some of my conversation with Rodrigo to Beto. "It's his opinion that Ezra was 'in thrall' to Alma, not in love with her or involved with her sexually."

"Could be. Maybe the Willoughby marriage was platonic. It's not that uncommon. Maybe that's why they adopted a kid."

"So, where does that leave us motive-wise with Ezra? If Ezra wasn't planning on replacing Fabiola with a new model, and assuming they did have an open marriage, what would be the point of Ezra doing away with Fabiola? Money?"

"No good. Prenuptial agreement. All finances were kept separate. And Fabiola left all she had to Max. But you've still got revenge, hate…"

Hate. The word brought Max to mind—and Rosanie, Nessa, and Rodrigo as well.

"I think you've hit the nail on the head." I told Beto of Rosanie's conviction that someone had it in for Sarah, and I repeated part of the conversation I'd had with Nessa on the day of the blackout. "Nessa said we sometimes hate the things we fear. We'd been talking about Ezra's aversion to cats, but I got the feeling that Nessa was referring to something else. Then, there's Rodrigo. Did you know he considers the portrait of Alma Montresor to be an abomination because it shows the true woman: an evil seductress?"

"So, you're saying that the spirit of Alma Montresor killed Fabiola Willoughby?"

"No. Don't be silly. My point is that hatred can grow and fester if not addressed head on. Allow me to bring Max back into the equation. Max is the only person to have openly and honestly expressed his hatred of Fabiola Willoughby. Everyone else, while perhaps secretly despising the woman, allowed themselves to be manipulated by her to some degree or other. Rosanie called her a bitch in an almost admiring way, but I think there's a lot of resentment simmering under the surface. And Rodrigo? He claims that his wife—who he loved—divorced him because of his loyalty to Fabiola. And he speaks of Fabiola as if she were Mother Teresa, Eleanor Roosevelt, and Evita Peron rolled into one."

"You think he doth protest too much?"

"I'm beginning to wonder."

"And Nessa Hanson?" Beto asked. "What did Santa Fabiola have on her? It was she who hired Mrs. Hanson."

"And who hooked Nessa up with the local theater company. Based on what I have been told, it's safe to say that Fabiola Willoughby never did anything for anyone without exacting a price for her favors. What was Nessa's? Or, like Max and Sarah, did Nessa have a natural immunity to Fabiola's head games?"

"That's for Nessa Hanson to know and you to find out," said Beto with a smile. "I'm glad we had this conversation. You've learned a lot and opened new avenues of investigation. From the get-go, we had opportunity. We now have the possibility of several motives. And I think your psychological point of view puts Max in the clear. Unfortunately, we're back to what brought in a verdict of accidental death: lack of evidence. Whatever we might suspect or believe, it is still quite possible that Fabiola Willoughby fell from that balcony due to the disorienting effects of one-too-many martinis. Unless someone confesses, we're still at a dead end. No pun intended. Have you visited the crime scene, by the way?"

"No. I've only looked at it from a distance. Why?"

"Modern building code would never allow it—a railing that low. An accident waiting to happen is what the ME called it."

"Convenient, if someone couldn't wait for that accident to happen."

"Exactly."

*

GUIDED BY MY responsibility to Max and my desire to preserve Sarah's legacy, I had set aside one afternoon a week for art class. More accurately, one afternoon a week when Max drew and painted while I read or graded papers and made the occasional critique of Max's work.

The weather had long since turned, and the chilly wet days were replaced by stretches of sun and humidity only occasionally relieved by a passing shower. On one such day, I sat in the shade of the pool portico pretending to read a novel as I watched Max work on a charcoal study of the Grove as well as his tan—remembering my own youthful days in the sun, painting on the boardwalk with Benedicta.

"Come in from the sun, Max," I called out, putting aside my book. "If you keep that up, by the time you're my age you'll look like a Brazil nut."

"I'm using sunscreen."

"Coconut oil is not sunscreen, and I was not making a suggestion."

Max produced the obligatory harrumph, but obeyed, donning his garish Hawaiian-style camp shirt, and joined me under the portico.

"What do you think?" Max asked, handing me his sketch pad.

I'd encouraged Max to experiment with the medium of charcoal as a means of weaning him from the rigid, architectural style of his graphite pencil work. While technically accurate, his previous efforts lacked personality. This one was different.

"I like it," I said. "This is how *you* see the Grove, not how the Grove is. If, indeed, the Grove has a fixed appearance."

"What do you mean?"

I leaned back in my chair and struck a Sherlockian attitude; my fingertips steepled and my gaze contemplative. "Perception," I said. "It's a concept that's been on my mind lately. If I said that everyone sees things differently, would you agree?"

"Yes."

"How is that possible?"

"I don't know… I mean, it depends. Are you talking about philosophy and psychiatry and stuff or about physical things?"

"Good question. Let's stick with the physical. So, then, how is it possible that everyone sees things differently?"

Max impressed me by not immediately giving whatever answer came into his head. He was learning the art of thinking before speaking.

"It should *not* be possible," Max said at last. "I mean, some people are nearsighted, and some people are farsighted. And some people are blind. So, like, they might see things with a different degree of clarity—or not at all—but that doesn't change the things they're seeing or not seeing. The objects are always the same."

"Really?" I ripped a sheet of paper from my notebook and set it on the table before Max. "What do you see?"

"A piece of white paper with blue horizontal lines."

I picked up the paper, stood, and walked out into the sunshine. Max followed. I held the paper up in the light toward the house. "Now, what do you see?"

"A piece of white paper with blue horizontal lines."

"Look closer."

Max squinted in concentration, then his eyes widened, and he smiled. "Now, I see a piece of white paper with blue horizontal lines and a shadowy image of the Grove. But it's still a piece of white paper with blue horizontal lines."

"Why?"

"What are you talking about, Prof? It just *is.*"

"Because that's what you need it to be. That is how you perceive it. But if a cat, say, Lulu, looks at it it's not a piece of paper. He doesn't understand the concept of *paper* the way a human does."

"But it's still a piece of paper," said Max stubbornly, "even if Lulu isn't intelligent enough to understand it."

"No, Max," I said. "I don't think a cat is less intelligent than a human. He's just intelligent in a different way, suited to his needs. His perception of the world we share is entirely different than ours. We may never fully understand his perception or know what he thinks or what he dreams of— where he goes during his long sleeps."

"You're starting to sound weird now, Prof."

"Sorry. I wandered from my point." I led Max back to the shade of the portico. "I'm not sure I had one to begin with," I said, sitting down and looking again at Max's rendering of the Grove. "I've just been rambling."

"I like when you ramble."

"Thanks." I poured some of Nessa's excellent iced tea and we sipped in silence for a few moments, then Max flipped the page of his sketch book, picked up his stylus, and began a drawing of me. I returned to my reading, studiously pretending nonchalance.

"Prof?" asked Max after working for five minutes or so.

"Yes?"

"Why don't you paint or draw anymore?"

I had been asked the same question many times. My answer was always two-pronged: I'd stopped painting when I realized I had no exceptional, marketable talent, and the exercise no longer fulfilled a creative need. Both were true statements, but neither was entirely truthful.

"Because it makes me sad, Max," I said, answering the question honestly for the first time. "Whenever I try to paint, I think of things I've done wrong in the past, mistakes I've made, people I've hurt. I think of my college roommate who I loved like no one I've known since, but who I lost because I was afraid to take a chance. I think of my parents—my father, haunted by the past and drunk all the time; my mother, loving but distant. Both gone. And Benedicta. Gone. Sarah…"

I didn't realize how much I'd said, or how close my emotions were to the surface until I felt Max's hand on top of mine, squeezing gently.

"Aren't you happy now, Prof?"

I saw in Max's eyes the need for an affirmative answer, but I also saw the need for honesty.

"I'm less sad than I've been in a very long time."

I wish it had been a cloudy day, so I could say that Max's smile made the sun come out. But I will swear that it shown brighter at that moment.

"Okay," said Max, letting go of my hand and pushing his pad and stylus toward me. "Show me what you got."

So moved was I that I didn't correct Max's English. I took up the stylus and began to draw.

Chapter Twelve

"YOU'RE A REGULAR little detective, aren't you?"

I thought I heard an edge to Nessa's words, but she followed them with a warm smile. I'd just asked her—casually, I thought—how long she'd been involved with the local theater group. "Sarah once told me that she'd been to a play at the PLP," I lied. "I recalled it the other day and looked up the theater on the internet. One of the first things I came across was a review of *Godspell* that mentioned your directorial debut and your star turn in Follies."

"Star turn? That's a bit of an exaggeration. Carlotta isn't a lead."

"True, but "I'm Still Here" is arguably the best number in the show."

"The show stinks," said Nessa, buttering her toast. We were enjoying breakfast à deux in the garden adjacent to the kitchen. "And I got that part by default, I'll have you know. It's meant to be sung by an alto, but our resident alto can't carry a tune."

I did not share Nessa's opinion of the Sondheim work, but I kept mine to myself. I wasn't in the mood for discussing musical theater. Instead, I refreshed Nessa's coffee and waited for her to properly answer my question, which she did presently.

"I've been with PLP for almost ten years. Mrs. Willoughby—she was a PLP board member—suggested I audition when she learned I'd studied theater and art in college. Before marriage, the ranch, and divorce."

"The ranch?"

"My husband and I owned a horse ranch in Montana. When he finally did something good for a change and died, I sold the place and moved to Florida. I had family in Miami then. Now, it's just me."

I wondered at Nessa's progression from aspiring performer and artist to rancher to housekeeper but sensed that she had said all she cared to say on the subject.

"On the morning we met," I said, "you left a comment about the Willoughbys unfinished and said it was a subject for another day. Could today be that day?"

"Why not? You've been here long enough to understand. What I had been about to say was that I often wonder why the Willoughbys adopted Max. I had just started here when he arrived, you know. Back then, when Max was a baby, it was different. Mr. and Mrs. Willoughby doted on him. But as Max grew older, they seemed to lose interest—as if they'd adopted a puppy who ceased to be cute when it became a dog. I know that's a horrible analogy, but—"

"It's a fair one. I understand exactly what you mean. I used to wonder the same thing about some of my students' parents. Boarding schools can be, unfortunately, a dumping ground for the unwanted. Many a boy has told me just what you have in one way or another. It wasn't that they were not loved, but they were no longer prized, cherished, as a child should be. It's a sad but common reality."

Nessa nodded her head slowly. "Yes. That's how it was with Max. Now, at least, things can be different."

I peeled a tangelo and asked, "What do you mean by 'now, at least'?"

"Well, as I said before, when Max was little, he got plenty of attention and affection from both of his parents, but when he started going to school, Mrs. Willoughby turned her focus to her television career and to her personal life: charity work, the arts, friends, whatever." Nessa shrugged and took a drink of coffee. I wondered if "whatever" included an ongoing affair with Rodrigo Velez. "The long and the short of it is that Mrs. Willoughby didn't have the time for Max—or for her husband. If you know what I mean."

The hint was less than subtle. "Interesting," I said. "I was under the impression that it was Mr. Willoughby's friendships—or one in particular—that upset the family harmony."

"Ezra Willoughby was devoted to his wife," said Nessa with the stubborn conviction of a witness under cross-examination. She toyed with her toast, then continued, "What I meant by 'now, at least' is that Ezra has the chance to rebuild his relationship with Max now that Fabiola is gone; to be something more than distantly kind—to be with us more often."

Nessa's words seemed to be spoken more to herself than to me, and I doubted that she realized how much her use of the Willoughbys' first names and the self-inclusiveness of her last sentence revealed about her relationship with Ezra Willoughby—or at least her view of that relationship. Had her many years of residency at the Grove engendered this familial possessiveness? Or was it affection for Ezra? Her digs at the deceased Mrs. Willoughby hinted at the latter.

"I understand from Mr. Willoughby," continued Nessa, returning to formal address, "that Max is doing quite well under your tutelage. I'm glad to hear it. He seemed unfocused in the care of Ms. Lewis. Of course, every teacher has their own style and methods. I'm sure that had Ms. Lewis continued in her position, Max would have profited from the experience in some way."

I was beginning to realize that Nessa was a mistress of the subtle put-down and the left-handed compliment. I was inclined to reevaluate my initial reading of her character.

"Anyway," said Nessa, "It's not a permanent solution, is it? Eventually, Max will have to return to *real* school." Nessa smiled as if she was totally unaware she'd just insulted me. "After the Grove is sold," she continued, "and Mr. Willoughby shifts his headquarters to his London office, I'm sure he'll return his son to a more conventional form of education. I understand that England has excellent boarding schools. Of course, you must know that already. I'm sure you'll prove invaluable in advising Mr. Willoughby on his choice."

Had Nessa intentionally dropped two bombshells, or was she speaking freely to a colleague whom she assumed to be in the know? To give Nessa the benefit of the doubt and save myself embarrassment, I said "I'm always willing to offer any advice to Mr. Willoughby that he might ask of me."

Nessa nodded, leaned back in her chair, closed her eyes, and sighed. "What a lovely day," she said. "I'm going to miss this place, you know. It grows on you. Then, again, I've never been to England. I'm looking forward to the change."

*

I WAS ADJUSTING my syllabus for the following week when I realized I'd left my handwritten notes on Sarah's desk. "Damn," I muttered under my breath. I could complete the changes from memory, but it would be unnecessarily time-consuming.

"What's wrong, Prof?" said my sharp-eared pupil, putting aside his hardcover copy of Isabel Allende's *City of the Beasts*. It was our weekly recreational reading hour. We would begin reading a work chosen alternately by Max or me and discuss it during following sessions as we progressed. Today, I was too preoccupied with Nessa's revelations to relax into reading.

"I've left my notes in the storeroom," I said, rising to leave.

"I'll get them, Prof. I'm a quarter of the way through the book and you haven't even started."

"Thank you, Max. I appreciate that." I handed him the key and described the notebook.

"Back in a flash."

More than a few flashes later, Max returned with my notes.

"Sorry I took so long, Prof, but the lock in the kitchen was jammed. No surprise. It's like a hundred years old. Anyway, I had to go through your place to get to the storeroom. I hope that was Okay. You left your door open."

"No problem," I said taking the notebook from Max. "I trust you. Besides, I always lock away my stash of cannabis."

Max's jaw did not actually drop, but his look of incredulity was comical.

"Seriously?"

"Come on, Max."

Max smiled. "You almost got me this time, Prof."

"I shall not cease in my endeavors." I made a chin jut toward Max's abandoned book. "Now, go back to the Amazon."

Max began to walk to the sofa by the window where he'd been reading, then turned around abruptly and said, "You know what you need, Prof?"

"Peace and quiet so I can finish planning your torture for next week?"

"No. Artwork."

"What *are* you talking about?"

"Your place. It's depressing. It's like a monk's cell."

"Monks' cells are not usually furnished with valuable antique furniture."

"You know what I mean. It needs color. Pictures and stuff."

"I'll make a note to take a trip to Hobby Lobby next week and pick up a few prints."

Max pulled a face. "You're cooking with gas today, Prof," he said, using the antiquated idiom he'd picked up from me.

"All right. I'll be serious. I happen to agree with you. What do you have in mind?"

Max reclined on the sofa, opened his book, and peered at me over the top of the spine. "It's a surprise," he said and then returned to his Amazonian adventure.

A few days later, following our last session of the afternoon, I followed Max to the crow's nest where he presented me with a bundle of artwork wrapped in brown paper and twine.

"Sorry. The only festive wrapping paper I could find had 'Happy Birthday' and balloons all over it. I figured the brown paper was more dignified. I mean, like, even if it was somehow randomly your birthday, that stuff was just too, you know, *seriously* childish."

"Max, your last sentence was painful to my ears, but I appreciate the sentiment. Thank you."

"You're welcome. When is your birthday, anyway?"

"December seventeenth. Yours?"

"November twenty-third. Wow. Maybe we have the same star sign. Do you know?" I shook my head. "I'll ask Rosanie. Open the middle-sized one first. It's the only one that's a real gift. The others I found around the house."

Dutifully, I unwrapped the dignified present and I could not have been more surprised or pleased at what I found. It was a framed enlargement of the snapshot I'd taken of Max and myself outside the lantern room of the lighthouse. "This is wonderful, Max. Thank you."

"I made the mat and the frame. And I tweaked the color in the photo just a little—nothing disrespectful to the photographer."

"I will treasure it," I said. "I think it will look much better on my fireplace mantel than my old books."

"Really?"

"Yes, indeed. I think it's time for a change. Now, what about the others? Are there further opening instructions?"

"No. They're nothing special. I just like them."

"That makes them special to *me*," I said. "Even if they're only mine temporarily." I unwrapped the largest first. It was a very nice lithograph of a painting of the Grove by a popular artist from the early part of the last century.

"That's from an exhibit I saw at the Tate Museum in London when I was little. It was so weird seeing my own house in a museum. It didn't cost me anything. It was a gift from Mr. Creswell because he was a friend of my dad. But Mr. Creswell is dead now, so it might be worth something."

I was impressed by Max's savvy—if not his rather callous practicality—and recalled Ezra's comment about the apple not falling far from the tree. A similar print by Ben Creswell had recently sold for over five hundred thousand at auction. At least I knew that Max could appreciate the lithograph's intrinsic as well as monetary value.

"Open the other one," said Max impatiently.

I did so and drew in a breath of appreciation. It was a spectacular landscape of a snow-blanketed valley, frosted pine forest, and majestic mountains. It was spectacular, yet not beautiful. There was a darkness to it—literal and figurative—that pulled me in and repelled me at the same time. The artist had succeeded in conveying the potential danger that lay beneath the prettiness of the white serenity and within the depths of the woods. And the almost photographic realism, the virtuosic use of shadow and light—the overall style—seemed familiar.

"It's cool, isn't it?" asked Max.

"I can practically feel the cold wind."

"Sarah told me that you like to ski. That's why I picked this one."

"Thank you. That was very thoughtful. But I have no idea where to put it. You'll have to help me." I took a longer look at the acrylic painting and said, "Don't you think it's a bit sinister?"

"Well, I guess so, but nature can be scary. Especially forests. I mean, fairy tales and everything; they always take place in a forest, right? I think she nailed it."

"She?"

"The painter. Mrs. Hanson."

"Nessa?" I asked, surprised.

"There's only one. Fortunately."

I examined the artist's signature for the first time. It was nearly illegible, but I could just make out the capital letters in the first and last name.

"A.H.," I read aloud. "Nessa doesn't start with an *A*."

"Well, duh. Nessa's what she calls herself. But her real name is Agnes."

*

I WAITED UNTIL the following Tuesday—Nessa's day off—to make an excursion with Max to the secret room. Choosing expedience over adventure, I allowed Max to employ his lock-picking skills (it was his house, after all), and within a matter of moments we stood in the music room. We swept aside the heavy drapes to reveal sunshine glowing though mullioned windows, and the chamber was transformed from the suffocating mausoleum of our first visit into a cheerful, welcoming salon. The only discordant note was the portrait mounted above the fireplace. "Now I understand what Rodrigo meant," I said, moving to face the painting.

"What are you talking about, Prof?" asked Max, sidling up to me.

We stood looking up at the portrait of Alma Montresor for several moments before I answered. "Rodrigo called this painting horrible. He's right. That painting you gave me of the snowy landscape is disturbing, in a way, because it examines the potential cruelty of nature—which is suitable for such a study. But this is a portrait. Portraits—at least those that are commissioned—usually flatter, not criticize. The viewer is meant to admire both the artist and the subject, not recoil. In the gloom in which I first saw it, this painting was seductive…beautiful. In broad daylight it's frightening—just like the landscape."

To Max's surprise, I removed my loafers, pulled one of the chairs at either side of the hearth to the center and mounted it.

"What are you doing?"

"Proving a theory." I scrutinized the artist's signature and whispered an F bomb.

"Prof?"

"Sorry. Pretend you didn't hear that. Max, did you know that Mrs. Hanson painted this portrait?"

"No. Why?"

"I'm just curious," I said. "I wonder if there are other examples of her work around somewhere."

"I don't know for sure. I found the snow painting when they were renovating the attic to make my new room. It was all covered up with old newspapers—the painting, I mean. I showed it to Sarah, and she said I should ask my dad if it was okay for me to keep it. He said he thought it was ugly, but if I wanted it, it was mine."

"How did you discover that Mrs. Hanson was the artist?"

"Sarah told me. I don't know how she knew, but she told me not to tell Mrs. Hanson, because it might upset her."

"I wonder what she meant by that."

Max shrugged. "Maybe Mrs. Hanson's like you."

"How so?"

"Maybe she doesn't paint anymore because it makes her sad."

Chapter Thirteen

MAX HAVING THROWN down the gauntlet, I rose to the challenge and approached artistic expression with newfound verve. I refined the sketch of Max I had begun, then bit the bullet—purchasing oil paints, good brushes, and the necessary accoutrements from an excellent purveyor in old Saint Augustine. If the shopkeeper thought me a retiree intent on rendering seascapes and domestic animals, I did nothing to dissuade her. To wax poetic about the desire to reclaim lost youth and squandered talent seemed a much more shameful alternative.

Alone in Sarah's workroom, I reconnected to my creative side and worked with enthusiasm on my portrait of Max. At times, I could feel Benedicta's presence—just as I had felt that of Sarah—and I considered reassessing my belief in spirits and the afterlife. They were both present with me as I worked. I could see Benedicta's smile, feel the touch of her hand on my shoulder. I could hear Sarah's laughter and smell the scent of her perfume. My mother, too, was with me. Since leaving Allerton and coming to the Grove, it seemed as if—little by little—a veil had been lifted. Outside of my accustomed comfort zone of so many years, I was growing, rediscovering myself and finding a new purpose in my life.

During our last Christmas together, Benedicta had anticipated just such a metamorphosis, as well as predicting the closure of Allerton and Sarah's marriage. Despite Benedicta's positive view of my future and the joy I always felt in her presence, the degree to which my dear mentor had deteriorated during a year of my absence had devastated me. I'd wished that Sarah and Victor had been with me as they had been in previous years but sensed that Benedicta had wanted the time to be just for us; that she had conspired with my friend and her fiancée to make it so.

Benedicta had been diagnosed with cancer three times throughout her life and had won the first two bouts against the disease, emerging victoriously in full remission. In the third bout, her opponent won. Benedicta refused treatment, placing her fate in the hands of Almighty God, rather than in those of the medical profession.

"But you've survived before," I pleaded. "Why give up now?"

"Because now is different, Neil. It wasn't my time before. Now, it is."

"How can you be sure?"

"Because everything is fading. Not visually—not like Bette Davis in Dark Victory—but emotionally. *Things* matter less. I'm losing my tether to this world. My new journey is beginning. I can't fight anymore. I don't *want* to fight anymore."

Had anyone else spoken to me in this manner, I would have told him or her to stop being silly, delivered the usual pep talk about the importance of the will to live, the power of the will to live. But I knew Benedicta. She was not giving up, not giving in. She was accepting the inevitable with grace and dignity. In her mind, there had been a reason for her previous victories, just as there was now a reason for her surrender.

"I almost asked you not to come," Benedicta said, as she poked the logs in the hearth. The gently undulating flames of the fire, the white lights, and the festive colors of the vintage Polish glass ornaments on the fragrant spruce Christmas tree lent a coziness and warmth to the small living room. The atmosphere was imbued with the love and faith of the person who had arranged each detail. Even in her weakened physical state, Benedicta exuded the spiritual strength that had been the hallmark of the life she had dedicated to the God in whom she completely, unconditionally believed.

"But you did ask me," I said, adjusting an ornament on a branch to better catch the light. "And I'm glad. Christmas will never be the same without you." I acknowledged the reality of her imminent absence with the practicality and realism she'd instilled in me during our long friendship, but thoughts of a life without Benedicta in it depressed me immensely.

"Of course, it won't, my boy," she said. "Everything must change, as the song goes. But it will not be better or worse, just different. My life on this earth is ending, but the next stage of yours is beginning. Life's cycles sometimes surprise us with the timing of these inevitable changes, but when the changes come, we need to accept them, grasp them. Only with acceptance can one find true happiness."

"You're right," I said. "As always. But I feel unprepared, lost. Sarah's planned her future: a new job, a husband. Why can't I do that? Why does the closure of Allerton seem like the end of the world?"

"Because you've allowed Allerton to become *your* world," said Benedicta, turning away from the fireplace, picking up her mug of eggnog and rising with an effort from her crouched position. "You've hidden there for nearly thirty years." She put up a thin hand to fend off the protest on my lips. "Yes, Neil, you've done good work. You've been blessed with the soul of a true educator, and you've touched so many young lives, helped so many boys find their path. But what about you? A life of service does not mean sacrificing oneself—one's inner self. That way is selfish and self-destructive."

"What do you suggest?"

"Stop."

"What?"

"Stop. Don't jump into another job simply because you feel useless or bored. Eventually, you will find a way to be useful, or it will find you. And boredom can be a good thing. It can stimulate your creativity. So, when Allerton finally shuts its doors come back here. Relax, think, dream. And wait."

"When God closes a door, He opens a window? Is that what you mean?"

"I dislike that saying. God doesn't do anything for us. He creates possibilities; it's up to us to act and make choices. In the Lord's realm, there are no doors or windows."

"You're getting mystic, Benedicta," I said. "I think I need to put more rum in the eggnog."

"I won't object. I have something very important I want to say to you before I move on, and I've been conflicted over whether I should say it."

I warmed the rum over the fire and added it to our mugs. Benedicta settled herself into her favorite club chair by the hearth and I sat cross-legged at her feet, like a child awaiting the telling of a fairy tale.

"Your mother was a brave woman," said Benedicta after a sip of her fortified drink. She stared thoughtfully into the fire for a few moments, and I experienced that odd tingling sensation I often felt when I anticipated something unpleasant was about to be said or done. "She was brave to finally break the chain of denial woven by your father and grandfather. In doing so, she risked losing you. And she did, for a little while. But she trusted in you, and her trust was rewarded with the close relationship you shared for the second phase of your lives. She passed on, knowing that you loved and admired her. And she was very proud of you."

I did not bother to dry my tears. Only Benedicta knew how much I missed my mother and how I regretted those years when I'd ostracized her out of stupidity and stubbornness.

"I've told you about her last moments, her 'deathbed confession.' But I did not tell you everything. She left it up to me, you see. She was brave, but what she feared more than anything was losing your love and respect. Eve's last words to me were *'tell him if you think it's right. I trust in your wisdom, Sister.'"* Benedicta reached into the left pocket of the bulky cardigan Sarah had knitted for her the previous Christmas and pulled out a cream-colored envelope folded in two. "I've held on to this for four years. I'm not as brave as Eve was."

Benedicta reached out her hand, and I returned the gesture, gripping the envelope between thumb and forefinger.

"Eve's letter is addressed to me," said my mentor, "but its contents were intended for you."

Benedicta leaned back and closed her eyes, knowing I would read it immediately, not wait for a moment of solitude; knowing I would need and appreciate her silent support. I unfolded the envelope, pulled out the letter, and read my mother's final message.

Dear Benedicta,

I thank you for all your years of love and devotion to my son. I can hear you saying that you simply did what God asked of you, but there is nothing simple about it. God asks many things of many people and often the call falls on deaf or uncaring ears. Accept my thanks as they are intended: from one mother to another.

I have never been strong in my faith, but now that I am dying, I have come to that stereotypical final moment of the faithless when you cling to the hope that God is indeed real and will welcome you with the open arms for which He is so famous. I do not pray for forgiveness but for understanding and leniency when my time for judgement arrives.

Although my upbringing was not a religious one, my parents stressed the importance of the principles of truth and honesty. They led by example, and I strived to follow it. As you know, at a difficult point in my years as a wife and mother, those learned principles were tested and found lacking. I put them aside in favor of love for my husband and fear for my son.

While, on some level, I felt betrayed by my husband, I understood why Jakob upheld the lies. What life could he have had if he had told the truth? But then, what life did he have holding it in, letting it grow form a shameful secret to a malignancy that slowly destroyed him? I want to believe that if he had told me the truth early on, I would have stood by him; would have judged him for the man he was, not for the sins of his father. Would I have? That I even raise the question provides the answer, I suppose.

Motives are subjective, aren't they? I'm about to explain to you what happened on the day my husband's father, Helmut Boehm, died. I have almost convinced myself I do so in order that Neil will one day understand. But that's not really the reason. The reason is that I need to justify my actions to myself. To write them down is to make them real, to own them.

It's important you understand that I once loved my father-in-law. My own parents passed away when I was a small girl, and I was raised by my godparents (a cousin of my mother and her husband) as if I were their own child. I grew up in a small ethnocentric, German-American town in Pennsylvania—the kind of place you now only see in films. The kind of place where you not only knew your neighbors but were quite likely related to them one way or another.

Jakob and I progressed from schoolmates, to

sweethearts, to newlyweds in a manner as outdated as our hometown. Although Jakob and his parents had immigrated from Germany toward the end of the war, by the time Jakob and I were married in 1959, the Boehms had established themselves—through family connections and wealth—as pillars of our community. By the midsixties, when Neil was born, Boehm Building and Supplies (BBS) had grown from a modest lumberyard into a major regional manufacturer of tract houses and strip malls. The business still thrives, and Neil retains a financial interest.

Although Jakob cared little for the family enterprise, his father recognized in me a talent for business, and I soon became his right hand and eventually a partner in the company. When the senior Mrs. Boehm died and Jakob's father lost not only his wife but his drive, I assumed control of BBS.

Before you become bored with backstory, suffice it to say that Helmut Boehm and I were in-laws, business partners, and friends. He was also my mentor. He encouraged me to pursue a college degree and gave me his blessing when I eventually stepped away from day-to-day operations at BBS to seek my fortune in advertising and marketing.

When Neil was still in kindergarten, we—husband,

father-in-law, and son moved to California. While pursuing my own dreams, I helped Jakob fulfill his aspirations of owning an antique shop. Jakob had impeccable taste and an encyclopedic knowledge of antiquities, collectibles, and artwork, but he was hopeless with finance. With my business acumen and monetary support, his dream was realized. Even if Jakob's Gems never turned a profit, it became a fixture in the community of Florentina Bay for many years and my husband found his niche and the place he could escape—if only briefly—from the demons that haunted him.

With my bourgeoning career at an advertising agency in San Francisco and Jakob's preoccupation with his shop, Helmut gradually assumed the role of caregiver for Neil. It happened so smoothly, so organically, that I hardly saw it coming or transpiring. By the time Neil entered grammar school, Helmut Boehm was my son's de facto parent. I considered myself lucky to have a father-in-law who loved and was loved by my son. Helmut had been generous, kind and loving to me, so it seemed only natural that that love should extend to my child.

Again, and again, I have asked myself how I could have been so completely and utterly fooled. How I could have lived with Helmut Boehm for so many years, how I could have loved the man without ever having an inkling of what he really was, what he had been. What evil occupied the soul of a man so outwardly gentle and caring?

Helmut Boehm's initial decline was rapid. A heart attack had partially disabled him—reducing his time spent tending his beloved garden and socializing with the small group of friends he'd met while working as a docent at the local public library—and a stroke less than a year later had nearly felled him. Yet the old man was the quintessential creaking door. Dr. Mitchell, our family doctor, advised that Helmut might have quite a few good years ahead of him with proper diet and exercise, or he could go at any moment. At the time, I found Mitchell's waffling prognosis irritating; unaware how well it would serve me in the future.

Eventually, Helmut spent more and more time in bed, and we were obliged to hire a nurse to look after him during the day. Meanwhile, the unexplained rift between my husband and his father became more pronounced. Jake seemed positively relieved at his father's confinement and never set foot in Helmut's room. It was Neil and I who sat with him, read to him, brought him his dinner and his bedtime tea.

It was on one such visit that I became aware of the album.

"Bring me my box, Liebling," Helmut said, laying a frail hand on my arm as I moved to take away his tea tray. He glanced toward the massive antique bureau that dominated the small room. 'There. In the bottom drawer."

"Of course, Vater." I placed the tray on the chair next to the nightstand and carried out my father-in-law's request. I found a good-sized metal strongbox under a layer of cashmere sweaters and cedar sachets and brought it to him. Helmut smiled his thanks, then settled the box on his lap, caressing the surface almost reverently as an old woman might caress the lid of a music box from her girlhood.

"Ein anderes Leben," murmured Helmut as he gazed at the box.

Burning with curiosity, I nearly asked him what was inside, but my respect for the old man kept my words unspoken.

"Thank you, Eve," said Helmut, turning a gentle gaze to me. "I'd like to be alone now."

I smiled, nodded, and kissed his scruffy cheek before picking up the tray and departing. As I turned the handle on the other side of the door and made to close it, I glanced up and watched Helmut through the narrowing gap between door and frame as he reached into his pajama top and extracted a chain from around his neck. From the chain hung a key.

At last, the mystery of the key my father-in-law had worn around his neck for as long as I'd known him was solved.

Ein anderes Leben. Another life. How sad, I thought, the old man alone with his box of memorabilia—love letters, photographs. A locket, perhaps. I washed the dishes, feeling a mixture of tenderness and melancholy. Later, after Jake and I had watched Johnny Carson and had a nightcap, I returned to Helmut's room for my habitual pre-bedtime check-in. A night owl, the old man would usually read well into the wee hours.

There was no answer when I knocked the first time nor the second. I entered the room quietly and found him fast asleep, the strongbox on one side of the bed and an open photo album on the other. I smiled indulgently at the scene as I approached the bed.

Then, I saw the pictures.

I can hardly describe how I felt, Benedicta. How the room seemed to sway, and how my breath caught in my chest. There before me, image after image of my beloved Vater, Helmut Boehm, in full Nazi regalia— medals, dashing cape and shiny boots. Images of Helmut with other officers—with Hitler himself—Helmut grinning proudly in each one. These were Helmut Boehm's keepsakes.

I looked at the Helmut I thought I knew as he lay there snoring gently. How could it be? But the evidence was incontrovertible. And all the little questions, all the little doubts that had nagged me during my early acquaintance with Jake and his family resurfaced and found answers. The whispering old ladies, the gossips after church:

"They're cousins, all right, but Boehm isn't their real family name."

"You don't say."

"Changed it after the war. All very hush-hush, of course. For the boy's sake."

"Poor thing."

I felt sick, but I managed to hold down the rising bile until I stumbled to the bathroom and vomited into the toilet.

Two days passed before I confronted Jake with my discovery. At first, he could say nothing but "I'm sorry" repeatedly as he cried, and I held him in my arms. "I didn't understand, Eve, I swear," he said at last. "I marched and saluted along with all the other officers' sons, but I didn't understand. I thought my father was a patriot. I admired him. God forgive me, Eve, I admired him."

I don't think I slept much for several days. I would lay awake beside my broken husband, reliving the last few years of our lives with Helmut Boehm under our roof. I would think about how I had loved the old man, how Neil had loved him. About his kindness to my son, his tenderness. About coming home to find Neil snuggled in his lap, fast asleep. Feelings of anger, hatred, betrayal, and disgust overcame me in these moments. The thought that the lips and hands of that monster had kissed and held my precious child made me physically ill. I forbade Neil to visit his grandfather, inventing orders from Dr. Mitchell. He obeyed, but I knew he saw through the lie. One lie begets another. Isn't that in the Bible somewhere? If it isn't, it should be. I began to lose my son's love with that lie, and I would compound it repeatedly in the years to come, believing I was acting in his best interests.

So, then, to the deed. Hitler had his "Final Solution." I had mine. Once I made my decision, feigning normality was much easier than I anticipated. I suppose I found strength in righteousness, in belief in my purpose. The irony that Helmut Boehm and his ilk had justified their actions with the same arguments was not lost on me. Indeed, I found comfort in it. I resumed my evening duties, laughed at Helmut's anecdotes, smiled as I poured his tea.

Jake must have seen what was in my mind because he began to eye me with the wary regard of a dog owner whose beloved companion has broken training and exhibits unexpected aggression. A look of fear and awe met my gaze whenever I made my nightly pilgrimage to Helmut's room. In the end, it was easy. A pillow held over the face—just like in the movies. No muss and little fuss.

Die, you fucking bastard!

I did not say it aloud. I thought it. I thought it for me, and for the millions of innocents who had perished because of Helmut Boehm and men and women like him. I thought it for my son, who would no longer be defiled by his touch. I thought it for my husband who had suffered for his father's sake for so many years.

Afterward, I cleared away the tea service, plumped the pillows and adjusted Helmut's dressing gown. I said "Goodnight, Vater" for the last time and left Helmut Boehm to his fate. When the nurse found him the next morning, she declared that he had died quietly in his sleep. Dr. Mitchell backed up her declaration with a death certificate stating basically the same thing. Yet over coffee later that day, Mitchell had regarded me with the same look I'd seen in my husband's eyes. He knew.

"It was for the best, Eve. Always remember that. His death was a kindness."

I suppressed hysterical laughter. Dr. Mitchell thought of me as an angel of mercy; a loving daughter-in-law who'd found the strength to relieve Helmut Boehm's suffering, who'd kindly closed the creaking door once and for all. I left Mitchell to his beliefs. I could not tell the good doctor that I was no angel of mercy. I was an executioner.

I trust in your judgement, Benedicta. I've made you my confessor twice now, without your consent. I hope you understand. I believe you will. And I believe that you will share my revelations with Neil when or if you think the right time has come.

I'm not sure how long I sat there, not painting, just thinking. Remembering. Was there a reason these memories should have come at such a moment? Was it the act of creating that allowed my thoughts to drift and take me away to another time and place?

Ein anderes Leben.

Turning my attention back to Max's portrait, I understood those words profoundly for the first time. My other life was over, its principal players dead. While I knew I would always cherish memories of them and hold a part of each of them in my heart, I also knew that Benedicta had been right. Everything must change. Myself, principally. I could not be the same person in my new life that I had been in my old—like an actor who continually plays himself rather than the character he is paid to portray. I needed to grow and to learn. And I felt it happening, slowly and surely.

I worked for about another hour, then returned to my room. I made some coffee, then stretched out on the sofa and looked for a long while at the framed photograph that now occupied the mantel of my fireplace. I thought not only of Max, but of the other occupants of the Grove—the *inmates* as I liked to call them. They all, like me, faced the challenge of a new world, a new life. The change had begun with the deaths of Fabiola Willoughby and Sarah and would continue inexorably whether Ezra Willoughby's plans played out as Nessa believed.

Nessa. Agnes Hanson, *né* Agnes Clotilde Montresor.

To be fair, Nessa hadn't lied to me about her identity. That she had not revealed to me her relationship to Alma was perfectly understandable, given that our acquaintance was thus far only one of amicable coworkers. Yet, the existence of the portrait and the music room to which only she was granted official access, spoke of deceit. Rodrigo had been forthcoming about his knowledge of the artist who'd painted Alma's portrait, but it did not necessarily follow that he knew the artist and Nessa Hanson were the same person.

I recalled what Max had said about his discovery of the winterscape. The work had been deliberately hidden, and Sarah had advised Max not to reveal his possession of it to Nessa as it might upset her. Maybe Max's guess had been accurate. Maybe Nessa Hanson had chosen to bury her past life as an artist because of painful associations, but the brilliant yet disturbing portrait of Alma remained because Ezra Willoughby owned it and would not be parted from it.

The Portrait of Alma Montresor. Convinced that the painting was at the heart of all that was and had been wrong at the Grove, I'd begun to think of it in capital letters. Something Max had said during our first visit to the music room came back to me. I had asked him if he knew who the woman in the painting was and he had said no; that it was someone from his father's past, someone from the time before he was adopted.

Of course!

I had been so intrigued by the enigma of Alma Montresor, her mysterious relationship with Ezra Willoughby, and the possibility that Max had been their love child, that I ignored one very important point. The portrait had been executed *before* Max's arrival. And now that I knew that Max was not the child of Alma Montresor, all my prior assumptions would need to be reexamined. I'd been thinking the wrong way around, looking at the results—the Grove as it was in the present—when I should have been looking at the Grove as it was *then*.

Before the advent of Max, Rodrigo, Rosanie, and, later, Nessa Hanson, Ezra and Fabiola Willoughby had been the only residents of the Grove, and each spent considerable time away—Ezra on business trips, Fabiola in Miami. Bits of my conversations with Rodrigo and Nessa came back to me with new significance.

Rodrigo: *"I met her in Miami at a museum fundraiser organized by Fabiola."*

Nessa: *"My husband and I owned a horse ranch in Montana. When he finally did something good for a change and died, I sold the place and moved to Florida. I had family in Miami then. Now, it's just me."*

Miami.

I rose from the sofa and returned to the workroom. Retrieving the stack of newspapers and periodicals I'd studied on the day of the blackout, I selected the opera magazine with the cover photo of Alma Montresor. A quick consultation of the photo credits confirmed my suspicion. The cover portrait had been taken at the diva's retreat on Star Island, Miami.

Cozy, as Beto might say. Three hundred or so miles separation was nothing for the likes of Montresor and the Willoughbys. Removing Max as a factor, a relationship still existed among Ezra, Fabiola, and Alma. Subtract one factor and add another: Agnes Hanson. Although she may not have begun living at the Grove until after her sister's disappearance and the Willoughby's adoption of a child, Agnes had been on intimate enough terms with the Willoughby-Montresor ménage to have painted a portrait of her sister in situ. Perhaps Agnes had been a long-term guest of the Willoughbys during the creation of the portrait, then, upon the death of her husband, returned to the fold as a live-in employee.

Pleased with my conjectures, I exchanged my coffee for wine and warmed leftover meatloaf and mashed potatoes in the microwave for my supper. After my meal, as I washed and dried my dishes and settled down for an evening of reading, my self-satisfaction waned. I'd really discovered nothing earth-shattering or incriminating—if indeed any crime had been committed. All I had were a set of circumstances and coincidences: perspectives and possibilities Still, I was certain that within that set was something significant. Something that would open a door. I heard Benedicta's voice in my head: *"God doesn't do anything for us. He creates possibilities; it's up to us to act and make choices.''*

Possibilities. Perspectives. Choices. I feel asleep with those words circling my mind.

Chapter Fourteen

NED WAVED WHEN he caught sight of me as he worked on the shrubbery outside the kitchen. I hadn't noticed him until then, as I'd been sipping my coffee and daydreaming.

"Hello, Ned," I called through the open casement window. "Join me for a coffee?"

Saturdays at the Grove were something of a potluck, population wise, and today was one of the days that I found myself alone in the house. I wondered if Ned was the only other person on the estate. I hadn't spoken more than a passing word to him since the day I'd arrived at the Grove, but Ned was no stranger to the kitchen where he came to gossip with Rosanie. I figured I'd try my hand at it.

"Don't mind if I do," said Ned, standing and removing his gloves and kneepads. "This here is Abel's job," he added, making a sweeping gesture at the shrubbery, "but the feller's been AWOL the last few days. Got a sick kid."

I met Ned at the mudroom door and ushered him in.

"Thank you kindly," he said as I set a place for him at the island. I served him his coffee and offered him a piece of the poppyseed cake I'd made the day before.

"Jack of all trades, eh?' he said, looking appreciatively at the cake. He took a bite and sighed with pleasure. "Goddamn! Haven't had a seed cake this good since my grandmama snuffed it. Real butter. That's the secret." He consumed the small slice before he even touched his coffee, so I served him another.

"Man," he said, finally tasting the coffee, "Nessa and Rodrigo got some serious competition in the kitchen since you come along. Miss Sarah, she was a sweet lady, but she wasn't the domesticated type."

Resisting the temptation to laugh at Ned's malapropism, I agreed. "No, she wasn't." We drank our coffee in silence for a few moments, both looking out at the lovely view of the kitchen garden.

"What were you thinking?" Ned asked, as I refreshed our coffee and cut another piece of cake and split it between us.

"I beg your pardon?"

"When I saw you at the window, you looked a million miles away."

"Actually, Ned, I was thinking about what you told me the day we met—about the jessamine. I was wondering what the Grove was like back then, before Mrs. Willoughby's uprooting of the vines. Before Max came along—before the household became what it is now. When it was just Mr. and Mrs. Willoughby."

"It was never just Mr. and Mrs. Willoughby," said Ned. "Not for long, at least. When they come back from their honeymoon, it was one party after another. House parties, Mrs. Willoughby called them. People coming to visit for the weekend or longer. Like it used to be in the old days when Mr. Ezra's parents were still alive. That's how Nessa and her sister come to be here."

"Nessa's sister?" I asked, feigning ignorance.

"Name of Alma. Alma Montresor. You heard of her? She was a big-time opera singer."

"Oh, yes. I have heard of her."

"One helluva a woman, I can tell you! Always decked out like Joan Collins in *Dynasty*. And drop-dead gorgeous. You wouldn't think to look at them that they were sisters. I mean, Nessa's a good-looking woman, but next to Alma, she was like a shadow."

"Now that you mention it," I said, as if the thought had just occurred to me, "I remember reading somewhere that Mr. Willoughby and Alma Montresor were friends, and that they shared an interest in art and philan-thropy."

"True, true. But he ain't the one invited the girls," said Ned.

Girls?

"That was Mrs. Willoughby's doing. It was her who introduced Alma to Mr. Willoughby. After that, they were like *The Three Musketeers*. Until peo-ple started spreadin' lies about Mr. Ezra and Alma."

"*Three* musketeers? How did Nessa fit in?"

"Well, it was just after she finished painting her sister's portrait that her husband fell ill, and she had to go back to Montana. Alma went after her."

"A portrait?" I was growing tired of pretending I didn't know. "I had no idea Nessa was an artist."

"And a damned good one, so I've been told. Mrs. Willoughby was thrilled with the portrait, but Nessa refused to take money for it."

"You mean it was Fabiola Willoughby who commissioned the portrait?"

"Yeah. She and Alma were that close. 'Course, there were folks said they were more than just friends. Gossip, it was, I reckon. Just like with Mr. Ezra. Still, I've always wondered. Because of the jessamine."

"The jessamine?"

"The plants are similar, you see. The same genus, different species. Most people think of the lavender-colored flowers, but hereabouts—and up north in Georgia and South Carolina—it's the yellow flower that's more common. Jessamine."

"And?"

"The perfume. Alma always wore jasmine perfume. It was her signature, like. So, when the Senora had all the jessamine torn out… Well, like I say, I wondered."

*

"BUT DOES ANY of it matter?" I put the question to Beto as we dined once more at La Cocina.

Beto shrugged and downed a shot of chicha. "Depends. Mrs. Hanson's relationship to Alma Montressor never came up during our preliminary investigation into Fabiola Willoughby's death. If Fabiola's death had been ruled a homicide, we would have dug further, and the relationship *might* have been discovered and *might* have come under scrutiny—if it was suspected that the relationship impacted any possible motive Mrs. Hanson may have had for doing away with her employer."

I'd eagerly presented Beto with the new information I'd managed to gather, only to be shot down.

"And" continued Beto, "as you say, Mrs. Hanson has not actively deceived anyone. There is no crime in being related to a famous person. If there was some relationship among the Willoughbys, Alma Montressor and Agnes Hanson, what of it?"

"Thanks a lot."

"I'm playing devil's advocate, Neil. I happen to share your disquiet. And so did Ms. Lewis, it seems. If Mrs. Hanson had nothing to hide, why should she be so upset about Ms. Lewis discovering her relation to Alma? Assuming that was the reason for Ms. Lewis's warning to Max. Yeah, maybe her sister's disappearance was traumatic at the time, but it's been many years since then, and from what you tell me, she seems quite happy in her new life."

"Yes," I agreed, "she does. Nessa told me that her late husband was a first-class bastard. So, it seems that his death did her a favor—gave her the opportunity to move and reinvent herself. If that's the case, why did she keep his name?"

"Good point. Maybe it's a case of a lesser of two evils."

"How so?"

"We know nothing about Mrs. Hanson's relationship with her sister. Maybe Alma Montressor was a first-class bitch of a sister—like Mrs. Hanson's first-class bastard of a husband. Bad blood could hurt deeper than a failed marriage. Alternately, changing your legal name is a pain in the ass. That could be all there is to it."

"You may be right. I've been thinking about an article I read on the investigation into Alma's disappearance. The police interviewed Nessa and her response to them was that what her sister did with her own life was her own fucking business. At the time I read the article, I took Nessa's words as a defense of her sister. They could just as easily be taken as a dismissal."

"But she hung out with her sister and the Willoughbys. She painted a magnificent portrait of Alma. Dismissal doesn't fit the profile I'm seeing."

"You haven't seen the portrait," I murmured, a spark of illumination igniting in my brain.

"What do you mean?"

"It's cruel, Beto. Mocking. Not in an obvious way. No. You need to study the portrait in different types of light, from different angles to understand. As far as it's possible to portray someone as evil and corrupting, while superficially beautiful and radiant, Nessa succeeded brilliantly in her study of Alma. It could just be that she was trying for brutal honesty, to reflect every aspect of Alma, but I don't think so." I poured myself more wine and swirled it. "I don't think that picture is labor of love, Beto. It's more like a labor of hate."

"That's cold, Neil. I thought you liked Nessa Hanson."

"I do. I did. I don't know. I'm trying not to let her news about Ezra's supposed relocation to London cloud my judgement. But its more than that. When I first met her, I read her as a little snarky but nice. Now I'm beginning to see a slick, two-faced side."

I thought about that day in the storeroom when Nessa had brought me the hurricane lamp. How, just for a moment, I'd seen cruelty, malevolence in her face. I'd put it down to a trick of the light. Now I wasn't so sure.

"She sounds like a piece of work." The waiter came to clear away the plates and we fell into a brief silence. "What's your take on Ned's allusion to a lesbian affair between Alma and Fabiola?" asked Beto once the server had retreated.

"He's a very observant man," I said. "He read my mood from a casual glance through the window. Ned lived on the estate back then. In his position as a gardener, he could have been just about anywhere without arousing suspicion. If there was something beyond friendship between Alma and Fabiola, I'm sure Ned would have noticed, and wondered, as he said. That his impression sticks with him after all these years speaks to its accuracy I believe."

"Okay. I'll buy that. But that whole ripping out the jessamine thing? I don't know. Are we supposed to believe that Fabiola was so grief-stricken by the disappearance of her lover that she destroyed the plants that reminded her of the woman's scent? A romantically over-the-top action like that doesn't seem to fit with what we've learned of Fabiola's personality."

"No. If it even *was* romantic. Ripping, tearing, destroying. The way Ned described the destruction of the jessamine, my first impression of the act was one of violence, of anger. Not sadness or grief."

"Grief can make people angry."

"I know. But it feels wrong. What about the music room? The portrait? If Fabiola was so grief stricken that she could decimate the vines that gave her home its name, how does one account for the shrine to Alma Montresor in the house itself? It makes no sense."

We turned away from the subject of Alma Montressor and her connection to the Grove as we ate our meal—talking instead of ourselves, our likes, and dislikes. Our love lives—or lack thereof. Our world views. Beto poured the last of the wine and said, "So, we're both Democrats, we both love to cook, we both…um…like both ends of the baguette. We're both Trekkies. What do you say to coming back to my place for some date-night videos? Voyager episodes or The Wrath of Khan? Popcorn, better wine than they've got here, and then…?"

"We get laid?"

"That's essentially my plan, yes."

"I like it."

*

I WAS DELICIOUSLY sated as I snuggled up to Beto, stroking the smooth skin of his muscular chest. The sex had been great. Beto was a sensitive, passionate lover. I'd experienced that indefinable spark that elevates a good fuck to something else entirely. And I had no desire to snuff it out and pretend it hadn't happened—as I had so often done in the past. I wanted more.

But I was also hungry.

"What about the promised popcorn?" I asked as Beto moaned and stretched. "And *Star Trek*? We skipped that part."

"And you have regrets?"

"No. But I could go for some extra-mega-buttered popcorn, a glass of merlot, and an adventure in the Delta Quadrant."

"*Extra mega*? I think Max is corrupting you."

Beto kissed me and then strode from the bedroom to rustle up the popcorn and wine.

As I watched the retreating globes of Beto's meaty backside, I wished he hadn't mentioned Max. Every doubt I'd harbored about the wisdom of intimacy with Beto returned in spades. If he'd been a total stranger, it might have been easier to think of this as a possible start of something good. But Beto was Max's father. Unknown to Max. What the heck was I doing?

Too late for that question, Neil. You've already done it.

"What's up?" asked Beto when he returned a few minutes later with big bowl of fragrant pan-popped corn kernels and a bottle of wine. "What happened to your dreamy, post-sex face?"

"I don't know."

"Come on, Neil. We're both too old and too intelligent for that kind of shit. Out with it."

"It's Max. After tonight, everything will be different. I care for you, Beto, and I think you feel the same about me." Beto nodded as he put the popcorn and wine on a side table, lay on his side next to me, and embraced me with one strong arm. "And I love Max. How can I go on not telling him that the man I…that my…er…romantic interest is his biological father? I see more and more similarities between the two of you day after day. But, as you pointed out before, he's Ezrah's son. How do we deal with this going forward—if there is a forward. How do *you* deal with it?"

Beto stroked my cheek gently and kissed me just as softly on my lips. "I think there's definitely a forward." He retrieved the bowl of popcorn and placed it between us, then opened the wine and served it. "There's an old movie—" Beto continued after some munching and sipping. "—I don't re-member the name of it. It's what they used to call a tear-jerker. About a poor, uneducated woman who has an affair with a wealthy man and has his child. He leaves her but comes back later and woos the daughter away with his wealth and social standing. The daughter becomes rich and famous—or rich anyway—when she marries some 'society guy.' The mother follows her daughter's social rise but never interferes because she doesn't want to ruin everything for her daughter. The final scene is the mother watching her daughter's wedding secretly from the street though a window and then walking away. Something like that. I haven't seen it in years."

"*Stella Dallas*," I said, "with Barbara Stanwyck."

"That's it. So, you're a classic film buff?"

"No. I was educated on the subject by Sarah. But I grew up watching old films on TV—like you, I guess—those and Japanese sci-fi shows and monster movies. Do you remember them?"

"Mothra? *Godzilla?* Ultraman? Oh, yeah. Don't repeat this to anyone, but I remember thinking Ultraman was hot."

I laughed and consumed my share of popcorn and wine. "For me, it was *Tarzan*. The really old movies—where you could see his ass peeking out from under the loincloth if you were paying attention. Which, of course, I was."

"Naughty boy." Beto kissed me again, and we sat back against the headboard, hands entwined over the bowl of popcorn, each to his own thoughts for a while.

"Is that how you see yourself?" I asked, turning to face Beto. "Like *Stella Dallas?*"

Beto sighed and squeezed my hand. "Sort of. Without the melodrama and the stirring music. I don't know my son like Stella knew her daughter, but since I've discovered who he is, I never stop thinking about him and praying that he's all right. And life will be good to him. I don't want to make a claim on him. It's too late for that. I made my choice. But I want to know about him—at least to see him through a window like Stella saw her daughter."

"It might not always have to be through a window, Beto. Things change. As devoted as Max is to Ezra, there's certainly going to come a time when he starts to wonder about his biological parents—when he wants to know them. Or at least know who they were or are. I don't think that time is far off."

"So what do I do?"

"We started this conversation with *me* asking *you* what to do." I took another sip of wine. "I think the answer for both of us is to wait. See how things work out and deal with them as they come."

Chapter Fifteen

I LEARNED HOW to read music and play piano when I was very young.

Of the good memories I have of my childhood, some of my fondest are of listening to my mother play the piano and sing. She wasn't particularly talented, but she applied herself with a devotion that impressed me and which I strove to emulate. While I never surpassed her much in skill at singing or playing the piano, I did learn how to read music and studied the subject as a minor in college.

Like my mother and I, Max showed little promise of ever being a professional pianist, but he grasped the language and structure of musical notation with the same ease as he did those of the spoken word. What truly impressed me—aside from his voice—was his amazing ear. Having heard a song only once or twice, he could sing it with impressive accuracy. He could identify a composer with only the briefest of musical clues.

"He's learned from listening and repeating," said Steven Ballas, as we discussed Max's progress over tea in the church vestry. "If Max went on some television talent show tomorrow, I've no doubt he could win, mimicking whatever is the pop flavor of the month. But if he wants to be a true artist, he needs to find his *own* voice. And he needs more than we can give him once a week for a couple of hours. Someone's got to get that father of his to pull his head out of his ass." He favored me with a long, significant look, before turning his attention back to his tea.

Steven's implication was clear. The someone he expected to affect the extraction of Ezra Willoughby's head from his rectum was me.

"Not so subtle hint taken," I said. "I'll see what I can do."

"I feel I've let Max down, not having pursued this earlier with Sarah. But Max is different now—less hesitant, less shy. That's down to you, I think. Sarah laid the groundwork, but you've built on it impressively in such a short time."

"Thank you."

"Not at all. If I'd had more cojones, I'd have put my two cents in long ago."

*

"HOW ARE YOUR plans going for the move to England?" I asked, as I reached for the mojito Ezra had prepared for me. We were at what had become our common ground—the pool—and I had just bested Ezra in a relay. I was feeling cocky.

Ezra made a toast and sipped his cocktail before responding. "Nessa?"

"She appeared to assume that I already knew."

"Damn her. I asked her to keep it under wraps until I knew it was a certainty. At which point, I would have informed you. I may as well have told Rosanie."

"I gather it's not a done deal."

"It's a dead deal. For the time being. I had my eye on a gallery, but I lost the bid to some Saudi prince."

"Max told me you never lose."

"I lose frequently, Neil. I just don't tell Max. Anyway, it would have required being on-site until things got going the way I'd want them. I figured it was good timing. You know, making a new start. Away from the Grove."

"You plan to sell the place?"

"Hell, no. Would the king of England sell Balmoral? This is the "Willoughby Memorial Museum," as Max likes to call it. It might even be one someday. That'll be up to the kid. But I doubt it. He likes to joke, but I know he really loves the place. I think he's the only one who does."

"Nessa remarked about the Grove that it 'grows on you.' I tend to agree."

"I hate that expression," said Ezra, turning on his side in his chaise to face me fully. "It's meant to be positive, to indicate the onset of a pleasant surprise, a warm and fuzzy feeling, right? Well, what it makes me think of is a fungal disease, or some nasty creeping plant like kudzu."

"Or jessamine? I remember Ned telling me on my first day here that the late Mrs. Willoughby had all the vines removed at some point."

"Ned holds a grudge," said Ezra. "And it wasn't Fabiola who—" Ezra stopped abruptly and placed his drink on the table between us. "Forget about it. Its none of Ned's damned business. And I'm not in the mood for talking about gardening."

Interesting. Ezra took a gulp of his mojito and lay back facing the sun. I followed suit and studied the passing clouds for a while before I worked up the courage to say, "You lied to me, Ezra."

I could hear Ezra turn in his chaise, and I imagined a what-the-fuck look on his face when he said, "Excuse me?"

"You lied to me," I repeated, facing Ezra once more. "You said that Max has no musical talent. Nothing could be farther from the truth."

Ezra inhaled and exhaled with a huff. "Are you trying to make me regret allowing you to take the kid to church? I can do a three sixty on that anytime."

"No. I'm trying to make you regret banning music study from your son's curriculum, and the playing of music in his own home. It's ludicrous that I need to take Max to church for him to learn how to express himself artistically. Your son has a gift, Ezra. I respect—though I do not understand—your personal aversion to the subject, but I can't sit idly by while you crush Max's spirit and hobble his talent. *Please,* don't do this to him."

I was prepared for an outburst. I was prepared for a summary dismissal. What I was not prepared for were Ezra Willoughby's tears.

My dad says crying is for sissies.

A dam broke before my eyes. How much sorrow, how much anger had been pent up and for how long, I did not know. But I had sensed it all along, I supposed. Beneath the veneer of charm, good looks, and studied bonhomie lay a broken man. I'd seen the cracks in the image but had put them down to grief. Only now did I realize it was much more than that.

When the quiet crying ceased, Ezra removed his hands from his face and said, "I'm sorry."

"For what?"

Benedicta's words of advice came back to me.

"You've got a lifetime ahead of you and you will do things that you will genuinely regret, so don't squander your apologies."

I wondered if Ezra Willoughby had squandered many. I doubted it.

"For hurting Max. It was never my intention. I didn't know. I swear, Neil, I didn't know. I mean, I knew he liked to sing, and Sarah convinced me that church would be a good outlet for him without…without breaking my rule. But Sarah never said that Max was gifted. If she had, it would have been different. At least, I want to believe that it would have been different.

"I made a promise once. And I've done things I've regretted in order to keep it. But I never intended to do so at the expense of Max's happiness. I *thought* he was happy. I *believed* he was happy. I guess I just wanted to believe it, rather than admit I was a failure as a father as well as a husband and lover."

"What do you mean?" I asked, realizing as I said it that it was the wrong question to ask. That I should have kept my mouth shut and given Ezra time to open up on his own. I was certain I'd been on the verge of finally finding answers to so many questions and I'd fucked up royally.

"It doesn't matter now. It's over. It's been over. I just couldn't accept it. Forget it, Neil. Like the jessamine. Just forget it."

"And Max?"

Ezra's expression changed. A light came on in his eyes. A light of hope through darkness. "He really is gifted?"

"You don't need to take my word for it, Ezra. Listen for yourself."

*

HOW LONG HAD it been since the drapes of the music room were fully drawn and the french doors open to the terrace? How long since the doors of the salon had been open to the rest of the house? Used as intended, it was a lovely space; the ghost of Alma Montresor quiescent if not irradicated. Her image remained above the fireplace, but its queer power was dimed by glorious sunshine, chattering voices, the clink of crystal glasses meeting in salute.

"I know the Lord moves in mysterious ways," said Mother Anne after we'd each taken a sip of our martinis, "but this is one for the books. Excellent work, Neil."

"If I'd not met you," I replied, "this day might never have come. I'm beginning to rethink my doubts about His existence."

"Then I've done some excellent work too. Here's to me." Mother Anne raised her glass and took a good swill. We shared a quiet laugh, and I surveyed the small gathering: Stephen Ballas huddled in consultation with Max at the harpsichord, old Mrs. Simmonds—decked out like minor royalty—being charmed by Rodrigo, Mother Anne's son, Evan, doing his best to charm Rosanie. Judging by Rosanie's coy smiles and hair flipping, the handsome redheaded young man was succeeding.

Ezra stood alone on the terrace, nursing a whiskey.

Mother Anne's gaze followed mine.

"Do you think he's ready?" she murmured.

"He's excited to hear Max sing," I replied, my inner thoughts going out to Beto, wishing he could have been present as well.

"Strange way of showing it. He's like a wallflower at a cotillion. And you know that's not what I meant."

"I remember you telling me that what is true and what is for the best are not always the same thing. I believe they usually are, in the long run."

Mother Anne smiled softly. "You're speaking from experience."

"Yes."

"Thought so." Mother Anne reached out and pressed her hand over mine.

"You remind me of someone," I said.

"Really? Who?"

"My best friend."

Steven Ballas stood and called the gathering to order. Ezra moved in from the terrace and I scanned the room again, looking for the one missing guest and feeling a mix of vindication and disappointment at not finding her. Nessa had barely spoken a word to me since Ezra had given me the key to the music room, and her presence at the Grove had become ghostlike. I took a sidelong glance at the portrait over the fireplace and heard Ned's voice in my head.

"You wouldn't think to look at them that they were sisters. I mean, Nessa's a good-looking woman, but next to Alma, she was like a shadow."

And to the shadows, Nessa had once more retreated.

I returned my attention to the harpsichord. Max looked to his father and then to me. Ezra smiled, I gave Max a thumbs-up and a wink; then Max nodded to Ballas, and the first notes of Zelenka's heartbreaking *"S'una sol lagrima"* filled the room.

I'd been present at all Max's rehearsals but watching and hearing him now was a revelation. He embodied the love and pain in the lyrics and offered himself up to his rapt audience. It was a performance mature beyond his years, the performance of a prodigy. Though Max was not Alma Montressor's child by blood, he was one with her in musical spirit.

As the final, gentle trills of the song faded into the ether under Ballas's skilled hands, we all rose and praised Max's performance with fulsome applause. Ezra came to his son, wrapped him in a tight embrace, and kissed his hair, his cheeks.

Then, as the applause died, retching sobs filled the salon. We turned, almost as one, to the open doorway, where Nessa Hanson stood, clutching the frame, her face a mask of sorrow.

"You promised, Ezra," said Nessa in a harsh whisper. Her voice rose as she advanced into the room and walked slowly toward Ezra Willoughby. "You promised!" The whisper had turned to a shrill scream. "You promised!" Nessa staggered, as if drunk. Ezra closed the distance between himself and Nessa, steadied her with firm hands on her shoulders, and said,

"Forgive me, Agnes, forgive me. I couldn't do it anymore. I couldn't...not anymore. It's over."

I heard my mother's voice in my head.

"Thank God, it's finally over."

Then, I heard my own voice.

"Leave it, Edward. It's over."

Over. A two-syllable word that pledged finality but rarely paid up.

Chapter Sixteen

"I SHOULD HAVE confided in Sarah."

Ezra Willoughby made this pronouncement with his gaze fixed on the french doors and the sunset over the grounds beyond, his right hand holding an empty tumbler. I took the glass from his unresisting hand, moved to the rolling bar, and filled it with a generous splash of whiskey. Ezra turned toward me at the sound of the shaker as I mixed myself a martini.

"I feel sorry for her fiancée," Ezra continued, as he approached me. "Sarah would have made a wonderful wife. If I'd met someone like her years ago…" He let his sentence trail off as he took his drink. "Thank you."

Ezra and I were alone in the library. Ezra had urbanely smoothed over Nessa's outburst—explaining it away as the result of stress over memories of her late sister and an excess of alcohol. Max's recital had continued successfully, and he was deservedly feted with a delicious luncheon catered by Mother Anne and her son.

I raised my glass in salute. "You're welcome."

"I don't mean for the drink. It's *my* whiskey. You just poured it. I'm talking about today. What you've done for Max. What you've done for me. You saved us, Neil."

"I just gave you a gentle push."

"You called me a liar, man. That is *not* a gentle push." Ezra huffed a laugh, then rubbed his head with what I now recognized as his characteristic show of frustration. "It worked," he continued. "That's what matters. Look, what I said about confiding in Sarah. The same goes for you. Even more so for you. You deserve to know the truth. My version of it anyway."

We sat on the chesterfield, Max's preferred reading spot, and Ezra commenced his apologia.

"Alma and Agnes. Two sides of a coin. Darkness and light. That's how I thought of them, though they were very much alike years ago. Physically, at least. Both with masses of glossy, wavy black hair, centerfold figures and intriguing faces. But where Alma was overtly passionate and exuberant, Agnes was quiet and shy. Brooding, I guess you'd call it. I put it down to what I believed was the artistic temperament of a painter…of a deep thinker, someone of a quiet, contemplative nature as opposed to a woman of Alma's theatrical glamour. Agnes was good at hiding the dark, cold depths beneath her placid surface.

"You need to understand that to Agnes, Alma was the alpha and the omega. She shone like the sun to Agnes's moon. Agnes catered to her sister's every whim, allowed herself to be treated like a paid companion or a poor relation. Alma says this, Alma wants that. Alma needs to rest. Alma is a star, she's not like us.

"As an only child myself, it's hard for me to image the youthful relationship between the sisters; how one became the controlling and the other the controlled. How Agnes, beautiful and talented in her own right, was content to fade into obscurity as Alma rose to fame and fortune.

"Of course, she was never content, as I would learn the hard way. Agnes's intense, obsessive love for Alma caused her to silence normal, natural tendencies to independence and self-fulfillment—to silence them but not to eradicate them. The more she fought those natural tendencies, the deeper they were buried, the more powerful they became and the more twisted. Like the roots of a tree planted in the wrong place."

I thought of my father, keeping the secrets of my grandfather's war crimes and his own involvement in the Hitler Youth buried for so many years. How even the death of my grandfather could not heal the damage of my father's own twisted roots.

Ezra stared at his drink for a few moments, then continued.

"I knew nothing about the physical abuse until after Alma's death. The emotional abuse, I only guessed at. That scar on Agnes's cheek? Alma gave her that when they were in high school. You see, they were both popular girls. Both high achievers; each talented in her own way. But Agnes would always follow Alma, would shine in her reflection. When Alma applied to the Julliard School, so did Agnes—so as not to be separated from her idol. When Agnes learned that they had both been accepted, she was over the moon. Alma was not so pleased. She took a knife from Agnes's art supplies and cut her sister's face, saying that there was only room for one star in the Montressor family. Afterward, Alma claimed it was a terrible accident, and Agnes, of course, defended her."

"Jesus Christ."

"I guess a shrink would call it a codependent relationship. Like the words from that old Eurythmics song. Some people need to use, and others need to be used. Something like that. It sounds crazy, I know, but I sometimes wonder if it wouldn't have been better if they just continued like that—each of them satisfied filling a role, fulfilling a need in the other. But Alma eventually outgrew the relationship. She stopped needing Agnes."

"She had the opera house and millions of adoring fans," I said.

"Exactly. Agnes became an annoyance. A hanger-on. Then, Agnes met Gregg Hanson."

"The crudivegan horse farmer."

"Yes. I really don't know much about their life together, but despite Agnes's snide remarks and putdowns whenever she mentions him, I get the sense that they found happiness of a sort. For a while. Agnes started painting in earnest. Had some successful showings. There was the beginning of some 'buzz' in the art world. It seemed Agnes had found her footing, a way to grow on her own.

"Her work from that time speaks for itself. What remains of it. What Agnes hasn't burned, given away, or hidden."

"What happened?" I asked, though I knew the answer.

"Alma. She couldn't bear the idea of her sister becoming a success, a celebrity. A rival." Ezra finally took a drink of his whiskey and shifted on the sofa so he faced me fully. "It was Fabiola who brought them together again, knowing nothing about their shared past. Fabiola was living in Miami then. I met her, Alma, and Agnes at the same function: a fundraiser for the opening of a new gallery dedicated to promoting the works of up-and-coming female artists. Agnes was a featured artist in the first exhibition. It was her chance to shine. But Alma stole her thunder.

"In some way, I can't blame her. I'm not trying to defend her, believe me, it's just…I mean…I can't say that it was intentional other than the fact that Alma was always the center of attention wherever she went. It just couldn't be any other way in her mind. Do you get what I mean?"

"That Alma Montressor was an egotistical bitch? Yes."

"She was that, but…"

"You were attracted to her anyway."

Ezra sighed. "That would have been simple. We would have fucked, had some fun, then moved on. No. It was Agnes that I fell in love with."

"But it was Fabiola who you married."

"Yes. I loved Fabiola, but I was never *in love* with her. I loved her mind, her body, her sense of humor. But I never had that ache, that… I don't know what to call it. That feeling when you meet someone, and you just know that somehow—one way or another—they're meant for you. Even if you never see them again, or a relationship doesn't work out— you'll know forever that they were the one. That no one else will ever give you that same feeling. That ache in your heart. And you know it from the moment you meet."

I recalled the day I'd walked down South Portland Avenue in Fort Green, Brooklyn, for the first time, a suitcase in one hand and my tackle box of painting supplies in the other. It was hot as hell, and I was terrified that my deodorant would fail me, and I would be stinky as well as embarrassingly wet in my armpits by the time I got to the apartment.

I heard the music before I saw him. Guitar fingering that made me think of Joni Mitchell. Then I smelled him. Patchouli with a middle note of weed. I checked the address, looked down at the lanky, slovenly dressed musician sitting on the stoop.

Wonderful, I thought. *Is this slacker my new roommate?*

"Edward?" I had asked, hoping to be wrong.

Edward Snow looked up and my life was changed. In those strange, pale green eyes I saw my past, my present, and my future. Edward smiled, and I knew instinctively I would love him forever and that his love would come with a cost. It was birth, life, and death in a matter of moments.

"I know what you mean, Ezra. I've been there." I took a drink from my martini. "And it never goes away. Something remains. Even if it's just a shadow; a voice in your head when you least expect it or a scent or a song that brings all the memories flooding back."

"You *do* understand," said Ezra quietly. "I felt doomed and ecstatic the first time I met Agnes. It was more than a year before I saw her again, but I knew it was inevitable." Ezra stood and began to pace, restless as he relived the past. "Fabiola and I were married a few months after that gallery opening. A whirlwind romance, the press called it. A perfect match."

"Except that Fabiola was bisexual."

"How the hell do you know?" Ezra raked his head again. "Doesn't matter. It's the truth. And it might not have made any difference to our marriage, but then there was Alma. I think Fabiola fell in love with Alma at the same time as I fell in love with Agnes. We were drawn together in some way, the four of us. But it was an unholy alliance."

I thought of Edward and Laura and wondered yet again what would have happened if I'd agreed to live with them.

"Fabiola invited Alma to the Grove and, of course, Agnes followed—and the old pattern of their relationship began to repeat itself."

"This was when Fabiola commissioned the portrait of Alma?"

"Yes. Agnes was a promising but obscure figure in the art world. Fabiola thought that a portrait of her famous sister would give Agnes's career the boost it needed, put her at the top. And Fabiola was right. Or would have been if the portrait had ever been seen outside the walls of the Grove. Alma hated it. She saw in it everything that Agnes had intended to show: her beauty, her glamour, as well as her cruelty and malevolence.

"I don't think Fabiola really had an inkling of the strange dynamic that underlay the relationship between Agnes and Alma until then. Nor did Fabiola understand the intense jealousy that Agnes felt toward her. How much Agnes resented Fabiola for the special place Alma held in Fabiola's heart—the place that was meant for Agnes.

"Shortly after Agnes completed the portrait, Gregg Hanson had a heart attack. Agnes went to him. Alma followed. Gregg passed away, and Alma remained with Agnes, for moral support, we assumed. Despite everything, I thought, they loved one another. Months passed, and we heard nothing from Agnes or Alma. I can't explain how those months were for Fabiola and me. It was as if we'd both lost the love of our lives—but we never talked about it. It was just there, under the surface.

"Then Alma disappeared. Agnes said that she just packed up and left without saying what her plans were. Agnes assumed she'd gone to New York or Paris or to her retreat in Miami. Agnes didn't ask. She'd never asked Alma to explain her actions and wasn't about to start. That was the last anyone saw of Alma."

What my sister does with her own life is her own fucking business.

"Agnes stayed on in Montana," continued Ezra. "When Max came, I convinced Fabiola to invite Agnes to stay with us. Work for us. Agnes accepted."

"Why?" I asked, incredulous. "You said she resented Fabiola."

"Because Agnes and I were in love. It was our chance to be together.

Even with the baby—maybe because of him—my relationship with Fabiola was on the skids. Motherhood was not what Fabiola expected. Once the novelty wore off, she lost interest. She even suggested that we return Max. Like an unwanted dog to the pound. If Fabiola could have done it without destroying her career, she probably would have tried. But I would never have let her take away my son.

"Divorce was out of the question. It would have been social suicide for both of us and I was afraid of losing Max. So, we lived together but apart. And Agnes and I, we made the best of it. I thought we were damned lucky. Fabiola suspected, but she really didn't care. Agnes was no threat to her, and I think in some way Fabiola felt responsible for Agnes. Because she was Alma's sister. I can't say they became friends, but I think the animosity between them faded over the years.

"The problem was," Ezra continued as he sat down once more beside me, "Agnes could never let go of Alma." He waived his tumbler in the direction of the music room. "That damned shrine. It was her one condition—that I keep that room locked and the memory of her sister preserved just as she was when she disappeared."

"And that no music could be played in this house," I added.

"Yes. I know it sounds bizarre—and it is, really. Agnes wanted to preserve her sister's memory but on her terms. She wanted…she wanted to *own* the memories. So that Alma could be hers alone just within that room. With Alma's portrait like a spiritual presence."

I shivered. I thought of my grandfather and his strongbox and his album of photos. His war trophies. His constant reminders of his glory days. I thought of the portrait of Alma Montresor, preserved just for Agnes. Her masterpiece, her crowning glory. Her victory.

Chapter Seventeen

THE ROOF TERRACE of the bar at the San Sebastian Winery was a few hours away from being inundated by sunset seekers. It was only Beto, me, the bartender, and a few tipsy wine-tasting tourists floating in and out of the air-conditioned interior lounge.

"Damn," said Beto, swirling his cabernet and giving me a somewhat leering once-over, "you've got great legs."

"Thank you." I recrossed my legs so Beto could have a better look at the other thigh, thinking that bar stools must have been invented for just such a movement. "You're only just noticing now?"

"I guess the last time I saw them I was too busy arranging them in different positions to fully appreciate them. And my…er…objective was elsewhere."

"You're forgiven."

Beto smiled. "You know, I've never seen you so dressed down: T-shirt, Bermudas, Jesus sandals. Professor Boehm in *sandals?*"

"They're Bottega Venetta."

"Whoever. They're still sandals, bro."

I pushed my empty glass toward Beto, and he refilled it. "So, what do you think of my scenario?" I asked, after a sip. I'd taken Beto through what I believed were the events that had led to the deaths of Alma Montresor and Fabiola Willoughby. Conjecture based on threads of conversations, rumor, and my own imagination.

"Okay. Let's take Alma first. According to your theory, Alma follows her newly widowed sister to Montana as moral support. But the reality is more like she goes so she can take advantage of her sister's weakened emotional state and take control of her life again. Sounds about right. Once reunited with her sister at the home on the range, the anger and resentment Agnes has held in check since her marriage break out and she kills her sister in a violent rage."

"I didn't say violent rage. But there is a history of violence between them. And we only have Agnes's side of the story about that scar. Alma may have been telling the truth all those years ago. Maybe it was an accident. The same thing could have happened in Montana. But this time it was fatal. And Agnes was free."

"Ten points for plausibility. Zero points for evidence."

"And Fabiola?"

"That's a tough one, Neil. You expect me to believe that Agnes, now free and triumphant, goes back to the Grove and her lover, Ezra, and just sits around quietly for almost eleven years before she finally decides to give old Fabiola the heave-ho?" Beto shook his head. "I don't buy it."

"It wasn't *necessary*, Beto. Not at first. Remember, Ezra and Fabiola's marriage was on the rocks—it was common knowledge. They kept separate residences. Agnes had every expectation that they would eventually get divorced. She just had to wait, like the proverbial spider."

"But *eleven years*, Neil?"

"I remember when Sarah first introduced me to Victor. It was obvious that they were made for each other, and it was easy to imagine them in the future, a retired couple living *la dolce vita* in some medieval town in Italy. But I couldn't see them married *then*. Neither could Sarah. She wasn't ready to give up the happiness and fulfillment of her current life for a future one. So, she and Victor remained long distance lovers for almost fifteen years. But eventually, the time came when neither of them wanted to wait anymore. The time came, and the timing was right. I think it was the same for Ezra and Agnes. They weren't in any rush. The right time would come."

"But it didn't."

"Not exactly. I think the turning point for Agnes was when Ezra decided to send Max to boarding school in France. Ezra told me that he and Fabiola stayed together because they wanted to maintain a public image as a solid nuclear family, regardless of their differences or how far apart they'd grown. Appearances were everything for them. Especially for Fabiola.

"If Ezra had his way, and Max was sent abroad for the rest of his education, there would have been an opening…a way to orchestrate the divorce in a manner that caused as little collateral damage as possible. I think that was Ezra's plan. And it became Agnes's dream. Suddenly, she wouldn't have to wait anymore. It was time. Everything was working out at last."

"But Fabiola screwed everything up by refusing to send Max abroad."

"Yes. And it was so unexpected, so totally out of character. You'd think it would have been the other way around—that Fabiola would have been more than happy to never see her child again except at holiday gatherings. Maybe some maternal instinct kicked in. Maybe she just did it to spite Ezra. Who knows? But whatever her motivation, that decision was her death sentence."

"And now Agnes Hanson is mistress of Jessamine Grove with a handsome billionaire husband-to-be. Am I correct in assuming that an engagement is soon to be announced?" I nodded. Ezra had made the announcement the day before. "What about Max?" Beto added, his slightly sarcastic tone softening.

"He's safe, Beto. Whatever Agnes may have done, Max is no threat to her. She's very fond of Max, I think. Maybe she believes that Alma really was Max's mother. And Max is fond of Agnes, in a grudging adolescent way. In the end, my suspicions are just that. Agnes could very well be the innocent victim Ezra believes her to be."

Beto signaled the errant bartender—who was lost in a cozy tete-a-tete with a nubile blonde and her cleavage—and ordered another bottle of wine.

"Well done, Professor," said Beto turning his attention back to me. He paused as the bartender reappeared with the wine and poured it. "You know, people in my line of work are paid to discover the truth. Meeting out justice is up to the courts. Unfortunately, in this case justice is going to have to be left to the Man Upstairs."

I thought of my mother, dispatching a man guilty of genocide. I thought of Alma Montresor, disfiguring her sister out of spite and jealousy. I thought of Fabiola Willoughby, a manipulative narcissist who used, rather than loved, and had been prepared to "return" her adopted child when the novelty wore off.

Perhaps justice had already been meted out.

Chapter Eighteen

"DOES IT REALLY rain *all* the time?"

Max asked me as I helped him pack for our trip to Florentina Bay. Max was to spend the remainder of the summer with me while Ezra and Agnes were to be married in Greece and spend the season in Europe.

"No. Not really. That's just the way I remember it from my childhood. Memories are funny things. I think I remember it as dark and gloomy because the dark and gloomy memories are the ones I chose to hold on to for so long. But there were plenty of sunny days, and now the sunny memories are the ones I want to treasure…and to share."

Max smiled and I felt truly happy for the first time in many years.

"You cannot possibly pack anything else, young man," I said as I watched Max stuff his telescope into an already bursting valise. "You may have the luxury of the cargo hold of a private jet, but there's not enough room in my house."

"Come on, Prof. I gotta take the scope! The stars are totally different in Florentina Bay. It's all about perception, remember?"

"Okay," I relented. "The telescope stays."

A knock on the frame of the open bedroom door called my attention away from packing.

It was Rodrigo.

"Excuse the interruption," he said, "but I need to have a word with you, Neil." He glanced at Max who smiled at his bodyguard and then returned to his work. "A word in private."

"Of course," I said, worried by Rodrigo's somber tone of voice. I turned to Max. "Carry on. I'll see you later."

I suggested my room, and Rodrigo agreed. Soon, we were comfortably ensconced in the same positions we'd occupied on Rodrigo's last visit—this time partaking of whiskey rather than tea.

"*Salud*," I said, lifting my glass to my guest.

"*Salud.*" Rodrigo took something larger than a sip and then continued. "I'm sorry to have interrupted your preparations. Ezra only informed me of his plans this morning. His wedding to Agnes on a Greek island. *Qué chévere*. You and Max on a retreat in California. *Qué bueno*. And me, I stay here to 'mind the store' as they say." Rodrigo smirked and it was not a pleasant sight, reminding me of Agnes's frightening visage by the light of the hurricane lamp.

"I didn't know," I said, genuinely surprised. "Ezra didn't say, but I thought…" I hadn't thought. I'd assumed that wherever Max went, Rodrigo would follow.

Rodrigo tilted his head and nodded; his bitter smirk replaced with a look of resignation. "I believe you. You are an honorable man. There are so few of your type in this degenerate world. Please forgive me thinking otherwise." He took another long drink and settled back in his chair. "I've always wanted to believe that I was not born a distrustful, deceitful person. That only my life experiences have made me that way. Now, I wonder. I do wonder… Nature or nurture? A debate that I do not think will ever be decided one way or the other." He shrugged. *"Pues nada,* I've decided that it is not necessary to kill you."

For a heartbeat or two I thought he was joking, but the look in his dark eyes indicated otherwise, and a horrible sense of understanding began to bloom in my brain.

"Ah," said Rodrigo, reading my thoughts, "finally, the brilliant professor begins to see the correct solution to the problem. *Felicitaciones."* He held out his near empty glass and raised his eyebrows. "May I?"

"Of course," I managed to answer equably as if I weren't alone with a madman.

As I poured the whiskey, I recalled Max's reiteration of my counsel: *"It's all about perception."* My own words of wisdom ignored. I'd been played expertly, but not by Ezra or Agnes.

"Gracias, my friend," said Rodrigo, accepting his drink with a regal tilt of his head.

"So now what?" I asked. "If you're not going to kill me, is this where you confess and tell me that you've slipped an untraceable poison into your drink?"

Rodrigo laughed merrily. "Don't be ridiculous. I will tell you everything—that's why I wanted to speak with you. That much of the stereotype of the criminal mind is true in my case: the desire to confess, to justify oneself. But suicide? No, no. I have no reason to take my own life. What good would it serve? As I pointed out before, you are an honorable man. I have nothing to fear from you. An honorable man would not risk ruining the lives of a boy he loves, a man he respects, that man's fiancé, or a young woman with her life ahead of her, only to avenge the deaths of two strangers."

As Mother Anne had said, what is true and what is for the best are not always the same thing. Even if there was compelling evidence to suggest Rodrigo was responsible for the deaths of Alma and Fabiola, I would not jeopardize my relationship with Max to prove it, nor would I upend the lives of Ezra, Agnes, or Rosanie in such a pursuit. If that was "honorable" was up for debate. But one thing was certain. Rodrigo had me by the short and curlies.

"You know something of my history," continued Rodrigo. "What I told you that day over cookies and tea. But I must apologize for not being entirely faithful to the true course of events during that narrative. I was yet unsure if I could rely upon your silence. I embellished somewhat to deflect attention away from myself and toward Alma and Fabiola, the two *brujas* in my story.

"For instance, my first daughter's illness and Fabiola's financial intercession did occur. But it was I, not my wife, Linda, who became skeptical of Fabiola's motives for offering help. It was my first hint of the kind of person Fabiola was. However, I was in love with her, so I ignored the signs. Also, any animosity between Linda and Fabiola was purely my invention. My wife never recovered from the loss of her first child, and she was more than willing to accept Fabiola, who she greatly admired, in the role of doting *tia*. By the time Rosanie began primary school, Linda had suffered a complete breakdown and was admitted to a psychiatric hospital. She has been there ever since."

I recalled the times that Rosanie and her father had taken the day off to visit a relative in a nursing home.

"Paid for by Fabiola Willoughby?"

"Yes. I owed her my life and that of my wife and daughter. But I refused to see any ulterior motive in her generosity. I loved her, and I believed that she returned that love. It was at this time that Alma came into Fabiola's life. At first, I believed that Fabiola's attraction to Alma was nothing more than fascination. It was impossible not to be charmed, enchanted when Alma chose to charm and enchant. I was too blind to see what Alma had in mind…how she seduced and corrupted Fabiola."

"They became lovers?"

"She poisoned Fabiola's soul. Turned her against me. I thought I would lose her. But then Agnes arrived in Miami, and Alma's intense friendship with Fabiola cooled as Fabiola and Ezra—through their mutual patronage of the arts—entered Agnes's orbit."

"And you?" I asked, reaching for my whiskey. I'd been so caught up in the Willoughby-Montressor menage that I'd forgotten that there was a fifth wheel: Rodrigo.

"I remained loyal to Fabiola. Even after she announced her engagement to Ezra. I could not be angry with her, since I knew that Alma's machinations had fostered the union. Ezra's true love was Agnes, and Alma did all she could to keep them apart—to prevent Agnes from having something she couldn't have. But Agnes had some degree of virtue. She remained faithful to her husband.

"When Agnes's husband passed away, she returned to their *estancia* in Montana. Alma followed, of course. But she did not travel alone. She insisted to Fabiola that she take me with her. *Take me*, Neil. As if I were a dog. Actually, the word she used was *borrow.*"

"And you acquiesced—like a dog—to your mistress, Fabiola."

Rodrigo's face hardened. With anger or shame?

"I did as my employer instructed," Rodrigo said. "Please do not interrupt again. As I was saying, I accompanied Alma to Montana. I made the arrangements for the funeral of Agnes's husband—Agnes being too distraught and Alma too uncaring to do so.

"Afterward, it was horrible to witness. The way Alma dominated Agnes. The way she belittled her, berated her, insulted her. When you read about domestic violence, it's always a husband, a wife, a partner, or a parent. You never read about siblings, do you? One day, I saw Alma strike Agnes. A hard, vicious strike to the side of her face—the side that is scarred. They did not see me, and I do not know what Alma had said to her sister. But I did hear Agnes's response: 'I'm sorry.' And she spoke the words as if she were a misbehaving child. It was chilling. I knew then for certain what Alma was, the truly evil creature she hid so well behind her façade of beauty and glamour.

"I arranged with Fabiola for Agnes to return to the Grove alone. I also saw to it that Agnes would never again be abused by her sister."

"You murdered Alma Montressor."

"Alma is alive, if not entirely well, living the life of a broken recluse. As you know, a professional boxer's goal is to take his opponent down, not kill him. Disguising myself as a home invader, I made certain that Alma would never sing again. A TKO. Her voice was her identity, her life. I took that from her.

"Fabiola and Ezra were crushed by the loss of the woman to whom they'd been so enthralled. But the magic eventually faded with her absence. Agnes, unfortunately, never stopped loving, idolizing her sister. Perhaps now that she is at last united with Ezra, she will move on and let go of the past. I sincerely hope so."

"Anyway, I must continue with my narrative. When I returned to the Grove, I received surprising news from Fabiola. She was pregnant. She told me that the child was mine. I was overjoyed. I believed that it was a sign from God."

"*Seriously?*" I asked, sounding like Max.

"Did I not ask you to refrain from interrupting? Although I begged Fabiola to reveal my paternity to Ezra and finally leave him, she refused. And she was terrified of childbirth. Her mother had had eight children before the Lord brought her home as she gave birth to Fabiola. I tried to assuage Fabiola's fears, but she would not listen. She had an abortion. She killed my child.

"I was devastated, Neil. But my love for Fabiola did not falter. I tried to empathize. I tried to put myself in her place. And even though I struggled with my faith, I succeeded. I forgave her. I waited. Then Ezra and Fabiola adopted Max. I suppose you think that must have angered me. It would have if I'd been a real man. But, as you have so accurately pointed out, I was not a man. I was a dog. A dog waiting for his treat. His reward for being a good boy.

"Time went by. I waited. It's amazing how time passes, isn't it? I had Rosanie to care for, I had the Willoughby household to attend to—Max to look after. And Linda. I settled into a groove. We all did. Then, Sarah came. She was, like you, an honorable person. A good person. And an inquisitive person. She questioned, she probed. Her natural curiosity awakened in me old doubts. Old questions. What if Fabiola had lied to me? What if she had never had an abortion? What if Max really was my son? Fabiola had spent so much time in Miami—months on end. Was it possible?

"When I confronted Fabiola with my suspicions, she laughed at me. She *laughed* at me! She told me not to be ridiculous. She told me that she never wanted children and had only adopted Max to have a hold over Ezra—to 'keep him in line.' And to promote her public image as a devoted wife. It was her coldness that broke me, Neil. After so many years of willful ignorance, I finally allowed myself to see the real Fabiola. Or maybe she was simply tired of acting, of playing mind games.

"Fabiola was drunk that night—the night she died. The network had canceled her show after more than twenty years on the air. She was devastated. To see her like that, defeated, pathetic, gave me such a sense of power, of righteousness. If she had turned to me for support, if she had admitted to some degree of wrongdoing, of sin, I would have forgiven her—just as our Lord forgives when genuine remorse is shown and penance carried out. I would have held her and comforted her. Renewed my devotion to her. But that was not to be.

"We stood on that balcony. Close enough that we could have kissed or embraced as we had so many times before. But when I reached out to her, Fabiola pushed me away. I told her that I loved her. That I'd always loved her. That, together, we could make things right. Make things better.

"Do you know what her answer was, Neil? What the woman I had adored, worshipped, been a dog for, said to me? She said, 'Fuck you!' Those were her last words, her dying words."

Words.

I felt sick as I realized that Fabiola's last words to Rodrigo had been the same as Edward's to me.

How often do we think about the power of our words before we speak? How often do we think about their consequences? My words, Edward's words, had they been different, could have healed rather than destroyed. Fabiola's words to Rodrigo had they been different could have saved her life. My father had kept words inside. Not speaking had killed him. Even unspoken, words have power.

I said nothing. I refilled my glass and then Rodrigo's. We drank in silence. When Rodrigo had finished his whiskey, he stood, thanked me for my time, and left.

Nessa's winterscape now hung above my desk. After Rodrigo departed, I turned my attention to it as I recounted everything Rodrigo had told me. I was glad I had misjudged Nessa. And though the jury in my head was still out over whether I liked her, I wished her happiness with Ezra. I also hoped she would return to painting, and that her great talent had not been utterly hobbled by her abusive relationship with her sister.

Had justice been served? Had Rodrigo, like my mother, been a righteous executioner?

As I studied Nessa's painting, I decided I knew what was true. I also believed I knew what was for the best. I washed the whiskey tumblers, made a pot of coffee, and then proceeded to make a list of what I would need to take with me to Florentina Bay.

Epilogue

September

Florentina Bay

I HAD ALWAYS loved blind contour drawing; both as an exercise in hand-eye coordination and as a form of artistic expression. Max came to the practice late in his art education, but it beautifully suited his cinematic and photographic tendencies in drawing. During our summer in Florentina Bay, Max produced some outstanding blind contour works which I encouraged him to develop further into watercolor studies.

Max was nearing the completion of one such painting as we enjoyed a sunny day at the beach. We were approaching the end of what Max called our "workcation"—though we had spent more time swimming, cycling, and taking road trips than working. As I observed Max painting, lost in his zone, I felt a sense of peace and closure that had been a long time in coming.

"So," said Max, putting aside his brush and looking at me with a frank, searching expression. "What happens now?"

"Lunch? Mother Anne's son gave me his recipe for carnitas, and I've yet to try it."

"That's not what I'm talking about, Prof. I mean you and me. Like, with you and Beto being boyfriends or whatever. What happens to us?"

There it was, at last. An answer to the anxiety and quietness I'd sensed in Max since I'd introduced him to Beto the week before. Though Beto had lodged at a bed and breakfast for the length of his stay, I made a point of including him in activities with Max so that Max could start to get to know him as he'd known Victor; that he would understand that I had a life of my own outside of our unique relationship. And so that Beto could get to know his son.

Tears welled in Max's eyes, then dripped onto the sand beneath his chair. "Are you guys going to get married and move away? Like Sarah and Mr. Adami were going to do?"

Shit! How stupid could I have been? Max thought I'd been setting him up for a goodbye.

"Look, Max," I said, turning away from my easel to face him fully. "I'm not sure what my future with Beto is going to be. Will we get married? Who knows? What I do know is that I care for him a lot, and I want our relationship to continue to grow. But that won't take away from the friendship you and I share. Remember when you asked me why I came to the Grove and why I stayed?" Max nodded. "I never answered the second part of that question. So, I'm answering it now. I stayed because of you. You have a very special place in my heart, Maximillian. And until I die, I promise

I will never leave you. I will always be there for you."

Max wiped his eyes and smiled. "I love you, Prof."

I was so overwhelmed I barely got my reply out. "I love you, too, Max."

We hugged and then began to pack up our gear. As I cleared away my paraphernalia, a wind gust kicked up and my can of water toppled over. When I reached to pick up the can and the scattered brushes, a movement in the periphery of my vision caught my attention.

I looked behind me toward the boardwalk and I could swear I saw Benedicta standing there at her easel, the sea breeze fluttering her habit as she worked. She looked up and smiled at me and then turned her gaze to Max. When her eyes met mine once more, she nodded slowly.

Then I blinked, and she was gone.

About the Author

Born in New York City and raised in the San Joaquin Valley of California, D.J. now divides his time between Brooklyn, New York, and Bogota, Colombia, where he lives with his husband, a cat, and a dog. D.J. has previously published under the pen name Zev de Valera.

Email

DJBlank176@gmail.com

Other NineStar books by this author

Left in the Dark, as Zev de Valera

www.ninestarpress.com

www.facebook.com/ninestarpress

www.facebook.com/groups/NineStarNiche

www.twitter.com/ninestarpress

www.instagram.com/ninestarpress

bsky.app/profile/ninestarpress.bsky.social

www.threads.net/@ninestarpress